helped me figure out w

thank you for all your a

My other beta readers also helped me

or not to go forward with this book. Sabrina Rawson, Christy Reyes, Tara Greseth and FL Hope. CDavid Gregory, you provided me with the male point of view that I needed so much. You guys rock my socks off.

And last but not least, thank you to Titan Publishing for giving me the chance to put my work out there. Chris Austin, Beverley Hollowed and the entire crew at Titan Publishing, you are an amazing team to work with and I look forward to continuing our relationship. Anthony Warren, you rocked the cover and put up with me making changes and then more changes, thanks for not losing your cool over all of my requests.

Chapter 1 1

Chapter 2 12

Chapter 3 25

Chapter 4 39

Chapter 5 55

Chapter 6 63

Chapter 7 84

Chapter 8 101

Chapter 9 115

Chapter 10 135

Chapter 11 155

Chapter 12 167

Chapter 13 189

Chapter 14 202

Chapter 15 217

Chapter 16 227

Chapter 17 240

Chapter 18 250

Chapter 19 266

Chapter 20 274

Chapter 21 288

Chapter 22 298

Chapter 23 322

Chapter 24 334

Running from Destiny 346

Copyright © Titan Publishing House 2013

Titan InKorp LTD © Company No: 8922529

All rights reserved.

Reprisal, A Dark, Erotic Thriller©

Christa Lynn has asserted her right under the Copyright, Designs and Patents Act 1988 to be identified as the author of this work.

Cover design by Titan InKorp LTD

Book design by Titan InKorp LTD

Editing by Titan InKorp LTD

No part of this book may be reproduced in any form or by any electronic or mechanical means including information storage and retrieval systems, without permission in writing from the publisher.

This book is a work of fiction. Names, characters, places, and incidents either are products of the author's imagination or are used fictitiously. Any resemblance to actual persons, living or dead, events, or locales is entirely coincidental.

Printed in the United States of America and United Kingdom

www.titanpublishinghouse.com

Titan InKorp LTD © is registered by the UK ISBN agency on the international ISBN Agency's Publisher Database

ISBN - 978-1-78520-061-8

Chapter 1
Sydney

The smell of chloroform invades my nostrils, closing my throat. I can't breathe and suddenly I'm choking on air. My mind starts spinning and as the darkness overwhelms me, I fall to the floor, gasping for my next breath. My heart rate increases and my limbs go numb. I can't move and.....

I sit straight up in bed, breathing heavy and sweating. Damn it, another freaking nightmare. I thought I was over this, but, they've started coming back. Guess it's time to call my shrink again, chuckling at the irony of that thought. The past few years have been fine, but all of a sudden the dreams have come back with a vengeance. I can't live this way, not again. These dreams took too much of my life before and I can't go back there.

The memories of my teenage years, held against my will, beaten and raped over and over come flooding back and I start to shake. No, not again. This can't be happening. "I'm over this." I tell myself repeatedly, "I'm stronger than this." I chant as I pull my knees up to my chest and rock back and forth.

I'm finally able to contain my emotions and make my way to the bathroom and splash cold water on my face. As I look at my reflection, I see fear and despair in my eyes. A look I haven't seen in twenty years. I look.....haunted, gaunt and weak. As I splash another handful of water on my face, I growl at myself in the mirror. "Never again, Sydney. You will never go there again.

Now, dry your eyes and get moving, because your patients won't treat themselves."

I sometimes wonder why I decided to major in Psychology, considering my history. Or maybe that's the reason, to help young girls in similar situations. All I know is it's the hardest job I could have chosen. So many times a young girl or boy comes in that has been raped, sodomized or beaten and I have to choke back my own fears and risk showing a side of me to my patients, that they don't need to see. If these kid's parents had any idea of my past, they would find another doctor real quick. But each day, I get through it with calming smiles and never let on that I have a similar past.

After taking a hot shower, I get ready to head to my office downtown. I only have three patients this morning, and then I'm taking the rest of the day to myself. As I make my way to my car, I call Doctor Phillips and schedule an appointment for this afternoon. I know I can't put this off any longer.

As I stand in front of my closed office door, I take in the name plate, Doctor Sydney DeCarlo, PsyD. I'm still amazed that I have a Doctorate in Psychology and Forensic Science. I spent ten gruelling years studying and never really had a life. I didn't party in school, I rarely dated and I spent my weekends in the University library cramming information in my head so I could graduate early. I completed my thesis and graduated with honors at twenty-nine years old, a feat not many can accomplish. I interned at Northwestern in Chicago before joining a colleague in private practice here in New York. After spending most of my life in Illinois, I ventured out of my comfort zone and moved up to the East Side of Manhattan. I love it here, really I do. But there are some crazy things that go on here.

I push open the front door and make my way to my office. I'm a little early, but that's a good thing. I can get some paperwork done before my receptionist, Beth, gets here. The first appointment is not until ten o'clock, so I have plenty of time.

At nine thirty, Beth comes in to let me know my appointment is also early and did I want to get a head start on the day? Always eager to close up shop early on a Friday, I nod my head.

Veronica comes in with her mother and they sit on the sofa in my office. She's a sweet girl and my heart breaks for her every time I see her. This is our fourth visit and she seems to be making progress, but she doesn't look good today.

"Hi Veronica, how are you today?" I ask the pale blonde girl, who has her eyes directed at the floor. She's fidgeting with her hands, so I know she's a bit nervous today. Her mother nudges her in the arm, "Answer Doctor DeCarlo, Veronica."

"It's okay, Mrs. Sawyer. She seems a bit scared today, give her a minute."

"I am not scared! I'm sick of coming here every week, I don't need her help anymore!"

Veronica screams as she runs out of the room. We both flinch as we hear the bathroom door slam closed.

"What's happened since our last visit, Mrs. Sawyer?" I ask her mother, who now has tears in her eyes.

"I don't know. She was fine until last weekend. She went to a school dance with some friends and then.....I don't know, she changed. Something happened at that dance and she won't tell me what. I'm afraid......" She releases a deep breath. "I'm afraid one of the boys she was meeting up with....." And the tears come more freely. "She came home early from the dance. I'm not even sure how she got home, to be honest with you. One of the other girl's mother took them and another was going to pick them up after the dance. She came barging into the apartment around nine o'clock, her makeup smudged and.......I fear she was raped again, but she won't talk about it."

Before I can respond, Veronica comes out of the bathroom, red faced and crying. She saunters back in my office and flops on the sofa, keeping her eyes to the floor. "Veronica, what was that about?" I ask her, but she doesn't look at me, swiping at her tears and looking down.

"I don't want to talk about it." She snaps, keeping her eyes down.

"Veronica, you came here to talk. Why don't you tell us what's going on?" I urge her on, but she still doesn't look up. "Would you like for your mother to leave the room? Will you tell me without her here?" I ask, nodding at her mother who stands up to leave the room.

"I'll be outside, honey. Talk to Dr. DeCarlo. Please." She pleads with her daughter as she backs out of the room.

Once she's closed the door, I move over from my chair and sit next to Veronica. Sometimes, you need to get in their space for them to feel comfortable enough to talk to you. I pause, giving her a moment to collect herself.

"Did something happen at your school dance?" I ask, figuring it's better to just cut to the chase instead of dancing around the issue.

She nods, but still doesn't speak.

"Tell me Veronica. Tell me what happened. Everything you say to me in here is confidential. Nothing will leave this room. Did a boy hurt you at the dance?"

She nods again and the tears start streaming again. Oh Lord, her mother was right. She was raped again. I'm not sure her psyche can handle a set back like this one. I keep quiet and let her gather her thoughts, not wanting to pressure her to tell me something she isn't ready to talk about.

She takes a deep breath and finally speaks. "Yes, a boy hurt me. But not the way you think. I wanted to......he didn't. He said I was damaged goods and that any boy would be nuts to get involved with me. I don't know how he knows about my past, but he said it in front of a big group of kids. I was mortified and humiliated, and he and all of his friends just laughed." She pauses for a second and wipes a stray tear from her cheek. "I thought he liked me, that......hell, I don't know what I thought."

"Veronica, it's okay. Boys can be real jerks at times." I say with a chuckle, hoping to lighten the mood a little. "There is no way he can know about your past unless you've told people. Have you told any of your friends your story?"

She shakes her head. "No. I can't even tell my best friend. So I have no idea what he's talking about, it just hurt that he turned me down in front of everyone. But somehow he seemed to know, like someone told him."

"I know, Veronica. It's not easy growing up. You've had to deal with a lot, but you are such strong girl." My voice catches in my throat. I want to tell her that she's not the only one, that she will recover and live a normal life. Hell, I'm living proof of that fact, but that isn't what she needs to hear right now. Kids can be mean and bullying should not be tolerated, but I can't step in and do anything. I took an oath when I graduated and I can't infringe on someone else's privacy. The only thing I can do is prompt her to tell her mother, then she can get involved.

"Tell me why it hurt so badly for him to reject you. If you get your feelings out and make it known to me, you'll feel better. Don't bottle it up."

"Why do you think it hurt? It hurt because he's right, I AM damaged goods! No boy will ever want to get involved with me. I'm going to grow up to be an old maid, alone."

"No you won't, Veronica. Trust me on that, even if you don't trust me with anything else.

I've been doing this a long time and I can assure you, you'll be fine. You'll be stronger because of it."

I know now it's time for Veronica's treatment to continue with a Child Psychiatrist and I mentally take note of a few people to recommend, though approval will have to go through the court system, since she is a victim of sexual assault. What she's going through now is beyond my realm of expertise. I handle the criminal side of things and once the investigation is complete, the victims are referred to other professionals.

Veronica was assaulted by an uncle when she was left in his care. Her father passed away when she was four years old and Mrs. Sawyer's brother stepped in to help, only he was a closet child molester that had been under the legal system's radar for many years. He had a way of coaxing young boys and girls to submit to him and he put so much fear in to their heads that they never told anyone. His first, and only mistake was abusing his own niece. That personal connection was his final downfall. After Veronica came forward, so did eleven other children.

I was pulled in to the investigation by NYPD and the FBI to assist with the scientific side of things, the investigation in to the actual act of abuse. Veronica was such a vulnerable girl that officials asked me to counsel her. Veronica was comfortable with me, so I agreed. But now, her mental stability has elevated to more than I can do.

"Veronica, sit here for a few minutes, I'm going to talk to your mother." I say as I stand to leave. A look of panic crosses her face and her eyes well up with tears again. "It's okay, Veronica, I'm not going to tell your mother, but I do need to go over some things with her. She needs to know what you are feeling, but only you can tell her that. Okay?" She nods as I exit my office to the waiting room.

Mrs. Sawyer is sitting on the sofa with her hand in her face, sobbing. I sit down next to her and gently place my hand on her thigh. "Mrs. Sawyer, I think it's time Veronica visits a child Psychiatrist. My expertise is on the forensic side of criminal investigations. I believe she is recovering from the trauma of what happened, but she is........hmm, she is a teenage girl and I think it's time she is referred to someone better trained in what she needs at the moment."

"Did she tell you what happened? Was she r-r-raped again?"

"You know I can't tell you that. Even though Veronica is a minor, I took an oath of confidentiality. Only Veronica can tell you what the issue is. I will make the necessary referral to the courts for her treatment." I say as Mrs. Sawyer nods.

"Thank you, Dr. DeCarlo. Thank you for all that you've done for my baby girl." She says on a sob.

"Mrs. Sawyer, can I make another recommendation?"

"Yes, of course."

"I'm going to refer you as well to someone to talk to, to help you better help Veronica. I know you have guilt issues for putting her in her uncle's care that day, but you had no idea that he was a sexual predator. Please, seek some advice yourself. Your therapist and Veronica's can work together to bring you both closure.

Nodding her head, "Okay. I'll do whatever I need to do to help Veronica. I'll take that referral. Thank you."

After they leave, I sit behind my desk staring at my computer and shaking my head. That poor girl, I know what she's going through. The same things happened to me, only more than once.

Veronica came forward after the one and only time her uncle raped her, so she was saved from the horrible torture I endured by the hands of my own father.

Chapter 2
Sydney

"Tell me about your dreams, Sydney." Dr. Phillips asks me at my appointment that afternoon.

I'm still shaken up by my last patient of the day, a young boy. But as my job requires, I have to let it go and move on until our next visit.

"It's dark and cold. Dampness is in the air and the smell......the smell of chloroform fills my throat and I can't breathe. I know he's there, but I can't see him. His presence sucks the remaining air out of the room and I wake up before he......." I drift off. "I wake up sucking in air and sweating, but it never goes further than that. It's him, I know it is. He's come back to haunt me and he wants me dead, I can feel it."

"What makes you think he wants you dead, Sydney? And how, he's dead himself?"

"I know, I know...but, it just seems so real. I can feel his body, smell his breath." I say as I shiver. "That smell has stayed with me, rotten and evil, burning my flesh, my mouth. The smell of death and decay overwhelms the air." I drop my head in my hands. "Why is this coming back to me now? It's been twenty years, I should be over this."

"Sydney, you're a doctor. You know these things can come back and overwhelm you at any time, any place. Memories and fears don't discriminate. What is your patient load like? Could you have one that is jarring these memories?"

"Yeah, a teenage girl. I think anyway, as the last one today is a young boy. Maybe her case is weighing on me more than I thought. Though, today I referred her to Dr. Casey for further treatment. Her issues have extended beyond the forensics now." I say.

"Well, now that she is moving along, maybe these dreams will stop. I'm going to give you some medication......"

"No, no drugs. You and I both know I can't take those."

"Relax, Sydney. Just something to help you sleep. You look retched." She says as she smiles at me.

"Gee, thanks." I smirk back at her. "If you haven't slept well for over a month, I can imagine what you would look like."

"This has been going on for a month already? You should have called me sooner, Syd." She says as she pulls out her prescription pad. "Just something to help you sleep, take it if you need it. Or don't, the choice is yours. But you have it now if you want it." She says as she tears the paper from the pad and hands it to me.

I fold it and place it in my purse, standing to leave. "Thank you for seeing me on such short notice. I really thought all of this was behind me."

"Anytime, Syd. But next time, don't wait a month. You call me as soon as the dream wakes you and I can either come over, or we can talk on the phone. I'm always here for you." Dr. Phillips pulls me in to a hug.

"Thanks Leslie." I call her by her first name, because our meeting is now over. I've known Dr. Leslie Phillips for fifteen years or so, we even shared classes in Chicago. So, not only is she my doctor, but she is my friend too, and right now I think that's what I really need.

"You wanna go for a drink? Get some of this psychoanalysis bullshit out of our minds for a bit? There's a new pub that just opened around the corner." Les asks me, a glint of humor in her eyes.

"Sure, I can go for one drink and that's it. But we go as friends, not doctor - patient - deal? I could use a break, so no work talk. Got it?" I say as I move towards the door. She shuts down her computer and grabs her bag, following me out the door.

Since this is New York City, we walk. Everywhere. It's the best way to get around, unless you are going far and then you grab a cab. As we make our way through the bar, we locate an empty table in the back and are immediately greeted by a waitress. "What can I get you ladies?"

I order a glass of moscato and Les orders a beer. "Beer?" I ask her, surprised.

"Yeah, it's Friday and the game is on." She says as she motions her head towards the big screen TV hanging on the wall. "Beer and baseball. Nothing like it." She waggles her eyebrows as the waitress brings our drinks. At the same time, the Yankee's pitcher throws out a Met's player on first. "Nice, love these 'Subway Series'. Yankees and Mets in the same bar. Keep your eyes open, cause we may get to see a fight tonight." Les says as she lifts the bottle to her full lips.

"So, what's up with you and Joe?" I ask her. Joe is her long-time boyfriend, but they never talk about getting married. "Ummm, He's......Joe." She responds nonchalantly and tips her beer back again.

"No ring yet?"

"Nope."

"You think he'll ever propose?"

"Nope. Don't want him to either."

"Why not? You guys have been together since college. What's going on?"

"He's fucking around." She answers without emotion.

"What? How do you know?" I ask her, totally blown away that Joe would cheat on Les. And amazed at how Les doesn't seem to care.

"Found her panties in the sofa last week."

"You found her panties? Are you sure they aren't yours?" I ask.

"Nope. I wear a small. These were a medium....and a thong. You know me, no butt floss. I'd spend more time tugging those bastards out of the crack of my ass than anything else."

"And you're.....okay with this?"

She shrugs her shoulders and set her beer down. "Things haven't been right for some time, I think. I'm just waiting on the right moment to kick him out. The lease on our sublet is up at the end of the month. I've already talked to the owner and his name will be removed from the lease and I'll kick him out."

"Geez, I'm sorry Les. How long have you known?"

"Well, I was suspicious for about three weeks when he kept coming home late reeking of cheap perfume. I pretended not to notice, but after about the third time I knew. He hasn't touched me in over a month and has started sleeping in the guest room, saying he can't sleep and he doesn't want to wake me. I called bullshit....inside. I figured I'd let him tie his own rope and once he has it nicely slipped around his neck, I'll yank it tighter. He won't know what hit him."

Her evil laugh barrelling out of her throat.

"Well, good luck. I hope I don't run into him on the street or he may never be able to have children." I tell her as I nudge her shin with my foot. "I'll kick him so hard in the balls, he won't be able to walk for a week." I laugh.

"No doubt, Syd. No doubt. If I were him, I wouldn't want to meet you in a dark alley." She chuckles as she raises her hand, motioning for the waitress. We order another round and continue our chat, having a good time.

The crowd is getting rambunctious and as loud as the game when it hits the end of the ninth inning.

Yanks are up five to four and the Mets fans are not happy. It seems they're chanting at each other and when I see a bottle fly through the bar, I know the hockey game is about to break out.

Les and I sit and watch the battle unfold before us. Shouting, screaming and some cuss words I've never heard before fill the room. You can no longer hear the game over the shouting. One guy is the instigator, apparently a Mets fan and he tells the Yankee fan to suck his.......CRASH!

"Oh shit, I think it's time to dip, Les." I say as I stand and grab my bag, throwing the long strap over my shoulder. Mets fan has turned a table full of bottles and glasses over and is now climbing it to get to the other side.

"Yeah, let's get out of here before glass starts flying in this direction. All I need is a trip to the ER for stitches." Les says as she makes her way around me and we slither our way to the door.

"Fucking cunt!" We hear Mets fan's fist hit Yankee fan's face, the sound echoing throughout the now quiet bar. The fans have all stopped screaming and yelling and now it's dead silent. I look back towards the bar from the door and the two men are standing there, circling each other like ninjas, waiting for the other to make the next move.

Before the second punch is thrown, a security guard or cop or something jumps in between them and pushes them both back from each other. Les is tugging at my arm, trying to yank me out of the bar, but this man that has stepped in has caught my attention. "Hold on a sec." I tell Les as I pull my arm out of her grasp.

"What? Come on Syd, let's get out of here before the shit hits the fan."

"No, hold on. No shit is hitting any fan here." I say as I nudge my chin towards the commotion in the center of the bar.

"Fuck. Me. Who is that?" Les whispers in my ear as her eyes locate the bouncer.

"No clue, but I'm sticking around to find out." I say as I walk back into the bar, straight to our still vacant table. My glass of wine is still sitting there with one last swallow in it, so I chug it back and sit down.

Leslie reluctantly follows me back into the bar and sits down beside me, her eyes wide with panic, like a riot is going to break out and she's in the middle of it. "Relax." I tell her. "The fight is over, hot dude in the center has nipped this one in the bud."

I rake my eyes over this man's body. No wait, he is not a man. He's a God. Dark hair, almost black and messy with matching dark eyes and a scruffy chin. He's wearing a tight black t-shirt that hugs his arms and chest. Low riding jeans that invite your curiosity as to what's hiding under there. My face heats and I embarrass myself at the naughty thoughts going through my mind.

I've never seen a man in person that has made my brain go in to erotic overdrive. My typically vanilla mind has taken a severe left turn and is heading somewhere it's never been. I'll take these feelings home with me and store them somewhere for a rainy day. I've never been one to pick up guys in bars and take them home, so tonight will be no different. I'll just watch from the side-lines.

"Earth to Sydney." I hear Les to my left jarring me out of my thoughts.

"What?"

"Where'd you go? Are you okay?" She asks, poking her finger in my arm trying to get my attention.

"Yeah, Les. I'm right here, just watching."

"Well, I got worried for a second when you didn't respond. What's got you all tied up?"

"Huh? Oh, nothing. Just waiting for the show to start. I wanna see what the bouncer does to those two coots that were squaring off." The bouncer that has caught my eye is big, but the two dudes going at it are bigger. Not beefier bigger, but fatter bigger. One squash and the bouncer could go down, though I doubt it.

Then, three of NYPD's finest show up and cuff the two brawlers, hauling them out of the bar.

The bouncer stays behind talking to who I think is probably the manager. I hear the bouncer laugh as he smacks the manager on the shoulder and turn towards the door, his smile lighting up the room. I can't take my eyes off of him, and I can feel Leslie's eyes on me, a smile cracking her lips. He glances around the bar and our eyes meet. He doesn't look away and neither do I, because I'm frozen solid. I feel Les nudge my leg under the table and I finally pull my eyes down. I know I'm blushing, I do that easily, but I don't look back up. I can still feel his eyes on me and I know now is the time to escape.

"Go talk to him." Les whispers in my ear.

"Ah, hell no. I wouldn't even know what to say without tripping over my own lips. Let's go, the show's over and I need to hit the bed. Been a long day." I say as I stand up and re-position my bag on my shoulder, which has since slid down my arm.

"Chicken." Les teases.

"Yep, that's me. Let's go."

I stand to move and Leslie falls in behind me, making me lead the way. I know what she's doing and I try to brush it off, making my way towards the door. I catch one more glance of the bouncer as we reach the door, but I make my exit in front of Leslie and the door shuts behind me.

Blue lights light up the street, no doubt with a drunk goon in each one. Leslie and I stand on the sidewalk while we contemplate our next move. Les lives close, so she can walk but I have to hail a cab. I live on the Upper East Side and she lives in Midtown. As a yellow taxi pulls up, I hug Les and tell her I'll call her tomorrow and of course, "be careful walking home. This ain't the suburbs girl."

"You too, sleep tight." She says as I close the door to the taxi.

It takes about fifteen minutes to get me to the door to the apartment I sublet from a friend of my mothers. It's a corner penthouse and totally out of my league, but I love it. As I unlock the door, my favorite scents of lavender and mint fill my nose and I take a deep breath. In my line of work, relaxation is a must during down time. You can't let the stresses of the day get to you or you'll go mad. This is my down time and I do what's needed to relieve the stress.

I drop my purse on the sofa and head to my bedroom, which is my oasis. Warm earth tones cover the large king size bed and dark furniture. It's warm and cozy and totally me. Since I live alone I was able to decorate just like I wanted. With a hectic schedule I knew I needed calm and comfortable at home. Simple decorations and a homey feeling.

I snap my iPhone in the docking station and turn it on to the jazz station as music fills the room. It's only ten thirty, so I fill the tub with hot water and chamomile and sink my tired, aching body down in to the bubbles. Thoughts of the bouncer fill my mind and I silently wonder if I should have introduced myself. I shake off that thought quickly, but I can't get his dark 'bedroom' eyes out of my mind. His eyes were seductive and sexy, just begging to be hovering over a willing female body. Or male, for all I know. Yeah, that's it. He's probably gay and I would never stand a chance. That's what I'll keep telling myself so I don't think about him anymore.

Les was right though, I am chicken shit. My tormented past prohibits me from making casual conversation with men, especially gorgeous men. I know I've probably missed out on a whole lot of fun in my younger days, but I stayed away from anything that could remotely be trouble. I've had enough of that in my life and now I focus on helping others get out of trouble. Maybe it's the wrong way to be, but it's me and I have to accept that.

Chapter 3
Gabe

"Man, did you see that woman and her friend that just left?" I ask Mark, the manager here.

"Nah man, women come and go through here like tornados, I hardly notice anymore. Why, what was so different about her?"

"Her eyes, dark and mysterious. You had to have seen her, because she was stunning. I watched her for a bit from the back bar and just her mannerisms were hypnotic. Long dark straight hair and those dark eyes, like she holds many a secret." I tell him as I stare towards the table where she sat with her friend. "After I broke up the fight, I planned to go to her table, but she and her friend disappeared out of the blue, almost like she was never here at all."

"Gabe, man. Snap out of it dude. You look like you've just lost your puppy. It's a bar, the women are a dime a dozen. Give it a few, another hottie will walk in shortly and you'll forget all about her." Mark says as he slaps me on the shoulder and heads back towards the bar, though I seriously doubt I'll be able to get her out of my mind anytime soon. My cock jumped at just the thought of having her underneath me.

Before I get too deep in to my daydream a woman squeals from the back of the bar. My eyes focus on the darkened room and I head back to where I heard the scream. As I enter the back billiard room, I see two men sandwiching a young woman, pressing her against the pool table. I watch for a second, because you never know when what you are looking at is consensual and you don't want to jump in too quickly. As one of the men turn, I see the fear in the woman's eyes and I know she's not asking for this. Being a cop by day and a bouncer by night, I have to make sure that what I think is happening is what is actually happening. New York has such a variety of people here that you never know when someone is actually acting out a scene.

Her eyes are wide and her skin is pale, so I know she is truly frightened and not acting. I step back a little to get some distance and grab my radio, letting Mark know I need NYPD back in the billiard room. Since I'm off duty, I can only do so much. I step back in to the room and clear my throat, making my presence known. "Back off man, this pretty little thing is ours tonight. Go find your own." The one guy says to me, but I hear the woman suck in a breath. Her eyes are now glazed over with moisture and I know she's about to cry. I step forward and grab the guy by the back of the collar and yank him backwards. He's a skinny guy without an inch of meat on his bones, so I know I can take him. I shove him back towards the wall and step towards the other dude, who's a bit bigger and might present me with a challenge. And I love a challenge. "Bring it on, man."

The bigger dude lets the girl go and steps back, assessing the situation. His eyes meet his friends' and his expression changes from a rapist glare to a murderer. "Dude, you're infringing on our territory here. I suggest you back off before I knock your head off." He says right in my face, the smell of beer and cigarettes flows from his mouth. I know he's drunk and one punch to the jaw and he'd go down like a dead fly. Yeah, I calculated this one down to two hits, me hitting him and him hitting the floor.

But the demon in his eyes has me taken aback just a little, and I witness his hand moving towards his pocket. I know then he has a weapon, but what is it? A knife? A gun? I decide that I have no time to try and figure that out, so I haul back and my fist connects with his face, crimson spewing all over the green felt of the pool table. The dude's body thunking on the floor. Yep, out like a light. I turn to his friend at the back wall behind me, but he's gone like the wind. I turn to the woman and confirm that she is in fact, okay.

"Thank you." She tells me as I pull her to a standing position, my eyes scanning her body for any injury. She's a tiny thing and would have never been able to defend herself against this man that now lies on the floor, blood seeping from his lip. His head is up and his eyes are open now and he's glaring up at me like he's thinking about taking me on, but as I step over his body he closes his eyes, an admission of defeat.

Two cops then come in, tugging the skinny guy behind them. "This the other one, Gabe?"

I look back and scan the scrawny man, "Yeah that's him. The other is lying here on the floor in a pool of his own blood." I say as I look back at the man at my feet. "Get up asshole, NYPD has some fancy jewelry for you." And I step back to allow the defeated man to get to his feet.

"I didn't do anything criminal......." He says and I cut him off, patting him down and locate the switchblade in his pocket.

"But you did attempt an assault on an officer of the law. That my friend, is a major crime. One that can have you sitting in a jail cell for a long time."

"You're a cop?" He asks like he is truly surprised.

I point to my badge attached on my belt and smile. "Next time, you need to pay more attention to your surroundings. Did you really think the law wouldn't be in here on a night like tonight? Plus, you were assaulting this young woman here, so you'd better be glad I stopped you when you did, because attempted rape is a lesser offense than rape. Haul him off, Gibbs." I say as I shove the guy towards Officer Gibbs, who waits patiently with his cuffs in his hand, ready to slap them on his wrists.

Gibbs drags the skinny dude out and Detective Scruggs drags the bigger guy out to their cruisers parked on the street. "Do you have someone that can come get you, Miss......"

"Jan. Yeah, my friends are in the bar. I'll just go find them." She says as she turns on her heel.

"Wait, you have friends here and they had no idea what was going on back here?" I ask, concern now lacing my voice.

"They're watching the game. I came back here to use the restroom and......"

"There you are Jan! Geez, what took you so long?" A young blonde asks from the entrance to the billiard room.

"Oh, NOW you come looking for me? Wow, thanks for nothing Stacey, nice to know my 'friends' are looking out for me." She says as she stomps her way out of the billiard room. Her friend stands at the door dazed and confused.

"What the hell happened?" She asks me.

"Well, apparently two men tried to attack your friend there." I say as I lift my chin towards where her friend just headed. "Maybe next time you visit the restroom in pairs. Safety in numbers girl." And I make my way out of the room, back to the bar.

Mark announces 'last call' and a mad rush for the bar begins. The bartender's frantically work to get their final drinks out so they can clean up and shut it down for the night. Night life sings in the city, but this bar closes at midnight so people drink up and then head to the next place. My night ends when the last person leaves and then I get about four hours sleep before I'm back at the precinct.

"Gabe!" I turn as I hear my name called from the door to the bar. Agent Jason Morrison, or Mo as we call him, is holding on to the door motioning me towards him. Seeing the FBI agent makes my stomach sink, because if he's here, then there's bad news somewhere in the city. I know then that sleep will have to wait.

"What's up man?" I ask, as he opens the door. I step out onto the still busy New York street scanning the area.

"We just got an alert for a missing young woman, age twenty. She was last seen getting in to a cab on Fifth Ave."

"Fifth Ave? Sure she wasn't just having a romp with one of the Wall Street's finest?"

"Maybe, but that was three days ago. Her dad is some hotshot bank executive and the authorities are wondering if this is random or not. A rope and chloroform cotton balls were found at the entrance to the Crown Heights station in Brooklyn. Trail cuts off there. Cab driver states he picked up a white man and a white woman, and dropped them off at Penn Station. She didn't appear scared, like she knew the guy but you never know what he had on her. He said her eyes were glassy, like maybe she'd been drugged."

"Shit. What took them so long to report her missing?" I ask Mo.

"Her parents said she was going to visit a friend on Long Island and didn't know until her roommate called them today to let them know she never came home. When her friend was contacted, she said the girl called her and cancelled, so she had no idea either."

"Damn, three days is a long time. Any word on a cell trace?"

"Yeah, located her phone on the bank of the Hudson, near Battery Park."

"Jesus, this guy's had her all over the place. Fifth Ave, Penn Station, Brooklyn and Battery Park. How long did this guy have her before they disappeared?"

"Don't know, seems as if the girl knows him."

"What's her name?"

"Sophia Fishman, daughter of Alex Fishman, CFO of NYB&T."

"Fuck, has to be about money. But why no ransom call?"

"No clue yet, but the Brooklyn looks like a war zone. Cops are everywhere, road blocks are set up on all bridges and throughout the streets. So far, nothing has been deemed suspicious."

Mo's phone buzzes and he presses the phone to his ear. "Mo here." I listen to his lack of words and watch his face as it turns ashen. He disconnects his phone without saying a word to whoever called him. He turns to me with a glum look in his eyes,

"Her body just washed up on the shore of the Hudson, about seventeen yards from her phone."

My mind travels back to last month when a girl vanished without a trace. Her body was found a week later, beaten and bruised. Multiple sexual assaults and.... I shiver at the thought of it. That girl vanished in the same manor, but no one ever reported her missing. She was a runaway out of Newark with no parents or family to speak of. Fled from a halfway house and wasn't found until her body washed up in the East River. I wonder silently if this is the same monster, coming out of the woodwork after a......wait, exactly one month. "Hold on a second. Do you remember the Samantha Brockwood case?" I asked Mo.

"Samantha Brockwood, the runaway that washed up on the riverbank of the East River? Yeah, why?"

"Check the dates, if I'm not mistaken it's been exactly one month since she appeared in the water. Could we have a serial rapist/murderer on the loose? I'll call Matthews and have him pull that folder, and let him know I'm coming in."

Twenty minutes later I bust through the doors to HQ, centered in Manhattan. Olivia is seated behind the check in table eyeing me suspiciously. "Detective Torres, what are you doing here so late in the evening?" She whispers, almost seductively.

She's a pretty little thing with a hot little body to go with it, and she's expressed an 'interest' in me, but I refuse to mix business and pleasure.

"Is Matthews in?" I ask, without acknowledging her smirk.

"Yeah, he's in his office." She replies while smiling at me like she wants to eat me. And, as frustrated as I am with the fact that I am at NYPD HQ at twelve thirty on a Friday night, her smirk is not helping. I had hoped to be naked and sweaty with a beautiful woman underneath me.

But, duty calls and here I am. I know I could have her at any time, but again - there is that business and pleasure combination.

I knock on the Chief's door and stand back, half expecting him to fling the door open. "It's open." He calls from the other side of the closed door. I walk in and close the door behind me, only to see he has his nose deep in to a folder. "You come looking for this?" He asks as he waves the folder at me.

"If that's the Samantha Brockwood file, then yes. You see anything interesting in it?"

He motions for me to sit in the chair opposite him, but I'm too fired up to sit. I continue to stand at his desk, glaring at the folder that I so badly want my hands on. "Sit, Torres." He says as he hands me the folder.

"Good call on this one, Gabe. Appears we may have a huge problem. Exactly one month ago today is when Miss Brockwood washed up on the shores of the East River. I've called in the investigators and profilers that worked this case and they should be here in the morning."

"Profilers?"

"Yeah, I've called in the FBI on this one." I nod because I figure that's why Mo grabbed me at Blazer's. "Based on the similarities in the crime, we may need their help. All of NYPD's forensic team is wrapped up in the Angelo/Meeney drug war. They've got their own issues and one of the FBI's profilers is........well, very knowledgeable. We had an abuse case a couple of years ago, a young girl kidnapped and raped. She helped bring the guy down and then counseled the young girl, who actually survived. His other victims didn't."

"You think it's the same guy?"

"No, that guy was gunned down by NYPD when he fired at the SWAT team. After the gas was tossed into the warehouse he was held up in, he came out swinging. Got off one shot before Preston took him out."

Preston is one of NYPD's sharpshooters, and he's damn good. Spent eight years as a SEAL and now proudly serves as NYPD's best. He can put a bullet in your head from six miles away.

"What's happening now though? Any leads on why this girl was taken?"

"Read the file, Gabe. Your intuition is always good. Scan it and tell me what you find. If you pick it up too, then we move forward."

As I scan the file, combing over notes on the Brockwood case and immediately notice both similarities and differences between this case and the Fishman case. Samantha was young and a runaway, with no family to speak of. Sophia is also young, but comes from a wealthy family.

But neither family knew the girls were missing right away. "Seems as if he's prying on their innocence. Money doesn't seem to be an issue, at least not on the Brockwood case, but....... wait.

Do you have pictures of these girls?" I ask Chief Matthews. He nods and slides another folder to me. As I open the file, two photos spill onto my lap. I suck in a breath at the similarities. Dark hair, dark eyes and stunning features. These girls are the epitome of beautiful. They look so alike they could be twins. "See if Rose can run a profile search on young girls between the ages of eighteen and twenty five with similar features. Both of these girls look so alike they could be sisters." I tell Matthews as I stare at the photos.

"There is one interesting thing."

"What's that?" I ask as I drag my eyes up to meet his.

"They're both adopted." Matthews says as he drops another folder at me.

I open the folder and scan the documents. "Both closed adoptions, but the file indicates they were.......shit. Both of their mothers were rape victims?"

"According to the court documents, both mothers were kidnapped and raped by the same man. The father is named as 'unknown' in the documents, but it appears they were both victims of the same man. Brockman's birth mother died during childbirth from her injuries and Fishman's birth mother committed suicide three days after she gave birth. Rose is already running a search for any other's that might fall into these parameters. Since the records are sealed, it's going to take an act of God to get a judge to open them. We'll have to get both families to consent before we can do anything, and if only one refuses to allow it then we are shit out of luck."

I stand to leave and head home after looking at my watch, one thirty. "Shit man, my shift starts in five hours. See if I can get copies of these files and I'll check in tomorrow. Sleep is calling my name."

Chapter 4
Sydney

The alarm goes off way too early, blaring in my ears. As I peel my eyes open and squint from the sun shining in through the blinds, I realize I managed to not have a nightmare last night. I feel rested and refreshed. But it's Saturday and I wonder why in the hell my alarm was set anyway. I guess in my exhaustion, I forgot to turn it off last night before falling into bed.

I kick off the covers and sit up, slinging my legs over the side of the bed. I stumble into the bathroom and see a different face than I did yesterday morning. My eyes are brighter and the dark circles under them faded. Amazing what a good night's sleep will do. I wash my face and brush my teeth. Not sure why I brush my teeth, since I haven't even had coffee yet, but I do it out of habit I guess.

After throwing on some yoga pants and a t-shirt, I make my way to the kitchen for that coffee. As it brews, I scroll through messages on my phone that I apparently missed last night.

Nothing interesting there, but I have one voice mail from a number I don't recognize. My finger hovers over the 'play' button, but I decide to wait. It's my day off and I won't let work interrupt my morning cup of liquid caffeine. I head out to my patio and sink down onto the chaise lounge and sip my coffee quietly while listening to the sounds of the city that never sleeps. Horns honking, cars zipping by and people milling about. I'm on the top floor out of fourteen floors of my building, so I am far enough up to have a decent view, but not far enough to drown out the city sounds.

After a few minutes of quiet time and a feeble attempt at waking up, my phone rings. As I look at the caller ID I see it's the same number that left me a message last night. I debate letting it to go voicemail, but since they're calling again it must be important. As I slide the answer button, I suddenly feel like I'm making a mistake answering the phone.

"Doctor DeCarlo." I answer, my voice still sounding sleepy.

"Sydney, this is Chuck Matthews with the NYPD, am I catching you at a bad time?" Does my voice really sound that bad? "No Chuck, what can I help you with?"

"The NYPD and the FBI need your help on a case. I know it's the weekend, but time is of the essence. Can you come down to the station and take a look at our files and see what you think?"

I shiver in my chair. Has to be another missing girl case, because that's the only time they call on me. Its times like this I second guess my choice of profession. "What's the case?"

"The daughter of a high profile bank CFO washed up on the Hudson and the similarities are......astonishing. I'd rather go over the details in person. Can you help?" He asks.

After thinking for just a few seconds, I decide that....yes, I need to help. If my experience can help one girl, then it's worth it."

"Sure, give me an hour or so and I'll be down."

"Thanks. See you then." He says as he disconnects the call.

Great, there goes my weekend. But, as I said earlier if I can help one girl, then it makes it worthwhile.

After taking a shower, I throw on jeans, a t-shirt and my Chucks. Yes, I know this is not professional, but it's Saturday and I figure I'm going to be there for a while, so I might as well be comfortable.

I catch a cab down to NYPD HQ and dodge the traffic trying to cross the street. It's a little cool today, so I pop the collar of my jacket up over my ears and enter the crowd of people crossing Lafayette Street. As I push the door open, a gust of wind blows through and almost knocks me down. As I sway to my right, I'm steadied by.....him. The man from the bar last night.

He towers above me and as I look up, I see him smiling. His eyes light up and his lips curve up into a sexy smirk. And what is that in his eyes? Recognition? I shake my head, no. Surely he doesn't remember me.

"I'm sorry, wind just about blew me over." I say as I straighten my jacket collar and try to compose myself.

"Well, you don't weigh but a buck fifty, so any gust of wind could blow you over." He says in a gravely, husky voice.

Embarrassed, I sneak under his arm that is now holding the door open and make my way to the reception desk. I know that was rude, but he totally threw me off guard. "Doctor Sydney DeCarlo here to see Chuck Matthews." I tell the older lady behind the counter.

"Have a seat, Doctor. I'll let him know you're here." She says.

I take a seat in the lobby and pull out my phone and call Les, letting her know who I just literally bumped in to.

"No way!" She squeals in to the phone. "Rock on girl!!"

"No no, Les. There will be no rocking on." I say as I scan the room. "He's nowhere to be found, so even if I wanted to 'rock on' with the man, he's long gone."

"Oh come on, Syd. He was hot! Oh, and what are you doing down at police HQ?"

"I got a call this morning from Chief Matthews. Something about a case they need help with.

And the guy from the bar is a cop, so it's no surprise I'd see him, I think."

"Oh no, not again. Another missing girl?"

"I think so, but don't know the details yet. That's typically why they call me. I'm seriously starting to re-think my career. I wonder if Starbucks is hiring baristas." I say quietly.

"I hear ya girl. Well, keep me posted. And if you see him again......"

"Stop it Les. I don't expect to see him again." I chuckle in to the phone.

"Doctor DeCarlo?" I hear the receptionist call my name.

"Gotta run Les. I'll call you later." And I end the call without saying goodbye.

I make my way towards the door where there is a uniformed officer standing there. "Doctor DeCarlo?"

"Yes, that's me."

"Follow me please." He says as he turns down a long hallway. The walls are cinder block and cold, much different than the warm and comfortable lobby area. I walk behind him, his night stick clinking against his handcuffs. That's the only noise I hear except our feet. We reach a metal door and the officer knocks once, before opening the door ushering me inside.

"Sydney, thank you for coming in." Chief Matthews stands and circles his desk, taking my hand.

"You're welcome, Chuck. What can I do to help you in this investigation?" I ask as I take the seat in front of his desk.

Chief Matthews is an older man, a little round in the belly. Thinning, grey hair and thin wired glasses. He's been on the force for probably twenty years or more, so we've known each other forever. He tries to keep it professional, but after so many years I'm comfortable around him. Comfortable enough to call him by his first name. The only thing that makes me nervous is the fact that he and my father used to be friends back in Chicago. I try to not let that get to me and keep our visits professional, but sometimes that can be difficult.

"Ah, Sydney." He says as he sits down. He shuffles some files and papers around on his desk before sliding a manila folder towards me. He nods towards the file and I slowly grasp it within my fingers. I look at his eyes, and they are full of worry. Whether it's worry for me or for the case, I can't be sure. He knows my past, thoroughly. Which I guess is why he continues to call on me for these cases.

I thumb through the documents one by one. Young women, probably eighteen, nineteen.

Dark hair and dark eyes....I suck in a breath. They look like.....me. "Sydney, as you can see by the photos of the girls....." He drifts off.

I know I must look like a deer caught in headlights, because he stops talking. I freeze momentarily just staring at the photos of these two girls. I close the file and stand up. "I don't know if I can do this Chuck."

I move towards the door. "Sydney, please. Hear me out on this one. I know.....I know these girls look...."

"Like me, Chuck. THEY LOOK LIKE ME!" I scream at him, my hands shaking and my voice unsteady.

Chief Matthews comes around his desk and stands next to me, placing his hand on my shoulder. "Sydney, we need your help on this case. The details are so.....so, shit how do I say this?"

"Similar? Creepy?" I answer with a bit of sarcasm in my voice.

"Yes. Which is why we need your expertise in this case."

About that time a knock on the metal door causes me to jump out of my skin. I'm thankful for the distraction, because my mind was about to go somewhere it doesn't need to go right now.

Chuck is right, they need me on this case and I need to wrap my head around it all in order to help him.

The door opens and HE walks in. All six feet, or so, of man. Our eyes meet and his lips quirk up in a half grin. His eyes appear confused this time. "Gabe, glad you're here. This is Doctor Sydney DeCarlo, the FBI profiler I told you about."

"Well, I'm not an official 'profiler' Chuck, and I'm not 'officially' with the FBI." I smile back at him. He has always thought I should have joined the FBI and not gone in to private practice, so he jokes with me all the time.

"A mere technicality, Sydney." He grins.

Gabe steps forward and holds out his hand in a friendly greeting. I take it and squeeze as hard as I can. Why? I have no idea, but he smiles and then lets my hand go. "So you're the famous Doctor DeCarlo?" He asks as his eyes travel over me.

"Yes, though nowhere near famous, Detective......"

"Torres, Gabriel Torres. The pleasure is all mine." He says and my eyes stay locked on his.

His eyes are a rich chocolate brown that appear to be hypnotising me. His face is tan from the sun, his jaw chiselled and a bit scruffy, like he neglected to shave this morning. My fingers are tingling from our handshake and the hairs stand up on the back of my neck.

Chuck just stands behind his desk, smirking before he clears his throat. The sound jolts us out of our staring contest. "Please, have a seat." He says as he sits behind his desk.

I sit down, thankful as my legs were starting to tremble. I have to remember I'm a professional and as gorgeous as the good detective may be, this is business and I never mix business and pleasure. I'm sure I'll have to keep telling myself this.

"Okay..." Chief Matthews starts to speak. "As you can see, we have two young woman, very similar in features, dark hair and dark eyes are the most common features. Both are about five feet four inches and slender build, athletic. One was a runaway and the other we aren't sure. He slides the photos of one of the girls towards me and Gabe and I both lean in at the same time, his knee brushing against mine. Gosh, I need to get my head straight or I will be no good to this investigation. Gabe senses my discomfort and backs up, but just a little.

I spread the photos of the girl across the desk. "This is Samantha Brockwood, the first victim that we know of. Her body washed up on the shore of the Hudson a month ago."

"A month ago?" I ask, trying to confirm the dates.

"Yes, exactly one month ago, on September 12th, which was a Friday. Some joggers saw her body floating in the river."

I scan the photos, taking it all in. Then he slides the photos of the second victim.

"This is Sophia Fishman, the second girl. She washed up on the banks of the East River, found by tourists, yesterday.

I look back and forth between the photos. Both are very pretty with dark hair. Samantha's is curly, while Sophia's is straight. They both have high cheekbones and creamy skin, at least from what I can tell by these photos. "Are they related?" I ask, without looking up from the pictures.

No one answers right away, so I peer up at Chuck who is glaring at Gabe. "What? What is it?"

Chuck leans back in his chair, crossing his arms over his chest. I can tell he's fighting with what he's about to tell me, but my eyes stay on his. "Both girls were adopted and the files are closed. But we do know they had the same father. Their mothers were rape victims and both died shortly after delivery." He says with a straight face. "We believe both women were raped by the same man."

I'm not sure how to process this information, but I try and also keep a straight face. As the realization hits me, I know this is the case that is going to blow my past right out of the water.

Taking a deep breath and leaning back in my chair, I ask the ultimate question. "How were they killed?"

Chuck looks at Gabe and Gabe looks at me. "Why do you keep looking at me like that? If you want my help, I need to know all the gory details." I stare back at Chuck, trying to ignore the heated stare of Gabe.

"They were both raped, multiple times. Once he got his fill of that, he strangled them with barbed wire."

I suck in a breath and my fingers unconsciously travel to the nape of my neck and the small scar that still remains. My fingertips brush the puckered skin and I immediately feel a chill in the air. "Sydney, are you all right?" I hear Gabe to my left, his hand brushing my shoulder.

I can't answer him though. All of those memories of 'that night' come rushing back to me in an instant. My skin gets clammy and my muscles tense up. My mouth has stopped working and all I can do is retreat. I can still hear Gabe and Chuck talking, but I can no longer understand what they're saying.

The smell of chloroform rolls across my nose again, and the piercing of metal on skin, MY skin, causes me to scream in pain. NO!!

"Sydney!" I hear a woman's voice. "Doctor DeCarlo? It's Dana Proffit. Sydney, can you hear me?"

I squirm and realize I'm on the floor, something under my head and a woman above me, shaking something under my nose. "No, no no!! Get that away from me!" I scream. She leans back on her ankles, but doesn't get up. As I shake off the smell and regain my focus, I see I'm still in Chuck's office, but there's a crowd around me and looks of sympathy are gracing the faces of everyone in the room, except the woman that sits above me. Hers is of concern, not sympathy.

Oh God, I've done it again. It's been three years since I've had a panic attack and based on the looks of the people around me, it was a doozy. I try and sit up, strong hands press against my shoulders as I rise up. I turn to look behind me and it's Gabe, sitting on the floor behind me. He's strong and steady, his warmth cradling my shivering body. "Grab her a blanket, Chuck. I think she may be in shock. Gabe we need to lay her back down." The woman says to him.

"No, I'm okay. I'm sorry." I say as my hands instinctively cover my face indicating the start of the sobbing. It always comes after one of these attacks, no matter how hard I fight it. A heavy blanket covers my legs as Gabe stands up, the loss of warmth immediate.

"Can you guys give us a few minutes?" The woman asks and the room immediately clears.

Now, it's just me and this woman, whom I don't know and is now sitting next to me on the floor.

"Sydney, my name is Dana Proffit, I'm the NYPD Psychologist. Can you tell me what happened?"

I shake my head, because I don't want to tell her. Right now, I want Leslie. She's the only one that knows my past and the hell I went through. She's brought me through so many of these panic attacks and as far as I know, she is the only one that can help now.

"I am so embarrassed, I'm sorry. I'm fine now, thank you." I say as I move to stand up. She doesn't try to stop me, and allows me to climb to my feet. I brush off the invisible dirt that now covers me and move to fold up the blanket that Chuck brought in.

"Sydney, you had an anxiety attack. Can you tell me what that was about?" Dana continues.

"No. I mean, yes, I can tell you. But I won't. It's.....it's personal and I have my own shrink to talk to. I'll call her this afternoon. Thank you for your help, but I'm good."

I cringe at my words calling Leslie a shrink, because that is what I am too. I chuckle inside at the remark, a sign that I'll pull through this attack like I have all of the others.

"Okay, but promise me you'll call her today. And feel free to come and see me any time." She says as she moves to the door. As she opens it, Gabe and Chuck come marching back in, concern written across their faces.

"Are you all right, Syd?" Chuck asks as he steps beside me.

"Yes, I'm sorry. I........" and I drift off. "I guess I need to enlighten you a bit, if I'm going to continue to assist on this case." I say as I sit down in my chair. "Please, guys. Sit."

"Sydney, you don't have to do this. I'm aware of your....situation. It isn't necessary to air your dirty laundry right now." Chuck says.

"Dirty laundry? You act like my sick and twisted past is something I did on purpose! Thanks for the support Chuck, you of all people were the one that I believed wouldn't judge me. You guys can solve this shit on your own!" And I stand and move towards the door, but before I exit I look back. "If you think you can solve this case on your own, you are sorely mistaken. But I will not be judged for my 'dirty laundry'. You know as well as I do, that my 'dirty laundry' was your best friend. You can go right to hell, Chuck." I fail to mention that his best friend was my father, because Gabe sure as hell doesn't need to know that.

I slam the door behind me and march down the cold, dark hallway shaking my head. "That asshole. He knows damn well what I went through and he's calling ME to the carpet? Well he can fuck the hell off."

"Sydney, wait!"

Gabe.

I keep walking, but I hear him coming up behind me quickly. He grabs my arm, effectively halting my steps. "What the hell happened back there?"

"Ask your friend, the good Chief." I say as I try to turn back towards the door.

"Would you wait a second? I don't want to hear what Chief Matthews says, I want to hear what you have to say. Tell me, what's going on?"

"Listen, I appreciate your concern, but this is personal. I have....a past, one that isn't pretty and one that I refuse to discuss with a perfect stranger. And I would appreciate it if you would let me go, I need to get out of here." I say and he lets my arm go.

"Have lunch with me. We can hit the deli around the corner and talk, get to know each other.

Then I won't be a perfect stranger anymore."

Yeah, you'll just be a perfect distraction.

"Fine, we can have lunch. But don't expect me to divulge any of my secrets." I tell him as I march towards the door, feeling just a bit better about all of this shit. I make a silent pact to myself to call Leslie later, because if I continue on this investigation, I'm going to need her a lot.

Chapter 5
Gabe

I'm not sure what to make of this, but I'm going to run with it. I get a distinct impression that she can help crack this case wide open, but I fear for her sanity. Chuck refused to tell me what their little altercation was about, so I decided to find out for myself. I grabbed the files off of his desk and took off after Sydney.

Sydney DeCarlo. DOCTOR Sydney DeCarlo. Wow, I had no idea when I spotted her at Blazer's last night that she was a doctor. She's beautiful and apparently damaged, so I may be making a huge mistake by asking her to lunch, but I find myself wanting to get closer. To get to know her, the woman. Though, I expect internally she'll be ripping me apart with her psychological bullshit. I'm not perfect by any means, but I know a beautiful and intriguing woman when I see one. And her eyes, yes. Those eyes I feel hold many secrets and I plan to dig deep to find them out. She's got this natural, wholesome beauty about her. Almost like innocence lost, and I pray that isn't the case. After her episode in Chuck's office, I know there is more to Doctor Sydney DeCarlo then she's making out to be. And I also plan to find out her connection to Chuck Matthews, Chief of the NYPD.

I follow her out the door onto the blustery New York streets. It's lunch time in the city, so the streets are full of taxi's and people on foot, rushing to get a quick bite to eat before heading back to the grindstone. That's one thing I love about this city, it never sleeps.

My eyes immediately travel to her backside and I feel my dick jump. Easy Gabe, this is not a pick up session. You're just getting to know her, try not to dry hump her as soon as you sit down.

I get my arousal in check and follow her to the corner. The wind blows her brown locks across her face, her dainty hands tuck the errant strands behind her ear as we wait to cross the street.

She's not paying me any attention, and I find that...shit, Gabe, get your mind out of the gutter.

It's lunch with a colleague. The light turns green and we join the crowd crossing the street and turn left towards the deli. As we approach the door, I see there is no line which is unusual for this time of day. I don't argue with it and we make our way to the counter.

"I'll have a turkey on wheat bread, light mayo and extra tomato." She orders. "Oh and a diet Coke." I start to wonder why she needs diet *anything* but I shake off those thoughts. I order the Rueben and we seek out a table in the back. Most people like to sit near the window and watch the craziness that is New York City. But being a cop, I prefer to hide myself from it as much as I can.

We sit down and stare at each other, the silence deafening. She smirks at me, like she's waiting on me to start grilling her, which I really want to do. But I have no plans to scare her off, especially since we really need her on this case. I just wonder what happened in her life to qualify her as an expert in these types of cases. Chuck says he's used her before as well as the FBI, but she's in private practice, I believe. I decide to just make friendly conversation. As she gets more comfortable with me, maybe she'll let her guard down.

"So, what brought you to New York?" I start out with the cheesy one liner for lack of anything better to ask.

"Work."

Wow, she's really going to make this hard on me.

"Private practice?" I ask.

She nods, not answering my questions.

"Where did you go to school?" Great, now I really sound lame.

"The University of Illinois, then I interned at Northwestern."

"Ahh, a Chicago girl. No wonder the wind didn't bother you outside."

She smiles at that, and boy is it a beautiful smile. Perfect full lips, white teeth with just a small gap between the top two. But those eyes, they light up when she smiles. I have to make sure I make her smile more often.

"No, I'm used to it. I grew up in Lincoln Park and decided to stay close to home for school....." She says as she looks down at her hands, which are balled up on her lap. I get the feeling she wants to tell me more, but she refrains and changes the subject to me. "Where are you from?" She asks.

"Born and raised in Brooklyn. Papi was a cop and mama stayed at home." I see the interest in her eyes, so I continue. "Mama raised three boys and one girl while Papi worked double shifts to keep food on the table." I know she can now see sadness in my eyes as I remember when Mama got sick. I was seventeen, and I'm the oldest. With Papi working, I ended up being the one to raise my siblings after she died. Not a job for a seventeen year old boy, but I did what I had to do. I debate briefly if I should tell her this, but I decide it's too much information right now.

"So you're a true New Yorker." She says in her Midwestern accent, attempting to sound like a New Yorker. I chuckle at her attempt, because no one can fake a New York accent. Well, lots of people try but very few succeed.

"Yeah, never lived anywhere else. Never wanted to. The Big Apple is inside me and this is home." I say, smiling at her.

The waitress brings our sandwiches and I watch her take a bite. She even makes eating a sandwich look sexy. I know she doesn't mean to, but she exudes sexy. Her personality is so nonchalant that I don't believe she even realizes how beautiful she is. I take a bite of my sandwich and freeze with a mouthful as her tongue sneaks out to lick a drop of mayo away. Oh good grief, I really need to get a grip, in more ways than one.

"What made you decide to be a psychologist?" I ask, then watch her face fall slowly. I can tell I've hit a nerve, but I keep a stoic face.

"Umm, I knew.....a girl growing up that went through a.....a traumatic.....ummmm, experience and.....well, she had someone that helped her through it....and I wanted.....I don't know. I wanted to help people in the same way." She stutters through her answer as she sets her sandwich down on the plate. Her fingers push her chips around, but she doesn't pick one up. She looks lost all of a sudden, and I figure it's time for a conversation change.

"So, not married?" I ask as I glance at her left hand and notice her ring finger is bare.

She jerks her head up and glares at me. "No, not married and no kids. I have one older brother and one older sister. Both of them, including my mother, still live in Lincoln Park.

There, is that all you want to know? Because frankly I'm tired of the inquisition." She wipes her mouth with her napkin and stands up. "Look, thank you for lunch but I really need to get home and go through these files. I'll be in touch." And she turns and leaves.

I'm left sitting there with my sandwich in my hands and my lower jaw resting on my chest.

What in the hell just happened here? Things were quiet and then....bam! I guess I crossed the line at asking if she was married. Something is broken in her and I plan to do my best to find out what that is. Whatever IT is, could hinder this investigation and I can't have that. I resign myself to keep a close eye on her and if I feel like she's in too deep, she's gone.

Grabbing my cell I hit the speed dial for Chuck. "Chief Matthews."

"Chuck, its Gabe. Just had an.....interesting lunch with Doctor Sydney DeCarlo.

She's.....um, how do I say this?"

"Unstable?"

"No, not unstable. Guarded? Like she's hiding something. What happened between you two at the office? If she's going to assist in this investigation, I need to know what's going on."

"Look Gabe, if Sydney wants to tell you then that is up to her, but it's not my place to....."

"DAMN IT CHUCK!" I scream in the phone as I slam my fist on the table. Everyone turns to look at me, so I lower my voice.

"Chuck, if she's going to assist in this, I need to know what her weaknesses are. She can hinder this investigation if she flips out again like she did in your office."

"We'll keep Dana close in case that happens. Her secrets are not mine to divulge, Gabe. You have to respect that. Would you want me spilling your secrets to a total stranger?"

"I don't have any secrets, Chuck. You know that, so think of something else."

Silence fills the other side of the phone and I wonder if he hung up on me.

"Look, she has.....a past. A very.....shit, just let it go Gabe. If she wants to tell you, then that is her decision."

Instead of waiting on him to hang up on me, I disconnect the call and place my phone on the table, probably a little heavier and louder than needed. I start to wonder if I can find out her secrets on my own, with a little help from Greyson down in archives. But this is New York.

Whatever happened must have happened in Chicago, damn it. I'll just have to keep pushing her, get her to trust me. Then maybe she'll clue me in, because if she can't get a grip on whatever happened to her, then this investigation will go straight down the toilet.

Chapter 6
Sydney

What in the hell is wrong with me? Never do I snap like that! But he just kept pushing and pushing. Shaking my head I realize, no he wasn't. He was just making conversation, but if I don't get these emotions in check, I'm going to fuck up this whole investigation. I grab my phone and call Leslie immediately after walking out of the deli.

"Hey, it's Syd. Can you meet me at La Cafe? I need coffee, and an ear."

"You okay Syd? You sound funny. Yes, I'll be there in fifteen."

"Yep, see you then."

I slide the phone back in my hipster bag that is draped across my body. I dare not carry a regular shoulder bag in NYC, because someone will run past and yank it off of me. After the day I've had, I might shoot someone. Speaking of, I'd better make sure my .45 is with me from here on out. Once this rapist gets word that I'm assisting in the investigation, I may become a target. Or, at least I was last time I got involved. Thankfully, the last guy missed his mark, by a mile.

But still, one can never been too prepared in New York.

October in New York is nice. Typically stays in the fifty degree range, but this wind is out of control, even for a girl from Chicago. I head into the wind and make my way to La Cafe, my favorite coffee shop. I grab a hot mocha and find a table in the back, but with a view of the door so I can see Leslie come in. And like clockwork, exactly fifteen minutes after our phone call, she comes walking in. She stops just inside the door and I wave her down. Without ordering a drink she marches back to me and sits down, her eyes glued to mine. She's in doctor mode right now, not friend mode.

"What is it Sydney? Is it the case you got called on?" She asks, not making casual conversation.

"I had an anxiety attack in Chief Matthews' office. This one wasn't pretty either, apparently I blacked out and when the police shrink stuck the smelling salts under my nose, I flipped out."

"Jesus, Syd. Why didn't you call me earlier?"

"Because I thought I was fine. But get this.....that guy from Blazer's last night? The one I ran into at HQ?" Leslie nods her head.

"Well, he's a detective with NYPD and he's in charge of this case."

She smiles, but I don't return the smile.

"Anyway, after my little 'escapade', I tried to do the mature thing and march my way out of Chief Matthews' office, but Gabe followed me out."

"Gabe?"

"Yeah, Detective Gabe Torres."

"Okay, so what happened?"

"He asked me to lunch." I say while looking down at my hands. I tend to twist my fingers when I get uneasy. Leslie knows this, so I look up to see her staring at my hands too.

"So, what's wrong with lunch?"

"He started asking questions. Personal questions that I'm not prepared to answer."

"Sydney, your business is your own. You don't have to tell anyone anything you don't want to, even me. But I'll kick your ass if you don't tell me what's really bothering you."

"It's this case, Leslie. The similarities are......frightening. I can't get into details and you know why, but let's just say I feel like my father is alive and well."

"Shit, really? Like a copycat killer or something?"

I just look at her, because I don't believe this is a copycat. I believe my father is really alive and has started torturing and raping young girls again. I know it's crazy, because I put the bullet in his head myself. I saw the blood splatter against the cold, cinder block wall of the basement he held me in. I can still hear the thunk of his body hitting the concrete floor. I can still smell the......

"Sydney? You all right?"

I focus on my friend and realize I've zoned out once again. "Yeah, this case....it's got me creeped out a bit."

"Can you tell me about it?"

"Not much to tell, and since it's an ongoing investigation I think I need to hold my tongue for a bit. So far it hasn't hit the press yet, but I fear for the panic when it does."

"Shit. Well, as your doctor you can tell me anything. I'm bound by......"

"I know, Les. So am I, remember? I may be a mess right now, but I'm still a doctor and I have to keep my wits about me. If

I freak out again like that at the station and I'm done. I think Gabe already wants me off the case."

"I think he wants in your panties."

I spew my mocha all over the table, even managing to get it all over Leslie. She grabs a napkin while glaring at me through squinty eyes.

"Damn it, I'm sorry." I say as, I too, grab some napkins and assist in wiping up my mess.

"Its fine, Syd. I didn't like these pants much anyway." She laughs.

"Yes you do, they're your favorite. So tell me, did Joe come home last night?"

"Ahh, classic change of subject Syd. And yes, he did. But I ignored him and that nasty perfume all evening. He slept in the guest room and I made sure to make plenty of noise when I woke up. He grumbled something about going to the gym and he left. Haven't seen him since. I plan to give him the unfortunate news soon."

"Which news is that?"

"The news that he's moving out. I can't take it anymore, so he's got to go."

"I'm sorry, Leslie. He's......"

"Don't Syd. It's been over for a while, I just need to get it over with."

"Well, I'm here if you need me. You can stay with me while he packs up."

"Oh hell no, you think I'm going to leave him alone in there to clean me out? Fuck that, I'll be hovering over him every step of the way. Hell, I may even pack his shit for him and toss it in the hallway."

I chuckle at that, because Leslie would do it and not care if anything broke in the process.

"Now, enough about me. What's got you so anxious, Syd? You called me down here for a reason, so let's talk."

I sigh, not sure I can get into the gritty details about this case. But she is a doctor and if I don't force someone to remind me that my father is dead, then.........

"I can only tell you the basics. Two young girls found dead. One washed up on the banks of the East River, the other in the Hudson exactly one month apart. Both around eighteen, nineteen years old. Raped and strangled." I leave out the barbed wire, because that will give too much away.

"Both were very pretty........but they look like.......me." I say as I look down. Leslie has heard so much over her years of counseling that nothing can shock her, but I hear her suck in a breath.

"Sydney, it's a coincidence. You, as a professional, have to know this. But that's why your father has come screaming back in to your conscience, right?"

My father's victims were all dark haired like me. My dad is Italian, so I take after him.

"Sydney? Stay with me girl."

"I'm here." I say as I smile. "I wish I could tell you more, but until I've gone through everything, that's all I can say."

Leslie takes my hand across the table. "I understand, but I'm here. Do you need something to help you sleep?"

"You gave me something yesterday, but I haven't filled it. I think I'll be fine. I managed to not have any nightmares last night, so I think I'm good."

"Well, you call me if you do. And fill that prescription, just in case. You don't have to take it, but it's better to be prepared than not."

"I'll be fine, but I'll fill it." She cocks her head at me, "I promise."

"So, tell me about Detective Torres."

"Not much to tell, native New Yorker - Brooklyn. Father was a cop and his mom died when he was seventeen."

"Wow, really getting to know each other eh?"

"I think it was his way to get me to open up. I guess he thought if he talked about his past, I'd talk about mine. But instead, I barged out after accusing him of an inquisition and ended up looking like an idiot." I say as I smack my forehead. "Gosh, what's wrong with me? Every time I get called in on a case like this, I totally freak. It doesn't help that he's rock star gorgeous either.

I was okay talking about school, but as soon as he asked about my family, I lost it."

"Sydney, your teenage years were very traumatic. Even though it's been twenty years, that never goes away. You've learned over the years how to deal with it the best way you can, but life is full of triggers and with being in the line of work you're in, well. Those triggers come more often."

"I know, speaking of careers, I wonder if they're hiring here." I say while glancing around the shop looking for a 'Help Wanted' sign.

"You are not changing careers, girl. You are too good at what you do. You have a gift my friend, a true gift. You'll bring down this asshole soon enough and then you can move on."

"We'll see I guess. Listen, thanks for coming down, but I need to get back to the station and get busy trying to solve this mystery. I barged out without the file I need, so I need to get back and do the walk of shame."

"There is no shame in what happened to you. I know this and you know it too. But call me when you get home and let me know how you are. I can squeeze you in next week if you need to come to the office."

"Thanks." I say as I stand and pull her into a hug. She grabs her purse and heads out the door while I order another mocha to go.

Once I have my warm drink in my hands, I too enter the busy sidewalk heading back towards HQ and Chief Matthews. As I walk, I think back to earlier and I get even angrier. How dare he accuse me of airing 'dirty laundry'? He knew my father, he knows what he did and he blames me? He's no better than my mom and brother. The bastard. If he thinks he is going to throw my past in my face, he's got another thing coming. I think this is good.

Anger. It's better to be angry than embarrassed. Hopefully Gabe won't be there and I can give good old Chuck a piece of my mind.

As I walk along, someone slams into me, which is not unusual in this city. But my scorching hot mocha goes flying and lands in a splatter on the sidewalk. I turn back to see who it was and to maybe give them a piece of my mind, but all I see is a young boy marching with his head down and his hands in his pockets. "Asshole." I murmur under my breath. I pick up the cup and toss it in to a trash can and keep walking.

Once I arrive at HQ I stop at the door and take a deep breath. I pull the door open and step in, the door slamming behind me in the wind. "Is Chief Matthews in?" I ask the girl behind the counter, who is not the same girl from earlier, thank goodness.

"Your name?"

"Doctor Sydney DeCarlo."

She picks up her phone and calls him, then hangs up and motions towards the door. As I reach it, I hear the electronic lock click and I tug the steel door open. "Third door on the right."

She says as the door closes behind me. I don't mention that I already know where I'm going.

I tap on the door and peek through the crack, "Chief?"

"Come on in Sydney. I'm glad you came back, you forgot your folder."

"I know. That's why I'm here." I say as I take the folder from his hand.

"Sit Sydney, we need to talk."

"No Chief, I've talked enough today. I want to go home and dig into this file and see what I can come up with."

"I'm sorry."

"What?" I reply in surprise.

"I said 'I'm sorry'." He repeats. "I put you on the spot earlier and I was wrong. I shouldn't have done that. I know what you went through, hell - I was there. I shouldn't have made a mockery of it and I'm sorry. It won't happen again."

Wow, just wow. Now, maybe he will apologize for making an ass of me in front of Gabe.

Course, then again, I made an ass out of myself in front of Gabe, so I'm no better. I just hate being put on the spot. I have a career of putting people on the spot, not the other way around.

I sit down in the chair across from his desk, laying the case file in my lap. My fingers pick at the edges as Chuck stares at me. He leans forward, setting his elbows on the desk and takes a deep breath. Great, here comes the speech.

"Sydney, if this case is too much for you......"

"No, Chuck. It isn't. I've already spoken to Leslie and she'll be there for me if I need her. It will be tough, because the details........"

"I know. The girls' appearance, their deaths....I know. And I know what you're thinking too."

"Oh really? Tell me Chuck, what am I thinking?" I ask as I lean forward cocking my head to one side.

"Sydney, your father is dead....."

"Hold up one second, Chuck. Don't you think I know this? I. Pulled. The. Trigger. I killed the bastard. He raped me, beat me to within an inch of my life and then strangled me with barbed wire. In our scuffle, I knocked his gun free and grabbed it. I put a bullet in his head at point blank range. I know he's dead, Chuck. I was there."

"Sydney, that isn't what I meant."

"Well, what pray tell did you mean then Chuck?"

His eyes drift up towards the door and I know immediately someone is standing in the threshold. "Damn it Gabe, can't you knock?"

Shit.

I drop my head in to my hands and hold still for what feels like hours. Guess I don't need to apologize for being an ass, as I have a feeling Gabe is about to beat me to the punch.

"Jesus, Syd. Why didn't........"

"No, Gabe. Let it go. You know more now than I ever intended for you to know. It's the past and......" I drift off again, because I don't know what else to say. Gabe now knows why I lost it earlier in this very office, and again at the deli. Damn it. I was hoping to keep my past in the past and not let it interfere with this investigation. Now he's going to be watching me like a hawk.

I shake it off and grab the files on Chuck's desk, fingering the pages and sorting through the photos. I move over to the conference table in the corner and start spreading out the photos.

Chuck and Gabe are still sitting, watching me. I can tell they are wondering what I'm doing, but I keep silent and go about putting the puzzle pieces together. I take the photos of Samantha Brockman and Sophia Fishman and lay them out, side by side in the best order I can see. Both are brunette, similar features and obviously related.

With my hands on my hips, I stand over the table staring. "Chuck, do you have a magnifying glass?" I don't look back at him, but I hear his desk drawer open and close. Within seconds I feel him standing to my right, and another warm body to my left. I don't look up from the photos because I don't want to miss what I think I might be seeing.

"What is it Syd?" I feel his warm breath in my ear, almost intimately. Shivers run up and down my spine, but I brush it off and get back to the task at hand. I know now I am going to struggle through this investigation, for more than one reason.

I take the magnifying glass from Chuck and lean into the photos, my eyes darting back and forth between the two girls. Sophia on the right and Samantha to the left. Both bodies in various states of decomposition and rot, but their features still show. Their hair is matted and clumps of it have been pulled out, leaving bare scalp showing. Samantha has one eye missing, but you can see the deep brown of the right one. Both of Sophia's eyes are closed, so I can't see their color. I scan the puncture wounds from the barbed wire that was tightly wrapped around their necks, severing the carotid artery. They both bled out from their wounds. My eyes scan their chest and the ripped clothing and travel down to their wrists, both bound with barbed wire. I can feel the bile rising in my throat as I remember my past, knowing these girls went through something amazingly similar.

I feel a warm hand press to my lower back and I relax, but only a little. I lean in with the glass to my eye and scan the photo of the first victim, Samantha Brockman. "Tell me about her."

I say, as I peruse the photos one by one.

"Runaway, found on the banks of the East River a month ago. No immediate family that we could locate, though we do know who her birth mother was. She was adopted, but was living in a half-way house." Chuck tells me as I continue scanning the photos. I move over to Sophia Fishman and begin the same process.

"And this one?" I ask, not looking up.

"We have a bit more information on her. She's the daughter of a high profile bank exec, disappeared a few days ago and then washed up on the banks of the Hudson."

"Hmm. Both tossed in the river, eh?"

"Yeah, bodies in similar condition."

My fingers trace the photos when something spots my eye. "Look at this." I say I as go back to the first set of photos and zone in on the same area, the right hip. "Both have a tattoo here." I whisper as I get closer to the pictures.

I take the magnifying glass from him and get closer to the pictures. My body starts shaking as I flash to my own kidnapping where I was strapped down and a tattoo carved in to my skin.

"It's him, Chuck. It has to be."

"Who, Sydney?"

I glare at him with steely eyes, full of anger because I can't believe he questions this. He stares back at me, his eyes full of confusion. "No Sydney, we've been over this. He's dead. You......."

"Look here." I point at the girl's hips. "Numbers. A number one on Samantha and a number two on Sophia, same place. Same font." I hear Chuck suck in a breath and I step back, my hands feeling behind me for a chair.

I sit down, as my legs are weak and if I don't get a grip on this, I'm not going to be worth shit. Gabe sits down next to me and I immediately soften. Not sure what it is about this guy, but he calms me. I don't even know him, but I find myself warming up to him. He's thick and strong, and his manly scent wafts across my nose. I can't do this, I decide. I stand to leave and look back at the two sets of eyes following me. I don't say anything and neither do they, they know.

As I travel down the cold hallway, towards reception I hear a voice behind me. No, don't follow me please. I need...space. I need time to think. I need Leslie, now. I grab my phone from my bag, not acknowledging Gabe behind me. I don't look back and I don't speak. I press the send button to get Leslie on the phone, but she doesn't answer. "Leslie, its Sydney. Call me as soon as you can." And I hang it up, never wavering in my steps towards the exit.

"Syd wait!" Gabe says as his footsteps increase in speed. He's now running behind me, because I too am running. Tears stream down my cheeks and I hit the door, shoving it open and almost falling onto the sidewalk. I gasp for air, struggling to breathe and collapse to my knees, my hands scraping across the concrete. People walk by me without speaking, without assisting.

This is New York and I'm sure they've seen stranger things, and most people don't want to get involved, so they turn a blind eye and pretend they don't see anything. I'm on my hands and knees and I watch the tears dampen the sidewalk, darkening the lighter color of the concrete. My mouth begins to water and I know instantly, I'm about to vomit all over the sidewalk. No, this can't be happening! My stomach heaves and I empty the contents all over the sidewalk, my hands and my bag. People scurry by, trying not to step in the puddle but no one tries to help, and for this I am thankful. Move on along, that's what they all need to do. Nothing to see here.

When I feel I'm done spewing my guts along the sidewalk, I rise up on shaky legs and wipe my mouth with the back of my hand. I take a deep breath and turn towards home, but slam right into a hard body. Gabe. "How long have you been standing there?" I ask, while trying to be nonchalant about the whole thing.

"Long enough. You okay?" He ask, his fingers under my chin tipping my head up.

"I think so. Sorry you had to see that." I say as I tug my chin out of his grip.

"I'm a cop, I've seen people puke before." He says on a chuckle.

"Well, that's typically something I prefer to do in private." And I turn on my heel to head the other direction, even though it's the wrong way.

"Wait, I'll walk you home."

"No, that's okay. I need to be alone." Is the best I can come up with? Because I don't want him knowing where I live.

"I'm not taking 'no' for an answer, Syd. Come on." And he takes my hand, spinning me around. I feel dizzy for a second and he catches me and pulls me in to his body. My cheek crashes against his hard chest and I then realize how much taller he is than me. I feel my knees give out and I start going down. My head starts spinning and the brightness of the day starts to darken a little. I feel strong arms around me and then my feet leave the ground. When I blink my eyes open, I find myself in Gabe's arms being cradled like a baby.

"But first, I need to feed you." He says as he turns and carries me down the sidewalk.

"You already fed me and look how well that turned out." I say as I struggle against him.

"And I can walk!"

"You sure? Because you looked like you were having trouble just standing. Walking might be a problem." He snickers as he keeps walking.

"GABE! PUT ME DOWN!" I scream as I beat my fists against his chest, which I realize right away is a mistake. Now my knuckles hurt.

I shake out the pain and squirm in his arms, but he just tightens his grip. A smirk curls on his lips and he keeps walking, looking straight ahead like I'm not even there. I give up, because I'm too weak to fight him. He stops at the entrance to a pizza place and softly puts me down, waiting to make sure I can stand on my own two feet without falling over.

"You good?" He asks.

"Yeah, thanks. I think." I respond as I move to enter the restaurant. But he jumps in front of me, opening the door like a gentleman. Been a long time since a man has done that for me. I smile at him as I step inside. The smell of garlic overwhelms me and my stomach takes a nose dive again. Ugh, maybe not the best place to go after a monster bout of barfing. But I suck in a deep breath and trudge ahead to the table where a young waitress awaits us. Her eyes smile at Gabe and he ignores it, pulling my chair out for me to sit.

"This place okay?" He asks?

"I think so, though I'll just have a salad. My stomach is still not at a hundred percent." I respond as I pick up the menu. Deciding to stick to my salad, I lay the menu back down and glance around the small eating area and realize I've never been here before. Red and white checked table cloths cover the tables with small red, lit candles. Italian paintings adorn the walls and lots of greenery fill the empty spaces. Cute.

"So, you want to tell me what happened back there?" Gabe asks as he sets his menu down, pressing his fingers together in a steeple.

"Um, no. Not really. It's....personal and....."

"Sydney, or shall I say Doctor DeCarlo.....even people in your profession need to talk sometimes. I'm here if you want to spill your guts....." And he pauses, reflecting on the last thirty minutes or so. "Errrr, if you want to talk." He grins.

"Very funny, Detective......" I pause this time, realizing I don't remember his last name. I'm sure he told me at some point, but my brain is no longer functioning properly.

"Torres, Gabriel Torres." He says as he holds his hand out for a handshake, as if we are just introducing ourselves. I take his large hand in mine and rest my fingers on his palm. Warm, callused and manly.

"Nice to meet you, Detective Torres." I say, finally able to smile.

Chapter 7
Gabe

I wasn't sure what to do when I saw her getting sick all over the sidewalk. I wanted to help her, to comfort her. But I knew she would push me away if I tried. So I stood there like a coward and watched in horror as she heaved and cried. Whatever happened to her in her past has come roaring back to her. This case isn't helping anything either, in fact I think it's what caused it to haunt her. I stood there and wondered exactly what happened to her, but was afraid to ask.

I watch her nurse her salad, almost afraid to eat. I wish she'd eat more, because after what I saw on the sidewalk, she needs to replenish quick. She's so tiny as it is, that she can't afford to lose any weight. In fact, if I have anything to say about it, I plan to plump her up a little.

I mentally shrug my shoulders, because I'm not real sure where that thought came from. I just met this woman, and she has a past, one I'm not completely sure of right now. We eat in companionable silence, the occasional flicker of her lashes as she looks up at me. I'd love to know what she's thinking, but I don't ask. She'll talk when she's ready.

"So how long have you been on the force?" She breaks the silence.

"Twelve years. Started as a beat cop right out of the academy. Moved up to Vice after about four years."

"You must enjoy it."

Great, this conversation is about me and I want to know about her. But I go along figuring if I open up, she will too. Didn't work last time, but maybe this time will be different.

"I guess, it's a lot of work. And I get to carry a gun." I smile as I pat my hip where my Glock sits, waiting patiently to blow the head off of some bad guy. Even though I'm technically off duty, I still carry my piece.

She laughs, and it's a beautiful sound. Husky and sweet, sexy. My dick gently reminds me that he's there, waiting patiently. I drop my napkin in my lap to hide the evidence, and grab another slice of pizza watching her intently. She's beautiful, I'll give her that. If I wasn't a cop I'd kidnap her and keep her to myself, though I'd never hurt her. Long, sleek brown hair, deep brown eyes and a perfect smile, even with the small space between her two front teeth. Creamy skin and tits to die for. Easy Gabe, you can't go there with her. Colleague......remember that.

"What made you decide to be a cop?"

Good, she's talking still. "My dad was a cop and I just followed in his footsteps I guess.

What made you decide to be a Forensic Psychologist?"

Wrong question. She drops her fork and gently wipes her mouth moving to stand. "Excuse me please, I need to use the restroom." And she's gone and I watch her ass sway......shit, stop it!

I need to remember not to ask her about herself, because she clammed up on me the last time I asked. Though now I know that there is a reason behind her avoidance, and I vow to find out everything there is to know about Doctor Sydney DeCarlo. She's mysterious and has some major secrets, secrets that she is fighting to keep hidden. When I overheard her talking to Chuck earlier, my heart sunk into my chest. I know she was kidnapped, raped and almost killed. I know it was her father that did this and that she blew his head off in the end. Good for her, cause if he was still alive I'd kill him myself. Something about this case is rattling her, something that isn't good.

The rape, the barbed wire.....the barbed wire, holy shit. I grab my phone and call Chuck, hoping to get this call out of the way before Sydney gets back.

"Chief Matthews." Good he answers on the first ring.

"It's Torres, Chief. Listen, I need to know what kind of publicity Doctor DeCarlo's story got in Chicago."

"For what reason?" Chief snaps, like he's being over protective of her or something.

"Because, I think we may have a copycat killer on our hands, someone who knows about Sydney's past. The barbed wire, the similar features. Hey, did any of her father's victims wash up anywhere?"

I hear him exhale a deep breath and then silence.

"Only one. Listen, I recently got a file up from the archives and this whole story just blew out of the water."

"What do you mean?"

"Not over the phone, when can you get here?"

"As soon as I'm done with dinner and get Sydney home, I'll be there."

"You're with Sydney?"

"Yeah, why?"

"Shit, don't bring her with you. And don't let on you're coming back here, I'm not sure we can keep her on this investigation after what I found out today. Take her home and get back here as soon as possible."

"Yeah Chief, anything else?"

"Yeah, keep your hands off of her."

"Wow, you really think I'd do that? Come on Chief, I just met her. I would never......."

"Yeah you would, Gabe. I know you and *you* know you. She's just your type, but stay away from her, at least until this case is over. Get her home and get back down here, that's an order."

Chuck barks into the phone.

"Yes sir." I say as I click the off button. Shit, now I have to figure out a way to get Sydney out of here and home safely, cause Chuck will kick my ass if don't. I silently wonder why he's so protective of her all of a sudden.

As I shove my phone back in the holster, Sydney comes back to the table and sits. She leans forward on her elbows and bats her eyelashes at me.

Keep your hands off of her.

Yeah, I will for now. But when this is all over, she's fair game.

"I'm ready to go." She says quietly. I can tell she's been crying by the redness in her eyes and the slight smudge of mascara. But I keep silent and nod for the check. The waitress brings it and a box for the leftover pizza. After it's boxed up and I pay, we head out.

I stroll alongside her, as I don't know where she lives but I'm about to find out.

But she turns to me and stops. "You don't need to walk me home, Gabe. I'm fine and would like to be alone."

"Nuh uh, you aren't walking these streets by yourself."

"Gabe, I've lived here for years. And, I have a Black belt in Sanshou. I know how to defend myself."

Wow, I am totally blown away by this. I don't know a lot about Sanshou, but I know it's a Chinese fighting technique, like kickboxing. "Where did you learn that?"

"There's a good school here in New York, I go once a week. Even teaching a bit now, so I'm not afraid. Plus, I own a gun too." She says as she glances at my Glock.

"Well then, if you insist. But I really don't mind walking you home. I'm enjoying spending time with you." I say this and immediately wish I could take it back, because she just stepped back about three steps.

"I do insist. Thank you for dinner and for carrying me there, but you have a big investigation to get through and I need to be alone. Thank you again." And she turns and leaves me in the dust.

I know I'll see her again at the station, unless Chuck boots her off of the case. I'm actually kind of relieved, because now I can find out what in the hell Chuck is talking about.

"Hey Sydney?" I call out to her.

She stops and turns around as I walk towards her. I pull out one of my business cards and hand it to her. "Will you call or text me when you get home, so I know you made it all right?"

She takes the card and smiles, tucking it in to her pocket. "Sure."

She walks away and I stand there a moment, breathless. Her smile lights up her entire face, I only wish she would smile more. Maybe once we catch this rat bastard that's raping and killing young girls, I'll see more of it.

Once she's out of sight, I turn back towards the station. I pick up my pace and get there as quickly as possible.

Rose is behind the glass window and looking the other way. I tap lightly and she glances up, pressing the button under her desk to unlock the door. Once I get to Chuck's office, I stop and stare at the back of the door. I want to know what this is about, but at the same time I have a feeling it's not going to be good news. I knock quietly, but with purpose.

"It's open!" I hear from the other side.

I step into Chief Matthews' office and take a seat in front of his desk, crossing my ankle over my knee and wait. Wait for what he has to say.

Chief Matthews pauses briefly before beginning to speak.

"I've already pulled Doctor DeCarlo's file." He says as he slides the thick folder to me.

"Chicago PD faxed it over to me today. You should look inside."

I take the folder and slowly open it, revealing pages and pages of incident reports and photos.

As my eyes focus on the photos, I realize it's Sydney. A very young Sydney DeCarlo. "Jesus, how old was she?"

"Thirteen."

"She was just a baby. Damn, no wonder she's so wounded. How does such a young girl survive something like this?"

"Lots of therapy." Chuck grumbles.

"What did you say?"

"Nothing. Look through that tonight at home." He stands to leave. "I've been here since four this morning and it's....." he looks at his watch, "seven. I'm out for the night. Read over all of that tonight and give me your thoughts in the morning. Be back here at nine tomorrow morning."

He grabs his jacket and as he gets to the door, he stops. "Sydney is.......fragile, Gabe. I think once you go through that file, you'll get it. I know you have that protective instinct, but Sydney can take care of herself. I believe we may need to remove her from this investigation, and maybe even put her in protective custody." He nods towards the file. "See you in the morning."

He leaves and I'm left sitting in his office dumbstruck. Protective custody? Surely, that isn't necessary. She seems to be tough as nails, but I guess everyone has a weakness. I flip through the incident reports and documents, knowing I'm going to need to spread these out to get a grip on them. I slide the folder under my arm and kill the light. Guess I have some major reading to do tonight.

As I exit the station onto Lafayette Street, the smell of exhaust and urine assault my senses.

The howling wind from earlier has died down, but it's cooled off. As I move to step into the crosswalk, my phone goes off.

It's Sydney, I'm home. Thanks again for dinner

Good girl, I'm glad to know she is safe and sound. But I ponder for a moment with what to say as a response without sounding over protective. She doesn't seem like the type of woman that wants a man paying homage to her all day and night, she's independent. Or that's what she wants everyone to think.

Thank you for letting me know. Good night.

There, plain and simple. Not condescending or patronizing, just....friendly. I want her to feel comfortable around me, not intimidated. But I also want her to know I'm here if she needs me.

And I have a feeling she is going to need me, sooner rather than later.

After arriving home in Brooklyn an hour later, I toss the folder on the table and grab a beer out of the kitchen. It's been a long day and I have feeling it's going to be a long night. I stand in the kitchen, staring out of the window, but that file is calling my name.

"Who are you, Doctor Sydney DeCarlo?" I ask to an empty room. "And who is this ass hat that's wreaking havoc on the young girls of this city?" Shaking my head, I toss back the rest of my beer and grab another one before tackling this file.

I slide my laptop over beside the file and stare at it for a moment. Google can be your friend, but it can also be a major enemy if you aren't careful. I have to be in the mind-set that not everything you read online is true. I thumb through the folders and glance in each one, deciding which to delve into first. There are three files sitting here, Sydney's file and both files on the current cases.

After another swig of my beer, I grab Syd's file and relax back into the sofa staring at the cover. I need to see this, but not sure I want to. Currently, all I know is that she was kidnapped and raped at the hands of her own father. That alone makes me want to kill someone. How a father can do that to his own child......I shiver at the thought. Thirteen years old and she went through what no one should never have to endure. And now, I plan to do whatever I can to protect her, since her own father failed her.

I flip open the file and scan the pages, looking for anything that might jump out at me.

Nothing. So I start at page one and go over the synopsis page.

Name: Sydney DeCarlo

Date of birth: 11/19/1982

Race: Italian American

Hair: Brown

Eyes: Brown

Mother: Gloria Watkins

Father: Luis DeCarlo

Brother: Franco DeCarlo

Date of birth: 5/23/1979

Sister: Sylvia DeCarlo

Date of birth: 3/9/1977

Hometown: Lincoln Park, Illinois

On July fourth 1995, Sydney DeCarlo left her home in Lincoln Park, IL to walk to a friend's house a few streets over. It was three o'clock in the afternoon. The weather was sunny and warm.

Her friend was having a party to celebrate Independence Day.

Once the sun set and the fireworks were over, Sydney was due back at home. When she didn't arrive, her mother, Gloria

Watkins DeCarlo contacted her friend's parents. Mrs. DeCarlo was informed that Sydney never arrived at their house and had not called.

Immediately, Mrs. DeCarlo set out on foot in the neighborhood along with her other children to look for her. After three hours, Mrs. DeCarlo contacted the Lincoln Park Police and a search party was dispatched.

The search party located a pink tennis shoe belonging to Sydney and foul play was then suspected. The Federal Bureau of Investigations and the Illinois Bureau of Investigations were called to the residence.

A tracking device was installed on the DeCarlo telephone and detectives were placed at the residence. The exterior search continued, but detectives had reason to believe that a possible kidnapping had taken place.

Detectives had reason to believe the incident stemmed from an outside source. The family's financial and social status were investigated. The family was comfortable, but not overly wealthy and it did not appear that any family member had any known enemies.

Approximately seventy-two hours later a call came into dispatch of gunshots fired at an empty house on South Halsted Street in Chicago.

Once officers arrived on the scene they located Sydney DeCarlo naked, unconscious and bleeding profusely from the neck and throat area. Her bare skin exposing bruises, cuts and dried blood. In her right hand was a .22 Calibre Ruger revolver. Her ankles bound to a metal chair laying on its side.

As detectives inspected the area, the body of a man, approximately thirty-five years old was discovered lying on the ground, a single gunshot to his head. EMT's and rescue personnel examined the male body and pronounced him dead at nineteen hundred hours.

Rescue personnel examined Miss DeCarlo and treated her wounds accordingly, quickly loading her into an ambulance.

The Chicago-Cook County Coroner arrived and loaded the male body in to a hearse and transported him to the coroner's office for an autopsy and identification. The entire face and head had been so damaged by the single bullet that visual ID was not possible. The left eye socket and nasal cavity completely shattered.

Jesus, this young girl was subjected to so much that I can't even read anymore. I make my way to the kitchen and grab another beer, enjoying the cold malt as it travels down my parched throat. My mind disappears to the house where this happened and I envision being the one to discover the scene. I've seen some gruesome things in my tenure as a cop and even more so as a detective, but the vision in my head is horrendous. I glance at the clock and realize its ten o'clock and I have to be back at HQ by nine, so I have a little more time to delve into these files.

The crime scene was scoured and the following evidence collected:

Wire cutters

Six rolls of duct tape

Approximately sixty-five feet of barbed wire

Sixteen discharged medical syringes

Twenty four unused syringes

Fourteen bottles of Chloroform

Three blankets - sent to the crime lab

Seven Automotive rags - sent to the crime lab

Two old mattresses

Approximately sixty-five feet of nylon rope

Various pieces of torn clothing - sent to the crime lab

Hair samples - sent to the crime lab

I sit here shaking my head. He tortured her. He beat her and raped her, his own flesh and blood. She was thirteen vulnerable years old. In anger, I throw my beer bottle across the room, the glass shattering against the wall. I stare at the hole now in the sheetrock and that makes me angrier. Suddenly, I have the urge to see what this man looks like, so I can memorize his face. I plan to go to Heaven one day, but in case I end up in Hell - I want to make sure I kill him again.

I shuffle through the stack of photos and come across a photo of Sydney, after the attack.

Her face is swollen and bruised, the skin cracked in places and a zig-zagged, bloody line across her neck. No wonder she freaked out when Chuck mentioned the wire, I probably would have too.

I scan the Medical Report for Sydney and take in all of the information there. Most of it I already knew, but what I find there is startling. She was repeatedly raped and sodomized, semen found everywhere, including her stomach. Good Lord, what did he do to her? Well, I can figure it out but how does a father do that to his own daughter? I'm thankful she shot him, killed him in cold blood. He deserved it.

But then something else catches my eye. In one of the other photos, I see the number four tattooed to her right hip. Fuck, I'm glad he's dead or I would be hunting him down and torturing him. Then something dawns on me. The other girls had also been marked on their hips with a number. Something about these tattoos has me concerned and I wonder if she had hers removed, or if it's still there. Tattoos. Something about tattoos. Could the creep be a tattoo artist? Nah, too easy. These predators don't make investigations easy, so I doubt it. But it's worth checking out.

Then I gather the DNA reports. I lay Sydney's report, Sofia's and Samantha's side by side and stare. Holy shit, can this really be happening?

The nucleotides match in all three reports. How is this possible? Sydney's attack was years ago, Sofia and Samantha more recent, though a month apart. So, the theory of a copycat killer was just thrown out the door. Now we have something bigger.

Chapter 8
Sydney

The sun shining through my blinds draws me out of my slumber. Thankfully, I made it another night without the nightmare. Sad really, when I get excited about a good night's sleep. I stretch and roll over to my side to see what time it is and jump when I see it's almost noon. My head hits the pillow again and I roll to my back and stare at the ceiling. Sunday. Sunday is me day, though my thoughts are far from me. They are with those two young girls that were brutally raped and killed. My body tenses up when I think back to the day that it could have been me.

Should have been me. I wanted to die back then, just to get it to stop. The pain and the humiliation of being tortured. The embarrassment suffered when I wasn't strong enough to stop it.

I know now, that I was strong enough. And I did stop it, but only because I refused to give my father the satisfaction of killing another girl. I saw the opportunity to grab his gun and I took it. I didn't think before I did it, I just did it. And, I knew I wasn't the first, he made sure I knew that. In fact, he branded it in to my skin. I was number four. The first three bodies were never found, that I know of. And if they were, they weren't connected to me at the time. I made sure the authorities knew it afterwards, though. The families of those young girls deserved closure.

My fingers absently trace the thick black number carved in to my skin. I've thought about having it removed, but decided to keep it as a reminder that I am a survivor. That I made it through a grueling experience that no one should have to go through. Ever.

But inside, I kind of envy those girls. They didn't have to go through life living with this nightmare like I have. It follows me everywhere I go. Sure, the memories have faded over time, but the pain is still there. Especially when I'm involved with a man. I've only had a few relationships over the years, because of that very reason. Being intimate is.....scary for me. After having been raped over and over, in more ways than one, it leads to severe intimacy problems.

Leslie has been great, but some things I have to overcome on my own.

That is why I chose this profession. I want to do what I can to prevent any girl, or boy for that matter, from ever having to suffer through what I have. I've managed to avoid explaining the tattoo on my hip for most of my life, and when a man starts getting too close I shove him away. Just so I don't have to spill my history. Hell, any man would run for the hills if they knew what I've been through. And, having to explain the nightmares.....well, that's another situation all together.

I finally kick the covers off and pull myself out of bed. Once in the kitchen I start the coffee and focus on waking up. And then it hits me.

Gabriel Torres.

What is it about that man that gets my blood pumping? I don't even know him, or much about him other than he's a true New Yorker, and a cop. I've never dated a cop and......no, I shake my head. Why am I thinking about this? I have a case to work on and shouldn't be thinking things like this. But it's been so long.......And those eyes. Those lips......stop it!

"Ugh, girl. Get a grip. You need to focus on these young girls that keep washing up, not on your sex life, or lack thereof. There's no time for that right now." I say to myself as I take a tentative sip of my coffee.

I grab the newspaper outside my door and glance around outside. All is quiet here today, which is good. As I open the paper, I almost knock my cup over. Great, the two murdered girls have made the front page. This is not good, as we needed to keep this a secret for a bit while we figure out what's going on. "Must be a leak at the police department." I whisper to myself as I scan the article. At least they've left out the major details and only stated who they are and where their bodies were located. Anything else could totally jeopardize the investigation. We don't need the perp to know we're on to him. But are we on to him? Not yet, I don't think. Not unless Gabe has come up with something.

Deciding I need to get busy, I shower and get dressed to head down to the station. So much for 'me day'. I should have been there earlier, but now is as good a time as any I guess. No one specified what time to be there, hell - they didn't even tell me to come back. But I am, because I plan to do whatever it takes to bring this asshole down, quickly.

My hand hits the door knob and I freeze, suddenly feeling a little nervous and scared. Today could be the day we bring this bastard down and I realize I am no longer safe. I head back to the bedroom and pull the metal box out from under my bed. I slowly open the lid, my fingers toiling with the canvas covering. I wrap my fingers around the S&W 9mm handgun and confirm that it is in fact, loaded. I slide my carry permit out of the envelope and the holster, and head back out into the living room.

Putting the permit in to my wallet, I strap the holster on, slide the gun in and cover it with my jacket. Now, I'm ready to face the world. If someone messes with me, all of those shooting classes will pay off. I can hit a bulls-eye from a hundred feet, so any potential attacker would be messing with the wrong girl. I learned my lesson early in life and I will never be unprepared again.

Heading into the busy New York streets, I head towards the station. It's not as windy today, but I snap the bottom two snaps on my jacket so that the wind doesn't expose my gun. Even though I have a permit to carry it, I don't need to draw attention to that fact, nor do I want to freak out everyone on the streets, seeing some broad with a gun. People draw too many conclusions in this day and age and all I need is a scene with someone thinking I'm a terrorist or something.

Within a few minutes I'm on LaFayette Street gazing at the entrance to NYPD Headquarters.

I realize I'm blocking the sidewalk when some douche bag slams into me, shoving me forward.

"ASSHOLE!" I scream back at him. He doesn't turn around but....wait. That's the same guy that knocked my coffee out of my hand yesterday. Surely......no, it's a big city.....and the chances of running into the same person two days in a row is unlikely, unless you know them personally.

His head is down and his hands are in his pockets, almost like he's trying not to be noticed.

"Well, then don't slam into people for no reason if you don't want to be noticed." I whisper to myself. But then the uneasiness hits me and I rush through the doors in to HQ and slam head on into a hard body. "I'm sorry." I say as I look up. Looking down at me are dark brown eyes and a smirk at the corner of his lips. "Gabe, hi." I say shyly.

"Sydney, are you all right?" He asks softly as he brushes a tendril of hair away from my face.

It's a tender gesture and totally takes me aback. I'm frozen to the spot and all I can do is stare up at him. He doesn't say anything else, but must see something in my eyes that I'm trying desperately not to show. He pulls me in to his arms and wraps his arms around me.

As my body presses up against his, his warmth spreads through me. But he releases me quickly and steps back, a major change in his facial expression. He looks at me now with concern, almost anger. He reaches forward and takes the hem of my jacket in each hand and forcefully rips it open. His eyes travel to my waist where he sees my 9mm Smith and Wesson secured to my hip. He stares at it for a moment and then brings his eyes up to mine, which are glued to his.

"What is this?" He asks as his thumbs caress the canvas strap holding the gun to me.

"It's a 9mm Smith and Wesson M&P9c hand gun. You like?" I respond while swinging my hips.

"I know what it is, Sydney. Maybe I need to rephrase the question. Why do you have it?" He asks, even more concern in his eyes.

"I told you yesterday, I have a gun. I decided......." And I drift off, because I'm not sure I want to disclose my insecurities.

"What happened, Sydney? Tell me. Now." He demands.

"Nothing, Gabe. Nothing yet anyway. I just felt a little...I don't know, uneasy this morning." I say as I step back and refasten my jacket. "Don't worry, Detective Torres, I have a permit to carry it." And I turn to head towards Chuck's office.

But before I can get my body completely turned, he grabs my arm at the elbow and spins me back around. "Are you trained to shoot it?" He asks, like he doesn't believe a girl can shoot a gun.

"Would you like to join me at the shooting range, Detective?"

Another smirk curls his lips and then turns into a drop dead smile. "You're on, Doctor DeCarlo. Let's go."

"Wait, now?" I ask.

"Yes, now is the best time. I want to see what you've got before I allow you to carry."

"Before you ALLOW me? Who do you think you are?"

"I am a cop and I'm committed to public safety, I need to make sure you know what you're doing." He grins.

"You're an ass, Detective. And yes, it's on. Let's go."

We make our way to the basement area of the old building and check in at the front desk.

Typically civilians don't get to use the range here, but Detective Torres checks us both in and we make our way to the range.

After donning our protective gear, we move to the lanes. I look down and see a paper target hanging from a clothes line. I hear it catch behind me and I prepare myself. I can feel Gabe behind me, watching me and I know I'd better nail this or I'll never hear the end of it.

I pull the gun up and aim it right towards the target. As it starts moving, I start firing. After I empty the cylinder, I lift my goggles to check out the results. Six out of seven shots blew a hole right through the heart. The seventh one piercing the head area. "Very nice." I hear Gabe behind me.

He steps into his firing lane and brings his Glock up and waits for the target to move. Once it starts, he fires off two shots, totally destroying the target. I hear him chuckle under his breath.

"Well, you have a bigger gun, Detective." I smile back at him. "And you only let off two shots. The others may have missed completely." I tease.

He laughs and steps beside me, pressing his Glock in to my hands. "Let's see how you do with the big guns."

Always being up for a challenge, I take the gun and examine it. I've never shot a Glock before, but it can't be that hard. As I aim the weapon and pull off my first shot, my body jerks back about three steps. He laughs again. "Uhh huh, too much for you?" He teases.

"Never too much." I snap back, determine to not let this gun get the best of me.

The target moves again and I plant my feet firmly on the ground and lock my knees. I refuse to let him win at this little game. I fire off three shots, hitting the center of the target dead on and manage to remain standing. The target is in pieces, with half of it hanging off.

"Wow." I hear Gabe whisper. "That's hot."

I pull the cans off my ears and the goggles off of my face and look back at him. "What did you say?"

He shakes his head as he takes the Glock from my fingers. "Well done, Sydney. You've proven to me that you can handle a weapon. Now, let's go handle a murderer."

And he walks off. Is he pissed? Yeah, he's pissed that I can shoot as good as he can, or better.

Arrogant bastard. But I follow behind him, smiling from ear to ear. That'll teach him to challenge me. He thought I would go all girly on him and not hit a damn thing. I laugh as I follow him up to Chuck's office, where the fun is gone. It's all business in here.

Gabe and I sit down and stare at Chuck for a few minutes. He's nose deep into his computer and doesn't appear to even realize we're sitting here. But neither Gabe nor I speak, we just sit there in silence until Chuck finally looks up.

"Ah, you're here. Good. Let's get busy. Gabe, what did you find in those files last night? Anything we can use?"

Gabe shifts uncomfortably in his seat but says nothing. I see him glance at me like he doesn't want me around for what he has to say.

"Gabe?"

"Um, yeah. Um....well, I......shit." He stumbles on his words as he looks at me.

"Spit it out Gabe. We don't all have day." I say, probably a little meaner than I should, but I can tell he's uncomfortable around me and he needs to know that if I'm going to be a part of this investigation, he needs to keep me informed.

He takes a deep breath and looks at Chuck. His eyes don't even glance towards me, like he doesn't want me to see what he's thinking.

"I went over all of the photos and reports and a few things struck me." He then finally turns and looks at me. "Sydney, we had your file pulled from Chicago PD, and I'm afraid some things just don't match up."

I suck in a breath and release it slowly. I'm pissed that he pulled my file without telling me, and now he knows everything. But, I realize that he is just doing his job and frankly, I was afraid of the same thing.

"What do you mean?" I say calmly, though I am far from calm inside.

"Well, the obvious similarities. The barbed wire for one. And....." He drifts off again.

"Spit it out, Gabe." I prod him.

"Both of the girls were adopted." He says.

"Yeah, and?"

He pauses before taking a deep breath and looks me dead in the eyes. "The DNA report from semen extracted from the girls stomachs match the DNA found during your exam, after......."

I suddenly feel the hair on my neck stand up and fear courses through my veins. "He can't be still alive. I killed him. Didn't I?" I look at Chuck and see the same thing in his eyes that I feel in mine.

"Yes, Sydney. You killed him. I have the coroner's report right here." He says as he slides it towards me.

I finger the folder and slowly open it and scan the contents.

Cause of death: Gunshot wound to the cranial cavity.

"Then.....how?" I ask.

"We don't know, yet. But we will Sydney, I promise." Gabe whispers to me as his fingers brush mine.

How can he promise me that? I look at him, tears pooling in my eyes. "Don't make promises you can't keep, Gabe."

"Oh, but I can promise you. We will get to the bottom of this and pull this predator off the streets."

I nod, but I know that's not possible. Is it? How can the DNA match......my father's DNA?

He's dead......he's been dead for years.

"There's another thing I noticed, though." Gabe says, bringing me out of my thoughts.

I look at him, but I can't speak.

"Tattoos. Both girls have tattoos on their right hip." Gabe says. I nod because we figured this out yesterday.

Gabe looks at me intently. He knows. I shake my head, because I don't want to talk about it, but if I keep it inside, it could jeopardize the case.

"We covered this yesterday, Gabe." Chuck states. I know I need to come clean here, because this is all too much.

"I have one on my right hip." I say quietly. "The number four. My father branded me as his fourth conquest."

No one says anything for a few minutes, but Gabe finally speaks up. Chuck knew about the marking, but for some reason he kept quiet too. Maybe waiting for me to speak up?

"You never had it removed?" Gabe asks.

"No, it's my reminder that I survived." I say as my fingers find my hip, lightly touching the area that is inked.

Gabe squeezes my fingers in a consoling gesture. Feeling the electric pulse that shoots through my fingertips, I snatch my hand back and look at him. I don't need consoling. I don't want pity or someone feeling sorry for me. I'm a survivor and I plan to stay that way, no matter what happens.

"Gabe, why don't you walk Sydney home?" Chuck says from behind his desk.

Gabe looks at me for confirmation and I nod, yes. "Yes, please take me…..home."

Chapter 9
Gabe

I silently thank Chuck for the early dismissal. I nod at him and stand, holding my hand out for Sydney to take it. She folds her small hand in to mine and I gently tug her out of her chair, pulling her close enough to smell her scent. But not close enough to where I'll get another "Keep your hands off of her" lecture from Chuck. She smiles up at me and a solitary tear rolls from her eye. I brush it away and as our eyes meet, I know.

I know I want to get to know this woman better. I want to know what it feels like to be buried inside her. To take all of her worries away, if only for a brief time. She's suffered through so much heartache and grief throughout her life, she deserves happiness. She deserves to feel loved and taken care of. She needs to know that not all men are like her father and that there is good out there.

Hell, *she's* good as gold. She spends her days counseling young boys and girls that have gone through similar things, helping them get through the trauma and pain. I know she doesn't want pity, I can see that. I admire her strength, her beauty. I want her to feel comfortable with me, to understand that I'll never hurt her.

Chuck clears his throat and I jerk my head to my left to look at him. He's smiling, but has that "Don't fuck with me look" in his eyes. I nod at him and look back to Sydney, "You ready?"

She nods and steps around me towards the door. I follow her out and we begin the walk down the cold, concrete hall towards the lobby.

She walks ahead of me and I watch her hips sway as she moves. She is simply stunning and doesn't even realize it. She's wearing tight jeans, ankle boots with a low heel. Her jacket covering her t-shirt, and her gun. Damn, she was so sexy shooting that gun, and damn good at it too. My Glock gave her a jolt the first time, but she stood her ground and made an ass out of me.

I damn sure don't want to be on the other side of that barrel when she's holding it.

She shoves through the heavy metal door and holds it open for me. I've managed to stay behind a bit, lost in my thoughts. "You coming?" She says anxiously.

"Yeah." I say as I pick up my pace.

I follow her out into the lobby and through the door, onto LaFayette Street.

She turns back to me, "Look, I know Chuck wanted you to walk me home, but I'm fine, really." She says, patting her hip, reminding me once again she's packing. Knowing that she can take care of herself turns me on. I know I shouldn't feel this way, but I can't help it. She. Affects. Me.

"I know you are. But I want to. You just found out some scary information and I don't want you being alone." I say as I look down into her eyes, my hand finding its way to her soft cheek.

I don't want her to go home by herself, I want her to go home with me. I know ways to take her mind off of everything, even if just for short time. Or all night long, if she'll let me. Her creamy skin, her smile, her everything. God, to lose myself in her, just for tonight.

We stare at each other for what feels like hours. She feels it too, I know she does. She shyly ducks her head and turns towards the sidewalk. I remember the last time we stood here, when I picked her up and carried her off. How much I'd like to do that again, only carry her to bed, or the kitchen...or whichever room we hit first.

But she's vulnerable and scared, so I know I need to proceed with caution. I can be an ass, but I won't be with her. She's special and I plan to do what I can to make sure she knows it.

As we walk along quietly, I take her hand and gently squeeze it. A symbol of reassurance. I know she thinks she doesn't need it, but I give it to her anyway. We make casual conversation as we stroll along as if there isn't a killer out there that could be coming after her next. Well, he's gonna have to go through me first and he won't win that fight. I'll hang him up by his nuts if he messes with Sydney. Not sure why I'm so protective of her, and I decide that now is not the time to try and figure that out, cause we are now standing outside of what I assume is her apartment building. Wow, she must do pretty well. Then I mentally smack myself upside the head. She's a Forensic Psychologist, of course she does well. And my dick jumps again, just knowing that she's self-sufficient and independent. That is a big turn on for me, though the undying urge to protect her envelopes me.

She punches in a code on the wall beside the glass door and it clicks. Good, she's secure in this building. No one can get in that doesn't belong here. I follow her inside like a lost puppy, because she didn't turn me away at the door like I thought she would. We get to the elevator and she turns to me.

"Coffee?" She asks.

I nod, because I can't speak. She's in her territory now and her beauty really hits me. She's smiling and comfortable, relaxed. Our eyes stay locked to each other's and the chime of the elevator shakes us both awake. We step inside and she pulls a card out of her pocket, scanning it and hitting the P on the wall. Penthouse? Whoa. I lean back against the wall of the elevator and watch her. She stands there staring at the floor indicator and groans when the door opens.

In steps an older woman with gray hair and a small white puppy in her arms.

"Mrs. Lancaster, how nice to see you." Sydney says.

"Doctor DeCarlo! How are you?" She asks Sydney as I watch Sydney rub the little dog behind the ears.

"Hello, Rocky boy. How's my favorite doggy."

The dog's tail wags frantically and he licks Sydney in the face. "Lucky dog."

Sydney turns to me with her eyebrows raised. She heard me. Good.

Mrs. Lancaster looks back to me as I lean against the back wall. She moves her body in such a way that forces Sydney back towards me, a twinkle in her eye as she moves. This little old lady knows exactly what she's doing, obviously playing Cupid. I wink at her and she blushes.

The elevator stops on another floor and three couples get in, dressed in bathing suits and carrying towels, pressing the R for the roof. Confused, I look at Sydney. "Roof top pool."

I nod in agreement as she moves back even closer to me while the six new guests file onto the elevator. Her ass is now pressed against me and her warm body is awakening mine. Mrs. Lancaster glances back at me and winks back, her eyes then traveling up and down our bodies that are now pressed together. If I don't get a grip on this quickly, Sydney's going to notice.

Finally, the elevator stops on the eleventh floor and Mrs. Lancaster steps out of the elevator, waving her hands and blowing me a kiss as she turns back. "She's a riot." Sydney says to me as she looks back over her shoulder at me. There are still six other people in here, but they are having an intense conversation about the Mars rover or something I have no interest in. I glance down at the dark headed beauty now purposely grinding her ass against me. I instantly harden completely and there's no way she doesn't feel that. She's teasing me and enjoying it.

We finally get to the top floor and the doors open ever so slowly. She sashays her ass right out and makes a turn to the right. I again, resemble the lost puppy following the only person that has paid it attention.

I trail behind her all the way down the hall and she stops at the corner penthouse, opening the door and walking in. As I follow her in, I take in the apartment. Very calm and comforting.

Creams, tans and dark woods. A mocha colored leather sectional sofa fills the room and faces a large screen television mounted to the wall. I hear the door click behind me and she stops at the small table by the door, removing her jacket and exposing her holster. Her breasts are packed in nicely behind her tight t-shirt, her nipples pressing through her bra and the thin material of her top.

I need to get myself under control or I'm going to blow right in my pants, without her even touching me. I mentally will my cock to behave and enter the spacious apartment. This place must take up the entire half of the building. I walk to the wall of windows and look down on Fifth Avenue. The city looks so peaceful and quiet from up here. I see her reflection behind me and she stands there staring at me. I can feel the heat of her eyes traveling up and down my body.

I watch her through the reflection in the glass and then turn to meet her gaze.

"Coffee? Or would you prefer a beer?"

"Coffee, please." As I need to keep my wits about me.

I follow her into the gourmet kitchen which is stark white. Stainless appliances and granite counter stops. She indulged in everything when she bought this place.

"Do you cook?" I ask as I look around the kitchen.

"Yeah, why? Are you hungry? I could whip up some spaghetti or something."

"Sure, I'm a man. I'm always hungry." I laugh and mentally smack myself. Nice line, Gabe.

Way to impress the lady.

She chuckles and starts removing pots and pans, "I hope you don't mind boxed noodles as I don't have the ingredients to make it fresh." She asks as she pulls a box out of the pantry.

"You make your own pasta?"

"You seem surprised. I am half Italian you know, so yeah. I can make my own pasta. I just ran out of flour last week and haven't been to the store."

She reaches in to the fridge and her ass is now......shit, stop it. She pulls out a whole bunch of things and starts chopping and dicing and mixing and I am totally impressed. She hands me a beer and I nurse it slowly, totally entertained watching her cook. She seems so comfortable in the kitchen that I wonder if maybe she missed her calling. "What happened to the coffee?" I ask her as she stirs the sauce.

"It's late, I figured you didn't need the caffeine." She responds as she opens up a beer for herself. And here I thought she would be a wine drinker, especially since that's what she was drinking at Blazer's the other night. She wraps her lips around the mouth of the bottle and I wish that it was me her lips were on. Later I think. I hope anyway, because I have to have her.

"What can I do to help?" I ask, trying to take my mind off of her lips.

"You can set the table." She replies as she points to the cabinet next to the kitchen table. I proceed with keeping myself busy setting the table. By the time I'm done, she brings in a big bowl of pasta covered in thick meat sauce. She goes back to the kitchen and brings out fresh parmesan cheese, fresh garlic bread and two more beers, then sits down right next to me. I expected her to sit across from me, but she sits immediately to my left.

I take my first bite and groan. I see her smile out of the corner of my eye as she takes her first bite. The smell of garlic and basil take over the room. "This is amazing." I tell her as I shovel my face. I feel like a barbarian that hasn't had food in weeks, but I can't stop. She leans forward to me and with her finger, wipes off a bit of sauce that has apparently found its way to my chin.

Then she sucks the sauce off of her finger in a seductive manner. It takes every bit of self-control I have not to take her on the table right here, right now.

I grin back at her, but proceed to finish eating because my mama taught me not to waste food, so I'll finish eating, then I will have her for dessert.

As we eat, I see a bit of sauce on her lower lip and decide to play her at her own game. I lean towards her and gently lick away the sauce. Her eyes flash and she presses her soft lips to mine, taking total control. I pull back and look deep into her eyes, she wants this as much as I do. But she will not take control of the situation, that's my job.

I pull her from her chair and plant her sexy ass right in my lap, knocking her fork onto the floor at the same time. The metal clangs on the tile and neither of us flinch. Her hands come up to my face and I slip my tongue in her mouth, dueling for control.

She shifts her body so she's now straddling me and I can feel her heat through two layers of denim. My fingers travel down her sides to the hem of her t-shirt and I slowly pull it up over her head, my lips feeling her loss immediately.

Her lace covered breasts are exposed and begging to be touched, her nipples poking proudly through the cups of her bra. I press my thumbs against the hardened nubs and gently pinch them between my fingers. I hear her suck in a breath and she removes her lips from mine, throwing her head back exposing her neck. My mouth finds her sweet spot and I kiss, lick and gently nip at the tender flesh of her neck while my fingers continue to torture her breasts.

She looks down at me, heat in her eyes and her breathing erratic. The heat from her pussy singeing my cock through their protective barriers, and she begins to grind her hips. My hips instinctively rise up to meet her thrust for thrust. I need to sink myself in to her awaiting heat, but not before she gets her release. I can tell by her frantic movements that she needs this, maybe more than I do.

I stand from my chair and hold her against me, her legs wrapping around my waist, and I move to the living room and gently lay her down on the sofa. She licks her lips and I lower myself over her, pressing my lips against hers. Her tongue meets mine lick for lick, stroke for stroke. I could drown in her kiss, and plan to do just that.

She pushed me back and mimics my actions earlier, pulling my shirt over my head. I'm left bare chested with my holster still attached at my hip. She flips the buckle and my Glock tumbles to the floor sliding under the coffee table.

Her eyes travel over my chest and I am thankful for my physique at this very moment. Her reaction to me makes my cock harden even more. Her fingers slide over my chest and down towards the clasp to my jeans. She thinks she's going to get me first, but I have news for her. I grab her fingers and slip one into my mouth, gently sucking on it. Then I scoot back and go for the clasp on her jeans, undoing the button and tugging on her belt loops to slowly drag them down over her legs. Once I have her jeans off, I stare at her perfect body, clad in nothing but a white lace bra and matching panties. Her caramel skin glows in the setting sun and the fire in her eyes burns through me. She reaches between her breasts and flips the clasp of her bra, spilling her ample mounds for my eyes, and hands. I cup each one of them, leaning in and taking a nipple in my mouth while toying with the other one. Her back arches and she pushes her nipple further in my mouth, cupping her breast and sighing.

I trail my lips between her breasts and down to her flat stomach, my heated breath causing goose bumps across her stomach. My tongue pauses at her belly button and I swirl it around, the skin left glistening. Her hips rise and I run my tongue under the elastic of her panties as my fingers begin the slow process of lowering them over her hips.

As I go lower, I see the tattoo of the number four on her hip. I feel her body tense up as the tattoo is exposed, but I gently kiss the inked flesh and continue my descent. I lean back on my heels after removing her panties and stare at her. She's looking back at me with the same fire in her eyes, her hands caressing her breasts. It's the hottest thing I've ever seen.

I lift her foot and start to kiss her inner calf, slowing working my way up to the apex of her thighs, leaving damp marks on my way up. I can tell the anticipation is killing her, but I drag it out. Finally, I reach her beautiful, pink pussy and press my tongue against her soft folds. Her smell and taste are intoxicating and I take a deep breath, hoping her scent stays with me after this is over.

I drag my tongue up and down, circling her clit but not quite touching it. She starts squirming underneath me, but I press down on her hips just enough to keep her still. I'm in charge here and she needs to just sit back and enjoy. "Gabe." Comes out of her lips on a rush.

"What Sydney?" I say against her cleft, the vibrations causing a sharp intake of breath. I can tell she's close, so I continue my torment of her pussy, sucking the now hardened bud in my mouth. I drag my middle finger through her now glistening flesh and slowly slide my finger in.

She's tight, but quickly relaxes around my finger. I pull it back and curl my finger up to stroke her inner wall and when her back arches off of the sofa, I know I've hit pay dirt. I continue to stroke her hot cavern and suck her clit, her body now vibrating underneath me. "Oh God!" She cries out, throwing her head back against the pillow.

Her hot tunnel contracts around my finger and the spasms suck my finger in further. Her head is back and her eyes are closed, a loud and almost painful growl comes roaring from her throat.

"That's it baby, cum for me." I mumble against her now soaking flesh and she moans in rhythm with the contractions around my finger. As I feel her body relaxing, I lift my face from her pussy and stand up to remove my jeans. She sits up and looks at me, "Allow me." She says as she hooks her fingers under the waist band and roughly shoves my jeans down.

Since I rarely wear underwear, my hard cock immediately bounces out and points proudly at her. Her eyes brighten and she smirks. Then, her pink tongue pokes out and catches the droplet of fluid at the seam. Her tongue is soft, firm and hot. Holy shit, I might cum right here and now, but I fight it off. She drags her tongue up my hard length and swirls it around the sensitive head of my dick, causing it to twitch. She peeks up at me through her long lashes as she sinks her hot mouth over my entire cock, my balls nudging her chin. I silently wonder if she has no gag reflex, because her lips are up against my abdomen and her eyes are still on me. She pulls up and wraps her fingers around the base of my cock, stroking and sucking, pulling me to the brink of complete explosion. "Baby, I need a condom." I say as I pull back. "I need to be inside you. Now." I say as I pull back and reach for my wallet. Thankfully, I have one nestled inside. She looks at me like, "you were pretty sure of yourself eh?" But I just smile back at her as I rip open the foil packet with my teeth. She reaches up and takes the rolled up condom from me and slowly and torturously rolls it down my length.

She lies back down, looking up at me with her deep brown eyes, begging me to take her. I position myself at her entrance and without warning, slam in to the hilt. She lets out a squeal, almost like she was in pain. So I pull back slowly, "Are you okay, baby?" I ask her, the tip of my cock still lodged just inside.

"Yeah, just.....it's been a while for me, so....I need a second to adjust." She smiles shyly back at me.

So I slowly push myself back in to her heated core, so slow that I think I might blow from the heat and snug fit. After a few strokes like this, I feel her body relax and her eyes close. "Open your eyes, Sydney. I want to see your face."

She opens her eyes, and I can tell it's a struggle for her. Her eyelids flutter and she manages to open them. The desire I see just about sends me over the edge, but I hold off because I plan to make sure she remembers this day, for a little while anyway.

I continue my rhythm, in and out, in and out. I can see she's holding back and I want her to cum again. I take her mouth, pressing my tongue between her lips in a heated kiss. She gives back as much as she takes, but something is missing.

I sit back on my heels and pull her up, so she is straddling me and I let her take control. She seems to enjoy this and by having her on me, it gives me access to her clit. As her ample breasts bounce in my face, I reach down and press my thumb against her heated nub and circle it. "Does that feel good baby?" I ask as my name falls from her lips on a moan. But she doesn't speak, she doesn't have to. I can see the orgasm in her face and feel her pussy clenching down on my cock, squeezing like a vise. Her bouncing gets faster, more forceful. I press harder on her clit and she explodes, her cream coating my cock and my thighs. Her undoing is mine and on a shout, I fill the condom with my release.

She falls forward onto my chest, my cock still lodged inside her. Her breathing is calming as is mine so I pull my legs out from under me and lie back, pulling her up on to my chest. I immediately feel the loss of her hot pussy as my cock dislodges from her. She sighs and relaxes against my chest, my fingers finding her hair.

We lay there for some time, just our naked bodies warming each other. She finally lifts her head and looks at me, a smile curves her lips. "Um....wow. I'm not sure what......." I cut her off.

"SHHHH, no talking. Just kiss me." I say as she brings her lips down on to mine softly and I realize then I could get used to having her lips on me.

My hands gently rub her back as she lays on me, her breasts pressed against my chest. Her weight gets heavy and I wonder if she's fallen asleep. But I stay still, my fingers lazily exploring her sensuous body. As my fingers reach her hip, I feel her body stiffen and she squirms off of me, grabbing her panties and frantically putting them back on.

"What is it, Sydney?" I ask as I sit up and remove the condom from my slowly hardening cock. There is something about this woman that makes me want to stay firmly lodged in side her.

She pulls her t-shirt over her head and walks off to the kitchen not saying a word. So I get up and tug my jeans back on and follow her. She was so open to me a few minutes ago and I don't want her closing off again, but I don't want to scare her away either. So I stand in the doorway as she cleans the dishes, placing them in the dishwasher.

She feels my presence and after a few minutes, she turns to me allowing me to see true sadness in her eyes, almost guilt. I move towards her and envelope her in my arms, and she comes willingly. "SHHH, it's okay, Sydney. I'm here baby, and I'm not going anywhere." I say as she pulls back, but her hands wrap around my waist.

"I'm sorry, Gabe. I'm a mess right now, you really don't want to get involved with me.

I'm.....I'm damaged goods, something you don't need in your life." She says, those damned tears threatening to spill out of her chocolate brown eyes.

"What are you talking about Sydney? You are a beautiful, smart and independent woman. I love those qualities. You have a past, yes - we all do, but you are far from damaged. I'm in awe of you, really." I say as my fingers find her chin, tipping her head up to look at me. "What happened to you was not your fault, you didn't ask for it and you survived it. That makes you amazing in my eyes."

That one solitary tear rolls down her cheek and lands on her lip. I lean in and gently lick the tear away, licking her upper lip and then pressing my lips to hers. I expect her to pull away, but she doesn't. This kiss is soft and sweet, not heated and passionate like earlier. I can feel her starting to give in, and I only hope I can help her overcome her pain.

She releases me and steps back towards the sink, wiping the next tear away. I walk up behind her and wrap my arms around her, pulling her back against me. My hands travel up her sides and I decide to take a chance and move my fingers over the tattoo again. Sure enough, her body tenses and she steps forward. "Tell me, Sydney. Tell me your story."

She turns to me and presses her lips against mine, "I can't. I'm sorry."

And she turns back to the sink and continues to rinse the dishes. She's visibly upset, so I let it go. For now.

I know what the police reports say, but I want to hear it from her lips. I want to know what happened to her while she was held captive. I want to be the one to heal her.

Chapter 10
Sydney

I stare in to the sink with tears rolling down my cheeks. Nice, Syd. Cry in front of the hot detective that just took away your pain, even if it was just for a moment. Could this be the guy that fixes me? I mentally shake my head because no, I don't think I can be fixed. I've tried over the years to overcome my insecurities and every time a man comes into my life, I push him away. I guess that's what I'm going to have to do this time, because this guy is getting too close.

But I don't want to push him away. I.....like him.

He comes up behind me and wraps his arms around me and I immediately feel secure and safe, like he would never let anyone hurt me again. But I know he can't make any promises, and neither can I. Right now, I have to focus on getting this bastard off the streets and either dead or behind bars. I prefer dead, but that's the cowardly way out. He needs to pay. He needs to suffer and if I have anything to do with it, he will suffer.

I lean my head back on Gabe's chest and exhale a deep breath. His body is hard and warm, his touch comforting. I haven't felt this in so long, that inside I'm freaking out.

"SHHH, just go with it, Sydney. It's okay, I won't let you fall."

And somehow I know this. He's strong while I am weak. No, I am not weak. I will not succumb to weakness. Not again.

"How are we going to catch this guy?" I ask Gabe while he holds me.

He releases me and turns back towards the living room.

"What Gabe? What is it?" I ask

"I'm not completely sure yet, but there are too many similarities with your case from years ago. While I know that your father is dead, something just doesn't seem right. The fact that the DNA found at the scene matches your father leads me to believe that he might be alive after all."

I shiver at the thought. Could it be possible? I was so young and so traumatized that maybe...... "Gabe, I shot him at point blank range. I don't see how it's possible that he survived that."

"Sydney, I'd like to think that's the case, but until we know more I want you protected at all times. No walking the streets by yourself, no going anywhere by yourself."

"No Gabe, I will not live in fear. If I give in to whoever this is, then he wins. And, we don't even know that I'm a target. Just because the details are similar, doesn't mean it's my father." I say this to him, but I'm not so sure I believe it. I think back to the day I killed him, the images still vivid in my memory. The blood, the flesh blown onto the wall behind him, the smell. He has to be dead.

"Sydney, I know you're a strong woman and I admire you, really. But until we know more, I want you to step back from the investigation."

"Who in the hell do you think you are? I fuck you ONCE and you think you own me? I don't think so, I am my own person. I will not allow this monster to rule my life, not again. Now, I think it's time you go."

I say this to him and turn back to the sink. How dare he dictate what I can and can't do! I've been living this nightmare for years, I'm not going to back down now.

"Sydney...."

"No, Gabe. I will not be a prisoner in my own home. I have friends, a career. I will not disappear into a hole while you and Chuck figure this shit out. I plan to do whatever I can to make sure this asshole never hurts another woman, even if I have to kill him myself."

Gabe doesn't say anything, he doesn't have to. He stares at me with pity and.....and I don't know what else, but he's pissed me off and he needs to go.

"Please Gabe, go home." I say, trying to fend off the anger that has enveloped me. "I'm covered, as I proved to you earlier. I have a gun and I know how to use it, no one will hurt me.

Not again. Now, I know you have an early shift so please go. I have early appointments in the morning as well."

He nods and continues back into the living room, putting on his shirt and strapping his gun back around his waist and then opening the door. He turns back to look at me, the look of torture in his eyes. I know he doesn't want to leave this way, but I need to get myself back under control and call Leslie. Or maybe not, because she'll agree with Gabe and I'll be on my own.

"I'll be in touch, Sydney. And please, stay safe. Call me if......"

"Don't say it Gabe. I won't get in to any trouble."

The door closes on a loud click and my heart beats double time, because I'm now alone. I should have been an actress, cause frankly I'm scared shitless to be alone. But I don't want Gabe knowing that. I stare at the door, mentally willing him to come back and throw himself in to my arms, but I know that won't happen. I hurt him, I know. But I'm so frazzled over this that I don't have time for anyone else. If I let myself go, how can I be any good to anyone else? I start chanting over and over in my head, 'I am strong, I am strong.....' as I wipe the next tear from my eyes.

What the fuck has my world come to? I thought this was over years ago, why can't my father's grip release me? Why does he have to torture me from the grave? Or is he even in a grave? What if it is him that has come back for me, the one that got away?

I grab my cell and call Leslie, because I need to nip this in the bud before I lose it. I'm a psychologist, a fucking doctor for Pete's sake. I can't let myself get beaten down or I'll be no good to my patients.

"Doctor Phillips." Leslie says as she answers her cell. Damn, I called her work cell instead of her personal cell. This will cost me.

"Les, it's me."

"Sydney? Why are you calling me on my work cell?"

"I don't know, pressed the wrong button I guess. Can you talk?"

"Sure honey, anything. What's going on?"

"Not now, tomorrow. In your office, can you squeeze me in?"

"Of course, but you know you can talk to me now."

"I know, but I need to do this face to face. I'll check my patient schedule in the morning and call you to set up a time."

"Okay, Sydney. But call me tonight if you need me."

"I will, thanks."

And I press the end button, mentally cursing myself for calling her. Damn it, I really need to get past this on my own, but she is a doctor and she's my best friend, so I need to do this. Get all of this out on the table and figure out how to deal with it, and quickly before it's too late. I have to be careful though, because I can't divulge details of the case. Not to her or anyone. If I were to do that and something leak, I'd never forgive myself. I do trust her though, but I must keep it to myself for now.

I head for the shower and turn the water on, but turn it back off. If I bathe, Gabe's smell will be washed from my body, and I want to keep it there. It's comforting and.......wow. What has he done to me? Instead I crawl into bed, pulling the covers up to my neck.

As I lie in bed, I see his face on the back of my eyelids, his smile and his warm brown eyes. I go over the days' events and smile. His soft warm lips, his strong hands commanding my body.

I feel the familiar tingle between my legs and I know I'd better put my mind on to something else before I'm reaching for my vibrator. After sleeping with him today, I can't imagine there would be any satisfaction in that. So I try and think about someone kicking a kitten, and then try and imagine a drunk guy puking on the sidewalk. Wait, maybe a......shit, it's no use. Gabe comes to rescue the kitten and hauls the drunk guy off to jail. I need to face it, he's not going anywhere anytime soon.

I reach for my cell and scroll through my contacts, starting a text message. I close it out and lay the phone down. No, I will not cave.

But after a few minutes I find myself staring at his name on the screen.

I need you

I quickly press the send button and then pull the covers over my head. I can't believe I just did that. Fuck! I feel like a horny teenager and I need to get a grip. Shit, what if he thinks something's wrong? No, I can't have that......so I grab the phone and before I can send another text he responds.

On my way

Wow. Shit, now what do I do? Do I text him and tell him 'never mind'? Do I let him know I'm okay? No, I shower. So I fly out of bed and jump in the shower, letting the hot water cascade down my body. I wash my hair and grab the body wash and loofah, giving my skin a good scrub.

The scent of jasmine and vanilla fills the bathroom and I find myself relaxed and calm.

That is until the door to my bathroom comes flying open and my name being called.

"Sydney?" I jump out of my skin and open the shower door to see a flustered and almost angry Gabe Torres standing in my bathroom.

"HOLY SHIT, YOU SCARED ME TO DEATH!" I yell out over the running water.

"You? You text me that you need me, so I come running over here and then you don't answer your phone. The door man couldn't reach you either."

"I'm sorry, I was taking a........." And he's on me. His lips come down hard on mine and his tongue snakes in my mouth in a frantic search for mine. He pushes me back in to the shower and reaches behind him, pulling the door shut. He's fully clothed and soaking wet, but I can't push him off me, the cold tiles on my back.

His hands come up and cup my face and he pulls back, brushing my bottom lip with his thumb. "What are you doing to me, Sydney?" He breathes.

"I was thinking the same thing earlier, Detective."

He steps back, but doesn't take his hands off of my face. "Is that why you texted me that you needed me?" I nod and he steps back closer, "I'm glad, because I need you too." And he presses his lips against mine again in a tender kiss. His tongue swipes across my bottom lip and he pulls me into him, my wet and naked breasts pressed up against his wet shirt.

My fingers instinctively go to the hem on his shirt and I peel the soaking material up and over his head. His tan skin glistens in the subtle lighting of the room, his eyes smoldering. I reach for the button on his jeans and deftly undo the button, but he pushes my hands back and lowers his soggy jeans and kicks them to the corner. He is now gloriously naked and his heated stare on my body has me on fire.

My fingers trace his chest and travel down his abdomen and I wrap my fingers around his now engorged cock. I shiver knowing I did this to him and that I affect him as much as he affects me. As I gently squeeze his cock, it throbs under my touch. Gabe sucks in a breath and he steps even closer to me, if that's even possible. He's so close, our bodies have become one. His mouth finds mine and our lips and tongues begin an intricate dance, heated and on the cusp of explosion.

He gently removes my hand from his cock and takes my other hand, raising my arms above my head. With one hand, he holds my wrists and presses the back of my hands against the tile.

He leans in and kisses my neck and slowly moves down my chest until he latches on to my nipple. It hardens under his lips and he tugs back, sending shockwaves down my body and a persistent throbbing between my legs. His other hand travels down my side sending goose bumps over my skin, even though the steaming water still streams over me. His fingers stop on my tattoo and I try hard not to tense up, knowing he knows it's there. He traces over the number four permanently etched in to my skin as his lips find mine once again. It's as if he's saying, "It's okay. I want you anyway."

I relax into his kiss and he moves his fingers to my stomach, causing me to suck in a breath.

His knee presses against my legs and he spreads them without removing his lips. He slips his fingers between my legs and strokes the sensitive flesh, pressing firmly against my clit. My hips start thrusting against his hand trying to coax him to press harder. But he's not catching on, or he's teasing me because I feel him smile against my mouth.

"Eager are we?" He asks, joking I think. But I'm desperate at this point. He must see this in my eyes because he slips a finger inside, firmly stroking as his thumb stays pressed against the now hardened nub.

"Gabe....." slips from my mouth as my head lolls back against the tile. He's apparently done this before and I shake that thought out of my head, because I suddenly don't want him touching another woman. He has me tied in knots and.........
"SHIT!" I scream as he brings me to orgasm, right there standing in the shower. The spasms start at my toes and crawl up my spine, throbbing and pulsating throughout my body. My legs weakening and threatening to give out from underneath me.

"That's it baby, let it out." He says as he removes his fingers and plant them right on my hips.

He gently lifts me up and my legs wrap around his waist as I'm impaled on his hard cock. He thrusts deep and it feels like he's hitting my cervix, but I don't care. The aftershocks of my orgasm keep going and going and I feel like I'm going to cum again. Only I fight it off, because I don't think I can handle another one right now. His face is buried in my neck as he holds both my legs on his hips, my back pressed against the shower wall. The steam is subsiding and the hot water is cooling so he reaches over and shuts the water off. He kicks open the shower door and carries me out of the shower, his cock never leaving the dark recesses of my core. He gently lays me on my bed, my ass almost hanging off the edge and slams into me. He leans in and he squeezes one breast while suckling the other. His free hand is between my legs and I'm overcome with feelings. Too much going on at once, but I can't bear to tell him stop, it feels too good.

His hips are frantic and his breathing gets heavier, his lips leaving my nipple as his release is coming. But he slows and pulls back, almost leaving my body completely before he slowly pushes back in. He was on the verge of losing control and I was ready to watch him do just that, but apparently he has other plans.

He pushes me back on the bed, towards the padded headboard and then flips us over, so I'm straddling him. I see torment in his eyes, like he is fighting to hold on. I rise up over him and slam back down, his hips meeting my thrusting. But I decide to shake things up, so I lift myself completely off his body and turn around, my ass facing him now and slowly lower myself on to his cock. "Jesus, Sydney." He sighs out as I slide slowly on to his cock, feeling every hard inch of him. He sits up a bit behind me and reaches around, pressing his fingers against my clit and placing his lips at my ear. "I'm not going to last like this baby. Cum for me." He whispers as he swirls his fingers through my damp, aching flesh. He hits the sweet spot and slams his hips upward and stills, spilling his seed inside me. He continues rubbing my clit and I unravel, the spasms taking over my body. Sweat mingling with the water still left on our bodies from the shower. I throw my head back against his shoulder and scream out his name, my hair across his face as he pulls us down on to the bed, my back on his chest.

I can hear his heart pounding and we both lie there for a minute, catching our breath. His arms wrap around me and he holds me, tight. I feel safe, secure and sated. Finally, I roll off of him and lay on my side, facing him and he turns to me as well. We are face to face, our breaths mingling and our eyes glued to each other's. He gently rests his hand on my hip and scoots closer, planting a soft kiss on my lips, his other hand brushing away strands of wet hair in my face.

It's then I realize we are still soaking wet, and so is my bed. The breeze from the ceiling fan cooling by body and I start to get cold. Gabe pulls me into his arms and his body heat instantly warms me. With my cheek pressed against his chest, I can hear his heart beat and feel the rise and fall of his body as his breathing calms.

He wraps his arm around me and his fingers trace my damp skin, relaxing me in to his embrace. We lay there for some time before his fingers find the tattoo on my hip. I know it's coming, so I brace myself for his question.

"Tell me about this." He asks quietly.

I try and wriggle my way out of his arms but he's too strong and he holds me closer. "No, Sydney, don't pull away this time. I want to know what happened to you, I need to know. For the investigation as well as……." And he drifts off.

"What Gabe, why do you need to know? It's not a pretty story and........" This time I fade off, not quite sure how to tell him what he wants to know, without giving too much away. I drift off and my mind goes back to the day my father branded me.

The rope is tight across my body, my chest firmly secured to the metal chair up against the wall. Each ankle bound to the chair legs, and I'm naked and cold. I can hardly breathe in the damp, mustiness of the basement. Water puddles in the corner from the rain and he stands in the corner, the tattoo needle in his hand, staring at me. My mouth is sealed by duct tape and blood trickles from my nose.

He stalks towards me, an evil smirk across his face and he's laughing. He stands to my side and grips my hair, yanking my head back. Pain sears through my scalp as he yanks a handful of my hair out, tossing it to the floor. Tears pool in my eyes, but I can't speak - I can only grunt at him.

I know he sees the fear in my eyes, and I try to mask it, but he loves it. He thrives on me being afraid.

He traces the needle along my neck, "Shall I put it here?" He says as the machine starts humming.

"Or here?" As he traces it down my chest, pressing it against my breast. The sharp needle pricking my skin.

"Or maybe here?" As he faces me, reaching his grimy hand between my legs.

"No, I want it where everyone will see it, because when I'm done with you, no one will ever get between these legs." He says as he places the needle against the skin on my hip. I can't see what he's doing, but I can feel the needle pricking my skin, injecting ink in to my flesh. I squirm, but I'm bound so tight to the chair that it's fruitless. *"Be still or you'll fuck it up."* He growls in to my ear.

I close my eyes, fighting off the tears. I need to be strong. I begin chanting in my mind, "I will survive this, I will survive this."

But in reality, I don't know this and I'm not sure I want to survive it right now. The pain coursing throughout my body though, reminds me that I'm still alive. And until that pain is gone, I must fight.

As he concentrates on marking me, I realize my hands are loose. I suck in a breath and try not to let on to him that I can move. I scan his body and see his gun tucked in to the waistband of his jeans.

My brain starts churning and I start trying to think of a way to get my hands on that gun. My heart starts racing because I know the end is near. Either he dies, or I die trying to kill him. My own father.

Right now, I can't think about that though. Right now, he's just an evil man intent on torturing me. But knowing the end is near, my attitude shifts and I decide that I will survive.

He turns his body a bit to get a better angle on me as the rope falls from my hands. It lands in a thunk and he turns to me, anger in his eyes. He grabs a pile of barbed wire on the floor and wraps it around my neck, the sharp ends piercing my skin. I reach up and shove him hard enough where he stumbles forward on to me.

With one hand grasping his face and my fingernails in his eyes, I grab his gun from his waistband. He senses the loss of the gun and gains his balance, standing back from me. He looks down on me with that evil look in his eyes.

"Go on baby, shoot me." He taunts as he steps closer to me. "You can't do it can you? You could never kill your daddy. Could you?" He smiles that wicked smile at me.

Without thinking, I aim and pull the trigger, the shot ringing off and echoing in my ears.

Blood splatters on the wall behind him and he reaches for me, pulling me over on to the ground, my head hitting the concrete floor.

As I come out of my dream, or nightmare - I realize that I've just told Gabe everything. I wasn't dreaming, I was talking. I know this by the look in his eyes. The pain, the sympathy, the anger.

I push back from him and turn my back against him. I can't look at him right now, nor do I want him seeing my face. I'm horrified and mortified that I just spilled my story to him, without even realizing it. But he sits up and moves behind me, pulling me in to his arms.

"SHHHH, it's okay, Sydney. He's dead. He can't hurt you anymore." He whispers.

"But he can, Gabe. He IS still hurting me! Even from the grave he's killing me. Why? Why can't this all just go away?" And I bury my face in to my hands and sob. I haven't cried like this in a long time, and Gabe just holds me, stroking his fingers through my hair. My body shakes and he just holds me. He doesn't speak, he just holds me, rocking me and comforting me.

Once the sobs subside, I turn to him. I know I must look a mess, because no girl is pretty after a good cry, but he smiles at me. He brushes his fingers across my cheek. "You're beautiful, you know that right?"

Shaking my head, I can't answer him right now. I see something in his eyes that I've never seen before, in any man's eyes. I see adoration, lust and.....love? No, I'm just a raging hormonal mess right now and I can't let myself get too deep. But he's the first man I've ever told that story to. I'm suddenly not embarrassed anymore, I'm relieved. I lean in and brush my lips against his and he pulls me down on top of him, so I'm looking down into his eyes.

"Thank you for telling me. I know that wasn't easy for you." He says.

"Honestly, I didn't even realize I was telling the story at the time. Whenever I think about it, I disappear mentally and I'm absorbed into the scene, like I'm still there. The fear never goes away, but I'm glad you know. Now you understand why I have to help, why I have to be a part of this. Don't shut me out of this investigation, please. I need to know everything so I can help bring this bastard down."

He cups my cheek with his large hand and I press against him. "Okay, Sydney. I'll keep you involved, but you have to promise me something."

I look at him waiting on him to continue.

"You need to let me know if anything gets too much for you. I'll keep you informed, but you must do the same. Okay?"

I nod against his hand, "Okay. I promise."

Chapter 11
Gabe

I'm totally stunned as I lay here holding Sydney in my arms. I had no idea what she went through and could only imagine. Most women I've known would have totally lost it and never gotten past it. But she did, or she's trying real hard to. She is one amazing woman and I plan to make sure she knows this, every day of my life if she'll let me. I know I've only known her a few days, but she has captured my heart already. I've never believed in love at first sight, but the moment I spotted her at Blazer's, I knew. It was fate that I ran into her again, only I wish it had been under different circumstances.

She's beautiful, successful and strong. But damaged in her own way and I can only pray she lets me in. I'll do whatever it takes to keep her close to me.

Her warm body is resting on mine and her hair is tickling my nose, but her breathing has calmed and I think she's actually asleep. I cock my head to the side and take in her face. Olive complexion, creamy and smooth. Her hair is a mess on her beautiful head and her almond shaped eyes closed.

I calmly move her off of me and make sure she's comfortable to my side before I slide out of bed. Glancing at the clock I realize it's two a.m. and I have to be at the station by six. But after what we went through this evening, sleep is the furthest from my mind. But I know if I don't get some shut-eye, I'll be useless and that is unacceptable. So I roll towards her and pull her in to my chest and close my eyes. She doesn't stir and I realize that she must be exhausted. Two rounds of explosive sex and then her confession must have worn her out. But I let her sleep and finally succumb to sleep myself.

Her alarm goes off at six a.m. and her hand reaches over, pressing the snooze button. I realize that I am officially late for work and I crawl out of bed and head to the bathroom to shower. As the water heats I call Chuck and let him know I'm running late.

"Uh huh, rough night Gabe?" He chuckles.

"A bit, but a good kind of rough. I'll be there within the hour." I tell him.

"Take your time, son. This case will still be here when you get here. You bringing Sydney with you?"

How did he know......never mind.

"Ummmm, I haven't talked to her this morning." Which is correct, since she's still asleep.

"Well, if she wakes up in time, bring her with you." Damn, he does know.

"Umm, sure." is all I can say. I don't want him knowing I'm with her, not yet anyway.

The door to the bathroom opens and in walks a sleepy Sydney. Her eyelids heavy and a little puffy from crying last night, but she looks beautiful.

"See you in a bit." And I disconnect the phone without saying goodbye, because frankly, Sydney takes my breath away.

"Morning sleepy head." I say as I press a kiss to her forehead.

She smiles, but says nothing while reaching around me to turn the shower on, not realizing it's already on. Okay, so she's not a morning person. I can deal with that.

The steam from the shower fills the room and Sydney steps in, giving me a sexy look as she does so. I'm not sure if she wants me to join her or if she's telling me to stay put. Hell with that, and I open the door and step in beside her. Her head is back in the stream of water and her breasts pushed forward, begging to be touched. Her nipples puckered and standing at attention.

So I reach for them, cupping them in both hands. She looks down at me, water dripping down her beautiful face. Her eyes are heated and as she licks her lips, my cock hardens painfully.

Her eyes move down and lock on to my cock, the bastard throbbing under her gaze. She scrapes her fingernails down my chest and stops just above my raging hard on. Her tongue pokes out and swipes across her upper lip as she lowers her body to her knees. I say a silent prayer that I don't blow all over her face before she even touches it.

She grips my cock in one hand as the other cups my balls, before she drags her tongue along the rigid underside of my cock. Her tongue is soft, hard and warm all at the same time and my head rolls back. "Shit, Sydney."

I feel her smile against me as her hot mouth sinks down over me, her lips hitting my abdomen. Damn, she really has no gag reflex and I'm sure I'm about to cum just watching her.

She peeks up at me through her long lashes and pulls back, only to deep throat me once again.

Her hand still on my sac and her fingers massaging the sensitive area behind it. I start to wonder where she learned this and decide that I really don't want to know.

As I feel my eminent orgasm coming, I step back and withdraw my cock from her mouth.

"No way am I going to cum like this, I want to be buried deep inside you when that happens." I tell her as I help her up. I move towards her and bury my face in her shoulder before tracing kisses down her chest and to her stomach. Lowering myself to my knees, I lift one foot and place it on my shoulder, exposing her pink pussy to my tongue.

Her flesh is glistening with moisture, both from the water as well as her own arousal. I lean in and press my nose to her flesh, taking a deep breath before stroking my tongue through her soft folds. I hear her suck in a breath as she lays her head back against the tile, her head thunking against the hard surface. I peek up at her to make sure she didn't hurt herself, but the look on her face tells me she feels no pain. Her eyes are closed and her mouth is open, her tongue darting out to moisten her lips. Jesus, she's beautiful. Long lashes flutter over her cheeks, rosy pink lips and high cheekbones. Her chest rises and falls with every shuttered breath as I keep stroking my tongue through her cleft. I thrust two fingers inside and I feel her body stiffen as her back arches against the wall, her breaths getting heavy. I keep those two fingers deep inside her, stroking her as I press my thumb against her hard pearl. I don't press hard, just enough to cause a multitude of sensations rocking her to her core.

"OH.......GOD!" She screams, her hips thrusting against my fingers as her juices spill on to my tongue. Her body convulses as I keep up the pressure on her clit, slowly circling it, my fingers stroking deep inside her. Her leg grips my shoulder, the bend of her knee squeezing my shoulder like a vice. I slow my thrusting and allow her to gather her bearings before I lower her leg and stand up. I press my fingers in to her hips and direct her to turn around, facing the shower wall.

I move up behind and slide my hard as steel cock against her firm ass. She bends a little at the waist and lines her pussy up against the tip of my cock. Then she slams backwards, impaling herself on my cock. "Shit!"

But she doesn't let up, she takes control and continues to pull forward, then slamming back down on to me. I let her get her rhythm, and then I join in her thrusts. The only sounds are the shower running, our heavy breathing and skin slapping against skin. Then Sydney lets out a moan, slow and low. Her reaction to me fucking her is my undoing, and I unload deep inside her.

As I thrust hard one last time, pressing my hips against her ass, she screams my name and I feel her pussy milking my cock.

We stay like that for what feels like hours, until the water starts running cold and chill bumps cover Sydney's back. I slowly extract my cock from her still throbbing pussy and reach over, turning the water off.

She straightens up and turns to face me. The look in her eyes is pure, unadulterated bliss.

Her facial muscles are relaxed and her skin is glowing, though I don't know if it's from the heat of the shower, or her orgasm. Course, the water was cold by the end so I assume the latter. Her lips curl up in a seductive smirk and my dick jumps at the sight.

"We're supposed to be down at the station. Chuck wants to see us."

"Us?" She asks.

"Umm, yeah, he told me to bring you with me."

"Does he know.......?" Her eyes drop to the floor. I reach up and gently nudge her chin to look up at me.

"I don't know, and I don't care. I didn't tell him, if that's what you're asking. But he's a smart man, he can figure stuff out on his own." I tell her.

"Shit, he's gonna freak out."

"Why would he freak out? He has no control over you, or me."

"I know, but we have to work together on this case, he might think our judgement will be cloudy if he knows."

"Well, we won't tell him. Keep him guessing, right? As long as we keep it professional while working, he won't have an issue."

"Okay, but........." She pauses.

"But what?"

"Did we make a mistake?" She asks, suddenly very somber.

"A mistake? Making each other feel good and taking our mind off of things? You think it was a mistake?" I step back from her, removing my fingers from her chin.

"I...I don't know, maybe? We need to be focused on this case, so that we can nab this guy before he hurts another girl. Feelings aren't a good thing to put in the middle." She says as she turns from me and walks to the bedroom. I watch her hips sway as she walks.

I shake my head and peel my eyes off of her ass and follow her to the bedroom, but she's not there. I grab my jeans and t-shirt and head out to follow her. I find her standing in the living room, staring over the New York streets. She's still naked, the curve of her hips sloping gently to her thighs.

I walk up behind her and put my arms around her, pulling her back against my chest. She leans her head back against my shoulder and my hands instinctively roam to her full breasts. But she stops me, placing my hands against her stomach.

"We need to go, Gabe. Chuck is waiting."

And she steps from my grasp and heads back to the bedroom.

I decide this time, not to follow. My boots and socks are out here, so I sit down on the sofa and tug them on. I can tell she has distanced herself from me, but I realize she's right. If we are going to work together, we need to keep our feelings out of this.

A few minutes later she comes out, fresh faced and dressed in khaki pants and a gauzy blouse. Simple, but elegant. A low heel boot tops it off. As she grabs her sweater and scarf out of the coat closet, I grab my jacket as well. She hasn't spoken, and neither have I. Maybe things are better left unsaid at this point.

"Are you hungry?" I ask as we walk out the door.

"A little. We can stop at the deli on the way, they serve bagels and other things in the mornings."

Funny, I had no idea. I typically skip breakfast and.........before I can finish that thought, she is out the door heading towards the elevator. I trudge behind her, following her like a lost puppy again. I realize then that I'll follow her anywhere. She takes her phone and presses a button, placing it to her ear. "Beth, it's Doctor DeCarlo. I need you to cancel all of my appointments today and tomorrow. Something's come up and I'll be out of the office. Take a few days' vacation, I'll see you on Wednesday." She tells what must be her receptionist, or assistant.

As the doors open into the lobby, her heels clicking on the marble floor, we head outside.

The temperature has dropped a bit since yesterday, and the wind is a bit stronger. Her hair flows frantically in the wind and she struggles to get it behind her ears. She reaches in to her bag and pulls out a hair tie, quickly wrapping it up and securing it behind her head. I admire the column of her neck and her creamy skin. Jesus, Gabe. You need to snap out of this and get back to the task at hand. There is no way you are going to be able to focus on this case if you keep getting a hard on over this woman.

After grabbing a bagel and coffee, we make our way to the station. We walk in companionable silence, just making small talk and not paying attention to our surroundings.

Which, as a cop, is a bad idea.

Suddenly a guy comes around the corner and slams right into Sydney, knocking her down.

Her coffee goes flying and the contents of her purse scatter across the sidewalk, including her gun. She lands in a thunk and immediately jumps for her gun, "WHAT THE FUCK!" She screams out.

But the guy who plowed into her kept going, no apologies or anything. I look back and see the guy, black sweatshirt with the hood pulled over his head, hands in his pockets. I start to go after him, but Sydney gets up, brushing the dirt and grime from the concrete off of her pants.

"Mother fucker." She says. "That's the third time in two days some asshole has bumped into me. These rude fuckers need to watch where they're going." She stands up chuckling.

"What did you say?"

She looks at me in confusion, a questioning look in her eyes.

"Did you say that's the third time that's happened?"

She nods, still looking confused.

"What? It's New York, Gabe. People get bumped into all the time, what's the issue?"

I stand back and try and focus on the asshole that just slammed into her and then walked the hell off. Shaking my head, I decide not to worry Syd with it right now. "Nothing, I guess.

Just.....people need to be nicer I guess."

Sure, lame I know. But I suddenly have a gut feeling, and my gut is usually right.

Chapter 12
Sydney

"Fucking idiot." I whisper to myself, but I know Gabe heard me. I flash back to the first time someone slammed into me, and then realize it was right in this same spot. Well, not exactly, but at the same corner right by my favorite coffee shop. "Son of a bitch." I say as I see the dark coffee stain on my pants. "Shit, I need to go back home and change, Gabe. You go on, I'll meet you there in a few. Probably not a bad idea that we don't show up together anyway."

I see a worrisome look in Gabe's eyes. "Relax, I'll be fine." I say as I gather the contents of my purse and shove them back in. "I'm packing, remember? And, I've shot someone before, so I'm not afraid to use it, Gabe. Go on, really. I'll be fine."

I can tell he doesn't want to go on without me, but I refuse to be a prisoner in my own city. I know self defense and I have a gun, a pretty powerful gun at that. I'm prepared and I refuse to allow myself to give in.

He leans in and presses a gentle kiss on my lips while tucking an errant strand of hair behind my ears. "You sure?" He asks, angst on his face.

"I'm positive. Go.....I'm just going to run up and change, then I'll meet you there. I'll be ten minutes behind you."

"Okay, but you call me if you notice anything out of the ordinary."

"Gabe, I'm a big girl. And this is New York. How can you tell if something isn't ordinary?

Nothing about this city is ordinary, Gabe. I'll be fine, see you in a few minutes." And I turn on my heel, headed back to my apartment. The wind blows a strand hair in my eyes, and I can feel Gabe's eyes on me. I know he's going to just wait here for me, but I don't turn back or acknowledge that I know he's still there.

I then hear his footsteps behind me, coming towards me rapidly as if he is running. I stop short and make an abrupt turn towards him, but my body is suddenly slammed to the ground again. Darkness covers my eyes and I feel a crack on the sidewalk, realizing that's my head. I flinch at the pain, but I keep my wits about me, rolling over and kicking my legs up, making contact with something, though I can't see through the blood in my eyes. I hear an 'oomph' from a male voice as well as a loud exhale of breath.

I hear my name called out from the distance and rapid footsteps coming closer to me.

Another 'oomph' sound and a crunching thunk on the pavement as two bodies hit the sidewalk next to me. Sounds of flesh hitting flesh and I feel wetness on my face. I realize it has started to rain and I lie there feeling the cold drops splash against my stinging face. I reach up to wipe my eyes, smearing a warm fluid across my face.

More sounds of fists hitting faces, rushing breaths as punches are taken in the gut. I can't see, so I can't tell who is fighting just to my right. A woman screams and then sits down next to me, a soft cloth presses against my head. "SHHH, it's okay lady. The police are on their way. Are you okay?" A soft female voice whispers against my ear.

I lazily nod my head, but I am unsure if I really am okay. My head hurts and I assume that warm fluid is blood gushing out of my head. I realize I no longer hear the sounds of fighting and I try and peek that direction, but my neck is stiff. Sirens fill the air and soon the sidewalk is a bustling area, full of police and first responders. The nice lady moves away and a man leans down towards me and starts asking me questions. A cervical collar is placed around my neck and cool saline is poured through my eyes, rinsing the blood away.

"Sydney?" I hear from my left.

"Gabe? Is that you?"

"Yeah, baby. Oh my God, are you all right?"

But before I can answer, a husky male voice interrupts. "Sir, you need to step aside and let us work please."

I hear a rustling and then Gabe speaks again, "Detective Gabriel Torres, NYPD."

"Oh yes sir, Detective. I'm sorry, I didn't know."

Gabe doesn't respond, but I feel his presence next to me. "What happened Gabe?" I ask, my voice scratchy and weak.

"Don't worry about that, Syd. Just lay back and let the EMT do his job."

"NO! Gabe, tell me what the fuck just happened."

"It seems as if your body slammer came back for more Syd. He jumped you from behind and tackled you to the ground. Thankfully I hadn't moved from where we were, and I jumped the guy. But after a few hits, he ran off."

"You didn't go after him?" I ask as I try to sit up.

"No, two beat cops were around the corner and they went after him on foot. The guy was quick, but he headed down towards the police station. Idiot as far as I'm concerned. They'll catch him."

I nod at him, but don't respond. My head hurts like a motherfucker and all I want to do is go to sleep. I close my eyes, but am immediately jarred awake by the EMT. "Ma'am, you need to try and stay awake. We're going to transport you to Mt. Sinai hospital to be checked out. We're going to slide this backboard under you and prep you for transport."

"No, I don't need a hospital. I'm fine." I say as I sit up all the way. I'm trying to convince myself that I'm fine, but at this point I can't say for sure.

"Ma'am....."

"NO! I am refusing transport. I'll take myself later if I........" and I proceed to vomit all over the sidewalk. Great, that's the second time in two days I've made a total lady of myself in public.

"Ugh, damn it!"

"Ma'am that is a classic sign of a concussion. We need to get you to the hospital to make sure it's nothing more serious. Plus, you need stitches in that gash. Detective Torres.....?"

"Sydney, let's get you checked out and make sure there isn't more damage than just a concussion, and get you stitched up. I'll make it up to you later." He says as he winks at me.

"Sydney?" I hear from a distance. As I glance over, I see Chuck walking up. "Jesus, Sydney.

Are you all right?" He says as he steps beside me, the EMT stepping aside.

"I think so, just got a fierce headache and......." And I barf again, all over Chuck's shoes.

"Shit, I'm sorry."

"No worries, Syd. We'll get you to the hospital."

And I nod, because I know he's right, but it doesn't mean I have to like it. They secure me to the back board and load me in.

"I'm going with her, Chuck. I'll check in once I know more."

"All right, but first tell me what happened."

I hear Gabe start to tell the story to Chuck as I'm loaded in to the ambulance. I close my eyes and try to go to sleep, but the EMT is right beside me telling me to keep my eyes open. This is really pissing me off, but inside I know he's right. I may not be a 'real' doctor, but I took enough classes in school to know you don't go to sleep with a concussion. I nod my head towards the EMT as I try and listen to what Gabe and Chuck are talking about.

By this point, the beat cops have come back to the scene and I can hear bits and pieces of the conversation. I don't need to hear any more than the fact that the body slammer got away. I sit up, suddenly frantic that he took my purse with my gun in it.

"Gabe?" I call out.

"Yeah babe." He responds from the doors to the ambulance.

Babe

That's the second time he's said that, and I have to admit....I kind of like it. "Where is my purse?" I ask, sounding like a whiney child missing his security blanket.

"I've got it right here. He didn't get it."

"Then I wonder what he wanted, if he didn't want my purse." I say.

"We'll figure that out Sydney." He says as he climbs in to the back of the ambulance, sitting down next to me. He takes my hand in his, brushing his thumb across the back of my knuckles.

"Gabe?"

"I'm right here." He responds and tingles travel up my spine.

"What do you think he wanted, if he didn't take my purse?"

"Sydney, I told you. We'll figure it out. The cops are still looking for him and once they can drag him in to the station by his nut sack, we'll know."

I chuckle at his response, but stop quickly when I realize laughing hurts my head.

"SHH, just lie back, Syd. But don't go to sleep, not yet." He says as the EMT climbs in and sits to the other side of me, the back door slamming shut. I jump a little at the sound, but Gabe quickly reassures me that it's okay. Two pats on the back door of the ambulance and it starts to move.

A few minutes later, I'm wheeled in to the emergency room at Mt. Sinai, the doctors and nurses hovering around me. "It's okay guys, nothing serious. I don't need the full staff tending to me." I joke, because it seems as if everyone has come to my rescue.

I hear chuckles behind me, and soon just one doctor is hovering over me. I open my eyes to a bright light being flashed in to my eyes. "Well having a sense of humor is a good sign, Miss DeCarlo." The doctor says to me. "Doctor Jamison will be here shortly to stitch you up. Looks like you need about six sutures.

I'm going to put some numbing ointment on the cut so you won't feel a thing. Then I want to get an x-ray just to confirm your concussion. Just lay here and relax, the nurse with be with you shortly."

And suddenly I'm alone. I scan the room and watch the others in action with other emergency issues. The nurse comes in and places a band aid on the cut and I wince at the pain, but soon after the pain goes away. I close my eyes and try to relax while waiting on the doc to come back in.

Finally, I'm stitched up and rolled away to x-ray. I silently wonder where Gabe is. He hasn't come by since I was brought in. But I shrug it off to police business. I'm sure Chuck had questions for him.

"Just a minor concussion, Miss DeCarlo. I'm releasing you, but you go home and rest. Do you have someone that can stay with you today and tonight?"

"Yes, she does."

Gabe.

"Gabe, you don't have to do that. I can get Leslie to come over."

"Nonsense, I want to. And you're in no condition to fight me, so deal with it." He says as he leans down and kisses my cheek. "Plus, until they find this guy you will not be left alone."

"Oh Gabe, really? He sucker punched me, jumped me from behind. He tries it again, he'll find the barrel of my gun down his throat."

He laughs, and I start to get pissed off. Who does this guy think he is?

"Sydney, that's my point. If he comes back, I'm afraid you'll kill him, and I want the bastard alive when we find him. I'll make sure the arresting officers take him to the station, the long way.

He'll never mess with another woman again." He laughs again.

"But before we go home, Chuck wants to ask you some questions. Are you up for it?"

"Yeah." I say as I try and sit up.

"Relax Syd. You're going to have a nasty headache for a while. If Chuck's questions are too much, just say so. He can wait until you're recovered if needed."

"No, I'm good. Let's get this over with."

He turns to go get Chuck and I ponder the words he said. *Home.* Surely he means my home, or his? No, I want to go to my apartment. I'm not sure I'm ready to go to his place yet, it's too soon.

Chuck comes in quietly and sits down next to me, taking my hand. "How ya feeling?" He asks quietly, as if any loud noises will be painful.

"As well as to be expected, I guess. Did you catch the guy?"

He shakes his head, "Not yet. But we will. I need to hear your side of the story, Syd. Can you tell me what happened?"

I think back, because it's kind of fuzzy. "Gabe and I were on our way to the station." And I stop, I just pretty much just told him we were together. Crap, now I bet he removes me from this case.

"A guy slammed against me, knocking me down. You know how the crowds are on the street, no one pays attention to what they're doing. Well, after I hit the ground, my coffee went flying and got all over my pants. I told Gabe to go on and I'd meet him there after I changed clothes.

He argued with me, but stubborn as I am......." He nodded as he smiled at me.

"Anyway, as I got close to my building I heard footsteps coming fast behind me. By the time I turned around, I hit the ground. I managed to turn over and kick my legs out, making contact.

But before I could get my gun out, he was body slammed by Gabe."

"Did you see his face?" He asks.

Shaking my head, "No. It all happened too fast and before I could focus, Gabe was on him.

Didn't he see his face?"

"No, the guy wrapped his gloved hand around his eyes, so he couldn't see him. Gabe got in a few punches before the street cops came running, then the guy ran off. The cops chased him, but he got away. Maybe he has some type of injury he is going to need seen to and will visit a hospital or doctor. I've put an APB out for him and all hospitals and clinics are on notice to call NYPD if he comes into their facility."

I nod, because I have nothing else to say really. Chuck stands up and turns to leave. "Call me if you think of anything else, okay?"

"Okay."

He moves towards the door before turning back to me. "Oh, and Syd?"

I look up.

"Gabe's a good guy. But if he hurts you, I'll kill him." He smirks as he exits the room. Shit, he does know. "Chuck?"

"Yeah." He turns back to me.

"Thanks."

He winks at me before he heads out.

I lay back on the bed and my head hits the pillow, a low throbbing persists and I close my eyes. Thankfully my neck isn't hurting and I remove the cervical collar that is still wrapped around me. I keep remembering the EMT stating to not go to sleep, but I can't help it. My eyelids get heavy and I exhale a deep breath and try to get as comfortable as I can, but before I drift off Gabe comes in with the doctor in tow.

"You ready to go Syd?"

My eyes pop open and I see the most gorgeous man hovering over me. "Hi Gabe." I whisper.

I'm so tired and drained that I can't hardly speak. Plus, he takes my breath away. As I look up into his chocolate brown eyes, I see warmth and comfort. He steps back and allows the doctor to get past him.

"Doctor, here are your discharge papers and a prescription for some pain meds." Oh now it's Doctor - not Miss - I laugh.

"I'm sorry, Doctor DeCarlo, I didn't realize who you were earlier." He smiles down at me.

"It's all good, doc." I say as I take the papers out of his hand. I scan them and then he hands me my discharge papers. I sign them and hand them back as Gabe rolls a wheelchair in.

"Oh now, I can walk. " I say as I swing my legs slowly to the side of the bed.

"Hospital rules, Doctor. "

"Fine." I huff out.

Gabe wheels me out and helps me in to the front seat of a black Crown Vic. My body molds to the soft, heated leather seats and I sigh in comfort. He buckles my seat belt, his strong body flexing over me. I catch a whiff of his spicy scent as he closes my door and I start talking to myself.......Wait Syd. You're just delirious after hitting your head. Get your mind out of the gutter and recover." I finish as he slides in to the driver's seat.

"Did you say something?" Gabe asks.

"Just talking to myself." I respond.

"Well, did you answer yourself?"

"No, smarty. I might have a head injury, but I'm not crazy." I laugh, the throbbing in my head persisting.

"Just lie back, I'll have us to your place in minutes." Gabe says as he pulls in to traffic.

"It's New York, Gabe. I may live only five minutes away, but it'll take us thirty to get there."

"Not the way I drive." He says as he flips the blues on and everyone parts like oil on water.

"That's cheating." I tell him, smiling.

"Who's going to tell, Sydney?" He asks as his eyes go back to the road and his right hand holds mine. I watch his face as he drives, zig zagging through traffic and driving recklessly.

"I'd like to make it to my apartment in one piece, if you don't mind."

He smiles, but slows down just a little, just in time to pull in to the parking garage of my building. He parks and rounds the hood, opening my door to help me out. I smirk at him, "Who says chivalry is dead?"

He doesn't say anything as he helps me out of the car. I debate smacking his hands, cause I can do this on my own, but as I stand up I get dizzy and I'm suddenly thankful Gabe is holding on to me. I steady myself as Gabe's arms wrap around me. "Easy

Syd. Hold on to me." But he's holding so tightly on to me, that I can't get my arms around him. He turns me in his arms and coaxes me towards the door.

The wind blows through the garage like a tornado and I start to shiver. Gabe pulls me even closer to his body as we walk, his warmth seeping through his jacket and enveloping my body.

As we get to the door, Gabe stops and takes a look around.

"What is it?"

"Mmm, nothing I don't think. Just making sure we weren't followed."

"Please don't scare me, Gabe. Surely he doesn't know where I live."

"Syd, you were attacked right outside your building. I'm thinking we get some of your things and go to my place."

"No, this building is secure. The guard is in the lobby and the elevator needs a card to get up to my floor."

"Sydney, you forget how easily I got up there yesterday."

"But you're a cop."

"Doesn't matter. The guard had stepped away for a bit and one of your neighbors got on the elevator at the same time. She didn't speak one word to me, but didn't kick me off the elevator.

It's too easy to get upstairs with half ass security."

"You got up there that easily?"

"Yep. That's why I don't want you here. We'll pack you a bag and go to my place in Brooklyn."

"Brooklyn? Ugh, I don't want to go to Brooklyn, Gabe. I want to stay at my own place."

"I don't think that's wise right now Syd. Let's get this guy off the street first."

I sigh, loudly.

"Sydney," Gabe stops me at the elevator door. "This guy knows where you live, and he's probably pissed that he wasn't successful in killing you...."

"Killing me? You think that's what he was trying to do?"

"Until he's in custody, we have to think the worst. And until that happens, you are under my protection."

"Good grief, Gabe. I don't need anyone's protection."

"You are the most stubborn woman I've ever met, Sydney. He got to you once...I will not let him get to you again."

"Since when were you named my protector?"

"Since I watched a man jump you from behind and tackle you to the ground, that's when."

His eyes are stern and I can tell he's dead serious. I back away from him slowly, the look in his eyes disconcerting.

"What aren't you telling me, Gabe?"

"Nothing Syd. Let's get upstairs and pack a bag."

"Fuck you, Gabe. Tell me what's really going on here." I say and I instantly regret it. I've never said that to someone out loud and the look on his face is....painful.

"Sorry, but I can tell you're hiding something."

"Upstairs, Syd."

He growls as the doors close and he presses the P.

The silence in the elevator echoes off the mirrored walls. We don't speak, we don't even look at each other. But his arms are still firmly wrapped around me so I don't fall. I know he's trying to protect me, and that pisses me off. Why? I'm not sure. Knowing I have someone on my side is comforting, but I refuse to be babied and coddled.

As the doors open, his arms get tighter around me and we move slowly, but deliberately towards my apartment. I reach in to my purse for my keys, but he takes them from me and unlocks the door.

We step in and he locks it behind me, throwing the deadbolt. The sound clicking louder than I've ever heard it. It almost feels as if I'm being locked away and the key being tossed. My injured brain flashes back to the basement at that house so many years ago. I heard that sound so many times during the few days I was there. I freeze in my tracks as the memories overload my mind. But before I can retreat completely, Gabe is wrapping his arms around me.

"Sydney?"

"Sorry, I'm okay."

"You sure?"

"Yeah, I just need to sit down."

He helps me to the sofa where I sit down slowly. You'd think by the way I'm moving that I had broken bones and severe injuries. I feel like I've been hit by a Mack truck. Well, I guess I sort of was, though it was a human truck. As soon as my body relaxes I hear Gabe in the other room on the phone. I try and listen in, but he's speaking too soft to hear clearly. I wait it out until he comes back in the room, then I plan to pounce.

I hear him come in behind me, though I can't see him. "Sit down, Gabe."

"Whoa, giving orders now?" He responds, a sexy smirk on his face.

"Yeah, now sit." I say again as I point to the chair across from me. I sit up and prop my feet on the table in front of me and glare at him. "Now, tell me what in the hell is going on."

"Sydney....."

"Stop! Quit trying to protect me! If I don't know what's going on, how can I be prepared?"

He closes his eyes for a minute and his face softens. He knows I'm right, but he hates it.

"Another young girl washed up in the Hudson, near the Holland Tunnel...." and he pauses.

"Damn it, Gabe. We've got to stop this guy."

"No Sydney, I have to stop him. The NYPD has to stop him, but you......"

"Spit it out Gabe."

"Chuck is relieving you of your duties. We no longer need your help."

"Fuck that, Gabe. You guys called me in on this case and I'll be damned if I'm stepping aside. I've been there Gabe. You know I have to do this."

"I'm sorry, Syd. But Chuck said....."

"I don't give a fuck what Chuck said......I'm not backing down!"

I sit back on a huff and look at Gabe. I know immediately there's something else he's not telling me. I lean forward and stare him straight in the eyes.

"Spill it Gabe, what else?"

He stands up and walks to the window looking over Fifth Avenue. He turns to look at me, and I can tell he doesn't want to tell me. "The girl has a tattoo......."

I stare at him, waiting for him to continue.

"It's the number three, Syd. This girl has a number three inked in to her right hip."

Silence. I can't speak or breathe at this point, and I feel like I'm going to hyperventilate so I lean back and take a few deep breaths.

At this point, I start heading for denial territory, but my over active imagination won't let me.

"If she had a three tattooed on her hip......does that mean.....?"

Gabe doesn't answer me, but I can see it in his face.

"What, damn it. What else?"

"Shit Sydney, I don't want to tell you this."

"GABE!!" I scream out in frustration. "TELL ME!! NOW!"

He sits down next to me, pulling me in to his arms, but I pull away.

"No Gabe, you will not distract me. Tell me everything."

"Fine. There was a note.....stapled to her hip covering the tattoo. It was......addressed to you."

"What do you mean, addressed to me?"

He pulls out his phone and shows me a photo texted to him by Chuck.

"It's a numbers game, Sydney."

I sit there and stare at the picture as I feel a prick of a tear in my eye. "My father."

Chapter 13
Sydney

"Sydney, it can't be your father. You killed him, I saw the records. It's not him."

"But who else could it be? You said our DNA matches, and the only killer in my family was him! I want to see those records Gabe, now. I want to see proof that he died when I put that bullet through his ugly head!"

"Well, then pack a bag cause the file is at my place. Get your stuff and let's get going. I'll call Chuck and have the building here secured as well as my house. We don't need to take any chances."

I nod at him, because now I'm ready to go. I want to see this supposed file on me. I want to see the proof that my father is dead. I remember pulling the trigger, the blood splattering across the wall. I remember the heavy thunk his body made as it hit the floor while he grabbed me and pulled me over. I remember everything. Almost. What I don't remember is actually seeing his dead body after I was rescued from that moldy basement. What I don't remember is a funeral for my father, a casket displaying his body. What I don't remember is my mother grieving. What I don't remember is my brother and sister crying. Wait.

"Gabe?"

"Yeah?"

"Has anyone followed up on the whereabouts of my brother, Franco?"

"Why?"

"Well, we would share DNA. And....I don't remember him crying or being upset when I came home, after I killed our father."

"I'll call Chuck from the car. Now let's get rolling."

I go to my bedroom, slowly as the dizziness overwhelms me again. Before I fall though, Gabe is behind me holding me up. "Sit on your bed. Where is your suitcase?"

"In the closet." I say as I point to the closed door.

He goes in and comes out with my large Luis Vuitton rolling bag. "Not that one, the smaller one." I say.

"You may be gone for a while, it's better to over pack than to under pack." He says as he flips the top open and sets in on the bed. He moves to my dresser and opens the top, smaller drawer and I flinch. "Not that drawer!" But it's too late.

He's located my lingerie drawer.

He stands there and stares into the drawer, his jaw ticking and his blood rushing through the veins on his neck. I sit there quietly and watch his reaction. I have some pretty......sexy things in there. But they're for me, I've never worn them for any man. Sometimes I just need to feel pretty and.....

I look up and he's holding my vibrator in his hand. He's staring at it like he's never seen one before, but he doesn't say anything. He sets it down on the top of the dresser and grabs the stack of under garments, moving to put them in the suit case. "Gabe, I don't need all that." I tell him.

But he just looks at me with a heated expression on his face.

He moves back to the dresser and grabs jeans, t-shirts and socks, stacking them neatly on the top before putting them in the suitcase. Then he goes to my closet and picks through the hanging dresses. He comes out with a little black dress, one I hardly wear. It's draped over his arm and my black stiletto heels hanging from his fingers.

"What's that for?" I ask.

He shrugs his shoulders, "In case I want to take you to dinner." He says without looking at me. He lays it across the bed and goes back to the closet and comes back with a garment bag, gently placing the dress in and zipping it up.

He then grabs my cosmetic case from the closet and goes into the bathroom. I know I should go in there and get what I need, but it sounds as if he's just throwing everything I own in the bag.

"Gabe, I don't need everything. I'll come in there and get that stuff." But as I stand up, my head starts spinning again and I sit right back down.

"I've got it. You ready?"

"Shoes."

"Shoes?"

"Yeah, you grabbed the black ones, but I need more shoes."

He shakes his head as he goes back into the closet. "Which ones?"

"The Reebok tennis shoes and the black ballet flats."

"These?" He dangles in front of me.

"Yes, those. Good job."

He rolls his eyes at me, but I can't help to jab at him while he packs a woman's suitcase. It's comical, really. But I can't even stand up without almost falling over. I lay back on the bed and close my eyes.

"Sydney."

I growl, because I'm tired and agitated. I look up at him standing over my bed "We need to go.

The building is secure and a car is waiting."

"You did that so quickly." I say as I sit up, rubbing my tired eyes.

"You've been asleep for two hours Sydney."

"What? Two hours?" I say as I look at the clock. "Shit, five o'clock?"

"Yeah, you needed the sleep."

"But two hours? Argh." I say as I get up, holding on to the table for fear of falling over.

Thankfully there is no dizziness this time and I'm able to walk on my own without stumbling.

As I make my way to the living room, I feel Gabe at my heels, probably making sure I'm not going to pass out on him. So I stop short for no reason and his hard body slams into mine.

"Jesus, Sydney." I hear him whisper behind me. But I chuckle and keep walking. I can almost hear him tsk-tsking behind me, shaking his finger like I've been a bad girl.

"Where's my suitcase?"

"Already in the car. You ready?"

"Yeah, I guess." I'm not ready to go to Gabe's house, but I am ready to see those reports he has there. So I suck it up and lock up the apartment.

The trip takes us about an hour and a half in traffic. We would decide to head out during the five o'clock hour, so it takes longer than it would have had I not fallen asleep. But I have to admit, I feel better since I had that nap.

Finally he pulls up to a gorgeous brownstone on Arlington Place. Silently, I'm impressed.

All of the homes are attached, but with private entrances and tall staircases to the front doors.

Lots of trees and greenery, something you don't see in Manhattan. Women walking down the sidewalks pushing strollers and walking their dogs. I hear children laughing and birds chirping.

It's then that I realize how much I hate the big city and how much I've missed this environment.

We didn't have brownstones in Lincoln Park, but we had yards and greenery. The only green in New York is Central Park and I rarely go down there.

"Penny for your thoughts." Gabe says after what feels like about five minutes of just sitting in the car.

"This is yours?"

"Yeah, you like it?"

"It's beautiful. I had no idea......" and I drift off because I have no idea what I was going to say. I'm not sure what I expected, but this is lovely.

"Well, let me show you the inside." And he opens the door to get out, moving to come and tug me out of the passenger seat. As I stand, I stretch my arms and legs and follow him to the door. I stand at the bottom of the stairs, looking up and I think I'm about to get a workout. There has to be ten steps to the door, and after the day I've had I'm not sure my legs will work. Before I step on the first one, Gabe hefts me up and throws me over his shoulder, fireman style. "GABE, PUT ME DOWN!" I scream, beating my fists against his back.

"Nuh uh. You've been through enough today, I got this." He says as he ascends the brick stairs to his front door. As he reaches the landing at the top, he lowers my body down, my breasts graze his chest as my feet finally touch the ground. His arms stay wrapped around my waist and he presses his lips softly against mine. "Welcome to my humble abode." He whispers against my lips. I smile back up at him, and in his eyes I see......so many things. Trust, patience and lust. He looks at me as if I'm the most beautiful woman he has ever seen and I start to ask questions, but he turns to unlock the door. He steps inside, pressing his security code on the wall and motions for me to step in. In my mind, I expect to see a typical bachelor pad with posters and beer signs all over the walls, clothing all over the floor and trash everywhere.

But as I step across the threshold, I see warmth and comfort. Black leather sectional sofa, contemporary furniture and a large screen TV mounted on the wall. The back wall of the living area is all windows, letting in the warm sunshine. I make my way inside and my feet immediately sink into thick, soft carpet. I stand and stare at the room around me and Gabe comes up behind me, wrapping his strong arms around me. I feel his lips against my ear, his heated breath tickling my neck. "You can go all the way inside, if you like." He chuckles against my skin, causing chill bumps to spread over my body.

As I step forward, he pulls my jacket off and hangs it on a coat tree by the door. He stands next to me as I take in my surroundings, then he breaks the silence. "Are you hungry? I can make some mean fajitas." He says as he walks towards what I assume is the kitchen. I follow him quietly to his kitchen.

As I step into the kitchen, I suck in a breath. All stainless steel appliances, black granite counter tops, a double sink and double oven. "Wow. This is a chef's dream." I whisper quietly.

"I like to cook. Even went to culinary school before joining the academy. Decided that I wanted to follow in my dad's footsteps and vowed to 'protect and serve.'

"A man of many talents, Detective Torres. I'm impressed."

"Well, you haven't tasted my food yet, so you might change your mind." He chuckles as he opens the refrigerator, pulling out peppers, onions, mushrooms, chicken and a large frying pan.

He places the pan on the stove and starts chopping vegetables. Once he's done, he tosses them in to the pan with the chicken, seasoning as he goes.

"What can I do to help?" I ask, suddenly feeling a little out of place.

"You can grab the sour cream, cheese and the container of guacamole out of the fridge."

I grab what I can find, but I can't locate the guac. "Where's the guac?"

"In the large plastic container, top shelf towards the back."

As I grab the bowl, I realize that it's homemade guacamole. "You made this?" I ask as I set the bowl on the table.

"Yeah, my mom's recipe. You seem surprised." He smirks.

"I guess I am. I've never met a man that can cook."

"Well, get used to it." He smiles, his pearly white teeth sparkling in the sunlight. This man is amazingly gorgeous and I can't take my eyes off of him. Rich, dark skin and those chocolate eyes.

He turns back to the stove and stirs the now sizzling veggies and chicken. He grabs another plastic container full of fresh tortillas and hands them to me. "Did you make these too?" I ask almost sarcastically.

He laughs, "Sadly, no. I can make them though, but these are store bought." I look at him with surprise. "Hey, you can make homemade pasta, I can make homemade tortillas. But this case has kept me away from home, so I've not had time to make any."

His mention of the case totally brings me back to the here and now. I look up at him and I know he can see the fear in my eyes. I'm struggling to be strong and get through this, but it's damn hard. Especially after hearing that another young girl has died. Then it dawns on me.

Four

There have been three girls so far and....... "I'm next aren't I? The note and........" I drop off, turning to look out the window.

"What Sydney?" He says as he turns the stove down and comes up behind me.

"How many girls have there been, total?"

"Three. The third washed up this morning."

I know, deep down inside that this guy is coming after me. My fingers absently brush against my hip where the number four is forever embedded in my skin. Silently I resolve to have that tattoo removed. Soon.

"Tell me Sydney, what are you thinking?"

I turn to him, fear and confusion filling my face. "I'm number four."

"What are you talking about?"

I pull the elastic down, exposing the tattoo. "Number four Gabe. He's making his way to ME! The note attached to the last girl....the fact that there have been three?"

"I know, Syd. That's why I brought you here. No one can bother you here, but you are not to leave this house without me."

"Great, nothing like being held prisoner again." I mumble, trying to be funny. But apparently, Gabe doesn't think it's very funny.

"Sydney, I'm trying to keep you safe. He can't find you here."

"How do you know, Gabe? How do you know we weren't followed?"

"I just know. No one knows where you are."

I reach in to my purse to get my phone and as I pull it out, Gabe takes it from me.

"Hey! You can't cut me off from the world completely!"

"Yes, I can. No one needs to know where you are just yet. Let the police do their job and catch this guy, Syd."

"You are the police!! Shouldn't you be doing something?"

"I am, Sydney. I've been put in charge of protecting YOU! And there's no place I'd rather be." He says as he wraps his arms around me. "No one - NO ONE, will get to you. That I can promise you."

"Don't make promises you can't keep, Gabe." I tell him again, as he likes to make promises.

"I have no intentions of breaking that promise, Syd. You. Are. Safe. With. Me." And his mouth rams down on mine, taking my breath away. His tongue licks in my mouth, taking what he wants, leaving me a heaving and panting mess. But he pulls back, brushing the hair out of my eyes.

"Let's eat."

Chapter 14
Gabe

We sit in silence as we eat and I'm enjoying watching her rolling her fajitas. Her lips wrap around the final product and I wish that was my cock her lips were wrapped around "Later." I tell myself. But after a bit, Sydney breaks the silence.

"I need to call Leslie. I was supposed to call her this morning and I can only imagine how freaked out she is right now."

"Chuck has already let her know what's going on, to an extent. She doesn't know everything, but she knows you're with me and that you're safe. Give it a day or so and you can call her, we just want to make sure no one knows where you are right now."

"What do you mean? You told me no one followed us, that I was safe here."

"You are, but the first twenty-four hours are critical. If someone knows you're here, we'll be made aware of it fairly quickly. These guys tend to make their move within a certain time frame thinking they're catching their victim off guard. That won't happen this time. The house is surrounded by off duty officers and a vacant home across the street has surveillance equipment installed. A camera is pointed right at the house constantly. No one will go unnoticed, please trust me."

"I'm trying, Gabe. But you must realize that I have trust issues. I trusted my father and we both know how that ended up."

"I'm not your father, Syd. I will never hurt you and I will never let anyone hurt you. You're safe here, I will guarantee that." I say, knowing there are no guarantees.

I watch her face after that comment, and I know she's not convinced. Hell, I'm not either for that matter. All I know is that I will do everything in my power to protect her. She's been let down before and that has happened for the last time in her life. I cringe at my own thoughts, because I can't be sure. Criminals like this have no regard for anyone else and will do whatever needed to get to the victim they want. If we can figure out who it is, then maybe we can nab him before he gets to Sydney.

"What did Chuck say about my brother? Is he accounted for?"

"Yes, he was working yesterday when the third victim washed up."

"What was her name?"

"Why?"

"I don't know, really. Just to put a name with the victim."

"Lacey Bennett. She was eighteen."

"Did she look like me too?"

"What do you mean?"

"Oh Gabe, don't play stupid with me. Did she look like me? Dark hair, dark eyes....you know?"

I shake my head, "No. This girl was blonde and blue eyed." And I know the question is coming. I'm not sure how much longer I can keep the biggest secret of them all. Something we have not made Sydney aware of.

"What Gabe? What aren't you telling me?"

I get up and gather our dishes, taking them to the kitchen. Before I can get there, Sydney grabs my arm and jerks me back, dishes go flying. "Shit, what the........!"

"DON'T 'WHAT THE HELL ME' GABERIAL TORRES!" Sydney starts screaming. "YOU KNOW MORE THAN YOU'RE LETTING ON, CHUCK TOO! AND DAMN IT, YOU WILL TELL ME! GIVE ME THE FUCKING FILE YOU HAVE ON ME! IF YOU WON'T TELL ME, THEN I'LL PUT THE PUZZLE PIECES TOGETHER MYSELF! IF I'M

SUPPOSED TO STAY SAFE, THEN I NEED TO KNOW WHAT I'M DEALING WITH!"

I really don't want her knowing all that I know. I wish that she could just trust me to keep her safe, but the details will come out soon enough. I pick the dishes up off of the floor while she stands there looking at me.

"If I give you these files......."

"Gabe?"

"I'll give you the files, but please....prepare yourself for what you find out."

And I walk away to my office to get the files and photos. Chuck is going to kill me, but Sydney is right. She deserves to know the truth. I just pray she can survive the truth.

I grab the files from my desk and contemplate removing some of the contents, so that she won't see them. But then I know, I can't lose her trust at this point. I want to keep her safe, now and always.

"Fuck." I say out loud.

"What is it, Gabe?" Sydney asks from behind me.

"Nothing, just thinking out loud."

She nods at me, but I can see by her reaction she doesn't believe me. "Those the files?"

"Yeah." I say as I hand them to her. "Let's go into the living room and spread them out over the coffee table, I can explain what it all is."

"No. Do you mind if I sit in here and go over them?" She asks as she sits down at my desk.

"I suppose not." I reply as I sit down in the chair across from her. She looks up at me and then back down at the folder, before lifting her eyes back to me.

"Umm, can I review these.....alone?"

I think, 'no way in hell' before nodding and leaving her alone. I know if I argue with her and try to bend the story any, she'll back away and I can't have that. She needs to know the truth, I know this. Though I don't want her knowing. But right now, it's not about me and I need to step back and let her do what she needs to do, hard as that might be.

I quietly close the door behind me as I leave my office and head back to the kitchen. I'll get the dishes done and out of the way. Maybe by that point she will be done reviewing the files and I can start trying to calm her down. Before I can get started, Chuck calls me with more details. I sit and listen to him intently, because I know Syd will want an update.

"The blonde is no relation to other girls. Seems to be just a random girl, but the DNA extracted from her matches the others." Chuck tells me. "Funny though, she doesn't appear to have been raped, no damage to the tissues and no bruising, almost as if it was consensual. She definitely had sex with the guy, but she wasn't raped. No skin found under her fingernails, no signs of trauma, with the exception of the snapped neck."

"Wait, he snapped her neck? What the hell, Chuck! Same DNA but different MO? This doesn't make any sense. Either he knows we're on to him and he's changing his signature, or he really knew this girl."

"We think he knew her, and maybe ran out of victims to kill until he can get his hands on Sydney. We're following up on that right now, but so far nothing else has come up. Is she all right?"

"I don't know, she's in my office going over the files on her and the others. She wanted to be alone when she went over them. I expect she'll come out of there pretty pissed off."

"Shit, I wish you had been with her while she went over them, to explain."

"I know, I tried. She's a stubborn woman so I didn't fight her. I'll be ready for her when she's done. Thank for the update." I say as I press the end button.

I get the dishes done and move to sit down on the sofa with a cold beer when she finally comes out of my office. I glance at my watch and realize she's been in there over an hour. Her face is white as a ghost and her hands are shaking. "Syd, are you all right?" I stand up and move towards her.

She glances at me, anger filling her eyes as a tear rolls down her cheek. She hold her hands up to me, keeping me at bay.

"YOU KEPT ALL OF THIS FROM ME! HOW COULD YOU?" She yells as she throws the folder at me. "I trusted you to.....hell, to keep me informed! Why didn't you tell me! I had a right to know that my father is in fact ALIVE!" And she storms off to the bathroom, slamming the door. The door lock clicking so loud that I think she might have broken it.

"SYDNEY, PLEASE. LET ME EXPLAIN!" I yell through the door. "Please come out and I can go over additional details."

The door flies open and she stands there glaring at me, "You mean there's more?"

"No, just more complete information. Those files were obtained early in the investigation. I talked to Chuck while you were in my office."

"Gabe, those girls......those girls were my......shit, I can't even say it." She says as she turns away from me, almost embarrassed.

"Your sisters, yes. Samantha and Sophia were your half-sisters. Syd, please come sit down and I can explain. I know more than the files show. Please."

She stalks into the living room, flopping down on the sofa. Her eyes are red and her face is puffy from crying. All I want to do is hold her in my arms and comfort her, but I know she'll push me away right now. She's hurt and angry and I hate that, so I refrain from touching her.

She looks at me, waiting and wondering.

"Syd, your father is dead. I read the coroner's report. This asshole is not your father, but we do believe he is related to you somehow."

"Well duh, Gabe. My DNA matches both girls AND the killer. Fuck! Why is this happening?" She cries in to her hands. "If it isn't my father, then who is it? You said my brother was working, are you sure it wasn't him?"

"Yes, he has an alibi for all three murders."

"The third one, is she a sister too?"

I shake my head, "Apparently not, but the same DNA was extracted from her body. We believe she had consensual sex with the unsub, so we feel that he knew her. There was no noticeable trauma on her body except the tattoo and......."

"And what Gabe?"

"Her neck was broken, but we don't believe he raped her."

I sit quietly and watch the expression on Sydney's face as she comes to the same realization Chuck and I came to earlier on the phone.

"He's changing his MO, Gabe. But if that's the case, why the tattoo of the number three on her hip? He knows we've linked it together and he's changing things up. But either way, he's after me next, I have no doubt. He's trying to throw us off course. But why kill an innocent girl? If he's after me, why not just come after me?"

"We aren't completely sure there are no other sisters. Chuck is looking into that right now, but I think what you said at dinner holds some truth." I tell her.

She sits quietly, contemplating her next words. "He needed a third victim before moving on to me, victim number four. Well I have news for you Detective, I will not be a victim again."

"No way, I'll make sure that never happens." And I step towards her, hoping her anger has dissipated and I can touch her, but she steps back from me.

"No, you aren't getting it Gabe. You need to put me in."

"What the fuck are you talking about?"

"He wants me, let him have me." She says, determination in her eyes.

"No fucking way, Syd. You've seen what this guy is capable of and I will not allow him to do it to you. No way." I shake my head and turn my back to her. I feel her small hand on my shoulder and my body tenses up. I will not allow myself to be distracted anymore. If she's volunteering to go and be killed, then I have to distance myself.

"Gabe, I wouldn't do it unprotected. Geez, I'm not a martyr. I'll have my gun and you won't be far away. I just have to figure out how to lure him to me without being obvious. Gabe, I need to go home. Now."

And she turns to get her jacket.

"Sydney, wait. Let's talk this through before jumping in."

"No, no more talking Gabe. Let's go."

And she walks out the door, slamming it behind her. I grab my keys and jacket, following her out. I lock up behind me and nod towards the house across the street, silently notifying them to be on the lookout.

But I look towards the car and Sydney's not there. She's gone. I hit the sidewalk and start turning in circles, looking up the street. Then down the street as I grasp for my phone. "What the fuck!" I ask the officer on the other end. "Who is this?" I ask.

"This is Detective Reynolds, sir. Are you leaving the house?"

"REALLY? DID YOU NOT JUST SEE US EXIT THE PROPERTY? WHICH WAY DID DOCTOR DECARLO GO?" I scream in to the phone.

"I...I...I'm sorry, Detective. I didn't see her leave, we thought she was locked up tight inside."

"Damn it! You had a job to do and you fucked it up! Now she's gone! Get Chuck Matthews, over here stat! I'm going searching on foot! You keep your God damn eyes on this house and you call me if she comes back, you got that? Can you handle that small task?"

"Yes sir."

Fuck, she's gone. FUCK! Why did she have to just barge out of the house like that? Damn, stupid!! She knew he was after her and she.....damn it, I have to get moving. I hike up the street and see one of my neighbors, Old Lady Thomason. I calm down and approach with caution, because she's a skittish old bird.

"Evening Mrs. Thomason."

She turns to look up at me, "Oh hi Detective Torres. Lovely evening isn't it?"

"Yes ma'am. Listen, did you see a young woman walk this way? She's about five foot five, long brown hair. She's wearing jeans and a yellow sweatshirt."

Her eyes glaze over as she thinks, "Well now, let me see. How long ago?"

"About two minutes ago, ma'am. Please, did you see her?"

"Ah now, Detective, running the ladies off already?" She tsks shaking her crooked finger at me.

"Apparently, ma'am. Did you see her or not?"

"Umm, no. I don't believe I did. But I will send her over if I see her."

"Thank you, Mrs. Thomason."

And I head back the other direction, scanning the street for unknown cars and people.

Nothing, I throw my hands in the air and scream about the time tires come screeching behind me.

Seeing it's the chief of the Brooklyn precinct, I march right over.

"Chief, you have a load of morons working for you. How in the hell can they......"

"Easy Torres, those are my men you're talking about."

"I don't give a FUCK about your men, Chief! They took their eyes off of my house and now Doctor DeCarlo is missing. If you want to claim those men, then go ahead because MY men wouldn't have slacked off on the job. Now, we need to get an APB out for Doctor Sydney DeCarlo, now! The first few hours are the most important."

"Don't tell me how to do my job, Torres. You brought this problem to Brooklyn from

Manhattan, you'll work on my terms here."

"Fuck you, I'm calling in the FBI."

"No you won't Torres. You have no jurisdiction here, now back off and let us do our job."

"Do your job? If your men had been doing their *job*, we wouldn't be standing here arguing."

"Torres, you don't know Jack Shit, now step down."

"Fuck you, Chief! Your men's ineptitude just caused a young woman to disappear!"

"Wait, what do you mean *disappear?*" He asks.

"REALLY? ASK YOUR FAITHFUL MEN WHAT HAPPENED!" I scream as I point over to the vacant house across the street. "I'm calling in the FBI and when you find out how stupid your *men* are, you'll be glad I did."

I march towards my house as the Chief gets on his radio. I hear him barking orders but I ignore him, dialing my own phone.

"Chuck Matthews."

"It's Torres, call in the FBI."

"Why, what's happened?"

"Idiots here not paying attention and Sydney's gone."

"WHAT THE FUCK?" Chuck screams in to the phone.

"Yeah, she got a wild hair up her ass to go home, to become a martyr and walked out the damned door. Before I could grab my keys and follow her, she vanished without a trace. Damn surveillance team fucked up."

"Obviously. No witnesses? No one saw her outside?"

"Not that I can locate. Street was pretty empty when I got out here. When I called the team across the street, they were like 'huh'. Fucking morons."

"Easy, Gabe. We'll find her. Calling Jason Morrison with the Feds right now. Stay put, I'm on my way too."

"Right, easy for you to say Chuck. She was in my protection and...FUCK!" I scream as I drag my fingers through my unruly hair. "Damn it Chuck, I failed her. She's never going to trust me again."

"Gabe, you and I both know this unsub is unpredictable, look at the last girl. He knows we're on to him so he's changing it up. We'll find her."

"We better, because I don't think we have much time."

"I know. I'll be there soon."

Chapter 15
Gabe

An hour and a half later, Chuck pulls in with Special Agent Jason Morrison of the FBI right behind him. Jason shakes my hand and nods towards the house across the street, "They still there?"

"Yeah, they're going through the video footage, looking for anything that might tell us what happened to Syd.....Doctor DeCarlo."

"Surely they had the camera on and saw where she went, right?" Mo says as he walks towards the surveillance house. "Let's go light a fire under them, eh?"

Chuck and I follow him as we ascend the stairs of the brownstone and cross the street. This house has been vacant for years, supposed rumors of a murder occurring there, and the owners have never been able to sell it. It's been up for rent now for a few weeks, but so far it remains empty, and right now I'm glad for that.

Mo opens the door and walks in without knocking, heading up the stairs to the master bedroom that overlooks the street. As we walk in, we see three NYPD officers staring at a blank screen and pressing buttons frantically on the recorder.

"Gentlemen? You have been relieved of your duties, you may be dismissed." Jason tells them as he marches into the room.

"Excuse me?" One of the officers stands up and faces him, nose to nose. "And who the fuck are you?"

"Special Agent Jason Morrison, Federal Bureau of Investigations. This is now a federal case, your services are no longer needed." He replies as he flashes his badge at the man. The officer moves to pack up the equipment but Jason quickly shuts that down, "No. Leave the equipment.

We're going to go over all of the footage you obtained to see if we can figure out what happened to Doctor De Carlo."

"Well, there's a problem with that." The officer says.

"Problem? There better not be a problem, Officer. And if there is, you'd better take care of it now, or you'll have even bigger problems."

Jason is a *no holds barred* kinda man, takes no prisoners and gets his point across quickly.

"Now, what appears to be the problem, and then tell me what you plan to do to correct the problem?"

"Umm, you see sir....." The officer stutters. "The camera, umm, it didn't capture anything."

"What do you mean it didn't capture *anything?*"

"It malfunctioned, or something, sir. That's what we were just trying to figure out."

"Show me." Jason says as he walks over to the small TV screen that the other two men are staring at.

"Nothing to show you, sir. Just a blank screen. Either the camera malfunctioned or......."

"WHAT DO YOU MEAN THE CAMERA *MALFUNCTIONED?*" I yell from behind Jason.

Jason turns to me, "Easy Gabe." Then he turns to the officer that appears to be in charge, though I doubt any of them have a fucking clue what they're doing. "What kind of malfunction?"

Damn, how can he be so calm? Sydney is out there somewhere, possibly being raped and......shit, I can't think that way. I let her down earlier buy letting this bastard get her, but I will make it up to her by saving her ass. God, I hope I can save her.

"OUT OF MY WAY, OFFICER!" I hear Jason scream at the dude blocking the TV. The skinny officer backs away slowly, fear crossing his eyes. Jason pulls up a chair and starts pressing buttons, adjusting the focus and after about ten minutes, the blurred screen comes in to view.......a beat up blue Honda parked on the curb, the door opening up and a young kid exiting the vehicle.

"You guys need to go back to the academy." Jason mumbled under his breath. I watch the three officers eyes dart between each other and the 'oh shit' looks they have on their faces. I silently chuckle as it appears they are amateurs at best. The three officers back away and I take one of the vacant seats next to Jason, Chuck standing behind me.

"Can you zoom in on the tag?"

"Yeah, but let's make sure this is the dude that got her." About that time my front door flies open and Sydney descends the stairs, hitting the sidewalk at a fast clip. Before she can even take in her surroundings the young guy that just exited the car slyly walks up behind her, pressing a white cotton cloth over her face, her body instantly collapsing in his arms. The guy moves quickly, shoving her in the back seat of his car and takes off about the time my door flies open again and I can been seen locking my door.

"Damn, he was quick. I never even saw his car pull away. He moved so fast!"

"Yeah, but at least we have a lead now." Jason says as he presses the rewind button, precisely stopping on the clearest view of the car. He spins the dials and presses more buttons, zooming in on the tag. It's not very clear, because the car was dirty and beat up. But after a few minutes we're able to get a clear enough shot of the tag, taken as the vehicle drove away.

"Shit!" I exclaim as I realize what I'm seeing.

"What?" Jason asks, turning to me.

"Can't you see that? That's not a New York tag."

Jason zooms in a little closer and sure enough, an Illinois tag.

"Does she have a connection to Illinois?" Jason asks as he ejects the CD and stands up.

"Yeah, she's from the Chicago area, Lincoln Park to be exact." And I'm suddenly thankful for the small bits of personal information she divulged during our previous conversations. She didn't give away much, but she gave away enough for the time being.

Then Mo freezes, his eyes on the television monitor. "Jesus." I hear him whisper as he glares at the officer standing behind him and pokes his finger in his chest. "You have no idea what a fuck-up you really are, do you?" Then his eyes meet the eyes of the two other officers in the room. "You guys better start praying." He says as he turns to me.

"Well, let's get to the local precinct and run this tag." He says as he exits the home, glaring at the clueless officers standing against the back wall. "Clean this shit up and meet us downtown, you have a meeting with your superiors."

It takes about eight minutes to get to the Sixty-Seventh precinct down on Snyder Ave, in late evening traffic. I follow Jason in through the doors and straight to Chief Andrew's office. Great, we've already had one altercation today and I have a feeling there's about to be another one.

He's not going to be thrilled that the FBI has been called in, especially after he defended his men.

I can't let that bother me at this point. Right now, I want that tag run so we can get an APB out on the vehicle. He couldn't have gotten far, but far enough to cause a substantial delay in finding Sydney. The first twenty-four hours are the most critical, and we're only three hours in. But, a lot of ground can be covered after three hours. If those idiots had been paying attention and doing their fucking jobs, we wouldn't be here right now. I'd be back at my place playing doctor with Sydney.

"ANDREWS!" Jason yells as he blasts past reception and straight down the hall towards the Chief's domain.

"Sir? You have to check in, please. Sir!" The dispatcher at the front desk hollers down at us, but we don't look back. The three of us march down the hall, single file, and on a mission.

"ANDREWS!" Jason calls out again. As we approach his office, he meets us in the hallway.

"What the fuck......shit, Morrison." He says, his eyes darting back and forth between the three of us.

"I told you I was calling in the Feds, now let's have a seat in your office, Andrews." I say as I step around Mo. Mo steps back and allows me this one moment before I'm sure he'll take over. I get up in his face, my finger poking his chest. Andrews may be six foot three and two hundred pounds, but he doesn't scare me. "Your men fucked up back there, Andrews. They're packing up that shit you call equipment and they'll be coming to see you, soon. Now, we've got work to do."

I say as I push him back into his office, somewhat gently, but probably a little harder than needed.

Morrison tosses the slip of paper on Andrews' desk with the tag number of the car. "I need this tag run, now. Had your men been paying attention and doing their fucking job, we wouldn't be here right now. But they didn't and we are, so you are at my mercy right now, Andrews."

I see a flash of fear cross Andrews' eyes as he reaches for the paper, his eyes never leaving mine. With his other hand, Andrews picks up his phone and presses a number. "King, it's Andrews. I need a tag run, stat." He says in to the phone and then rattles off the tag number.

"This is priority one man, I need it yesterday." And he hangs up the phone.

"Morrison......" Andrews speaks, but Mo cuts him off.

"Andrews, don't even try and pull rank here. Feds have jurisdiction over local PD and you know it. This is my case now, and you will do what I say." Mo says as he leans on to Andrews' desk, fire shooting from his eyes.

"Your 'so called' men back there allowed a marked woman to get out of their sights. They were put in place to watch and instead, they were jacking off and watching porn. Do you get that? They tried to cover it up, but MY MEN are smarter than yours." He screams at Andrews as he slams a CD on to his desk.

"Go ahead, fire it up." He says as he nudges his head towards the DVD player in the corner of his office. "I expect to hear about a mass firing here and if not, well....let's just say you don't want the press involved in this."

Andrews reluctantly picks up the disc and inserts it in to the machine while turning on the television. I stand back and watch his reaction as he sees what his men were watching. At first, you see the street and my house, and all is quiet. Then static covers the screen and a low budget porno fills the screen. I drop my head in embarrassment for the whole of NYPD. This is a scandal waiting to happen and I start to rethink my career choice. Maybe once this is over, I'll leave NYPD and join the bureau. I can't think about that right now, though. We need to find Sydney, and we need to find her now. Before it's too late.

I watch Andrews watch the video feed and redness creeps up his neck and I think I see smoke coming out of his ears. He looks furious, as he should. His men are douche bags and if they worked for me, they would be out of here. He grabs his phone and calls another number.

"Karen, get me Officers Flint, Miller and Sanchez. I want them in my office within the hour."

And he slams the phone down. He stares at the screen shaking his head, "I don't even know what to say, except this.....I need to call the academy and get some new recruits, because I'm down three men now."

Chapter 16
Sydney

A musty, moldy smell awakens me. Shit, it's happened again. As I blink away the cobwebs, I glance around the room. Fuck, it's the same damned basement. He brought me back to the scene of the original crime. The hairs stand up on the back of my neck and my body tenses up. My hands are bound behind my back and I'm sitting upright in a metal chair. THE metal chair.

But I'm alone. The only sounds are dripping water somewhere behind me. The air is stagnant and the smell.....the smell is the same, nothing has changed in almost twenty years. Gray cinder block walls, dirty concrete floor and only a trace of light drifting in under the door. I stare at it, waiting for it to open and my father to come walking in. I know deep inside that it's impossible, but if it isn't my brother......

The door opens and the bright light shines in, blinding me. In walks a young man. No, a boy.

I glare at him through squinty eyes, and can't quite focus on him. Dark hair, dark eyes and just a baby. Surely.....

"Well, well. The bitch is awake. How about that, Sydney? Or should I say, *Doctor?*"

"Who are you and what do you want from me?"

"In time, Doctor. All in good time."

He moves up closer. His face now right in mine. His breath smells rancid and rotten, so I try to hold it in without vomiting all over him. His grimy fingers brush across my face, "Beautiful. This is going to be fun." He breathes across my face and I shiver.

I jerk my head back and spit in his face. "MMMM, thanks for that. I needed a little taste of what I'm about to enjoy." He laughs as his tongue licks my saliva from his bottom lip. His fingers grip my chin hard as his dirty mouth comes crashing down on mine, the odor causing my stomach to flip. I fight him best I can, knowing his tongue is about to be bitten off if he even tries anything further.

But he knows better and pulls back, trailing his fingers down my chest. I search his body for a weapon of some sort, but he appears to be unarmed for now. My hands are tingling behind me from the tightness of the ropes binding them. I wriggle my wrists and fingers to try and get the blood pumping through them, but that's nearly impossible. My mind keeps flashing back to the first time I sat in this dungeon, begging for my life. I got out, I survived and I have to keep that close to my heart. I can get out again, I will survive. All I have to do is wait for this kid to do something stupid. And he will, and I must be ready.

"You recognize this place, Doctor?" He says as he walks around the room like he's taking a museum tour. He takes a deep breath, "The smell? You remember the smell Doctor?" He looks back at me with terror in his eyes. "Yes, you do don't you? By the look in your eyes, you remember it all too well."

"Who are you?" I ask again. But before he answers, I hear him behind me, the shrill sound of duct tape being ripped from the roll. His arms reach around me and he slams the tape across my mouth.

"No talking, Doctor. I will talk and you will listen." He growls as he bruises my face by the force. He grabs my hair and jerks my head back so that I'm looking back at him, upside down.

"You will sit here quietly until I'm ready for you. But be prepared bitch, because I've been ready for this for twenty years. I'm ready for my revenge Doctor. Are you ready to be number four again?" And he drops my face, pushing it forward so hard my chin hits my chest. "You sit here and remember being number four the last time, whore."

But as I scan his face trying to carve his features in to my mind, I see it. A strange tattoo engraved in to his neck. I can't make out what it is, but it appears to be a snake or other reptile, curling up in an "S" shape from his collar, up his neck, ending behind his ear. He turns and leaves the room, the door slamming behind him. I exhale a breath and scan the room frantically. Sure enough, there it is. The tattoo gun. It now taunts me, scares me. Paralyzes me. I realize he's going to mark me. Maybe not now, but at some point, he will mark me. Another ink portrait to go along with the other one, a constant memory to take with me everywhere. He plans to make sure I never forget.

But he mentioned revenge. Revenge for what? I'm the victim here, though I cringe at that thought. I never wanted to be a victim and I've refused to call myself that for so many years, but I guess I am. A poor, tortured victim, all because of my father.

I watched as the young boy left the basement, leaving me to my own devices. As he exits the room it hits me. The boy that slammed into me, three times, on the streets of New York. He's been watching me for……shit, who knows how long? He's the same boy that jumped me in the street, the one that got away. The lock clicks behind him and I struggle to free my hands. But it's no use, the ropes are too tight. He must have been a boy scout, because he sure knows how to tie a knot. But who is he and why is he after me? My eyes travel the room, looking for some hint as to who this asshole is and why he feels he needs revenge on me. I wonder silently if I counseled him as a young boy. Maybe he was abused and........yeah, that has to be it. Apparently, psychoanalysis didn't work on him. It does backfire sometimes, but I never imagined someone would come after me because of it.

But how did he know about this place? It then dawns on me that this place......is in Chicago.

I'm no longer in New York and the odds of someone finding me here are remote. At least not until I'm washing up in the Chicago River, or Lake Michigan. I shiver at the thought, and resign myself to getting out of here, alive.

I hear cluttering noises from outside the door, so I know he's still here. I close my eyes and try and take deep, calming breaths. But the smell is rancid and I struggle not to cough. I flash back to when I was here twenty years ago and the ending results. I know, that by the time this is over, there will be another dead body. I silently pray it won't be mine.

Glass shatters and curses fly out of my captor's mouth outside the door. My heart jumps into my throat and I try and swallow around the lump. After a few minutes of this, it goes quiet.

Eerily silent and all I hear are my shallow breaths and that dripping behind me. A car engine roars and tires squeal out of the driveway. He's gone. But for how long? My brain goes into overdrive and I start to panic, trying to think of a way to get out of here before he gets back. But my hands are tied so tight and my fingers are going numb from the lack of circulation. I make a futile attempt at wriggling them, but it feels like pins and needles stabbing through them. I fight through the pain and continue to wriggle them around, stretching them and bending them backwards best I can in their confines.

But before I can loosen the ropes any, I hear the same squeal of tires on the pavement outside. "Shit, he's back already. Fuck! I....need.....to.......loosen.....these.....ropes." I grunt out loud behind the duct tape, as I struggle to obtain a little give in this rope. The door to the house slams and I hear him right outside the door. His shoes blocking the light spilling into the room.

He's stopped right outside the door, as if he's listening. So I close my eyes and hold my breath, trying not to draw attention to myself.

Finally the shadows leave the light and he walks away from the door. I exhale through my nose again and begin to fiddle with the ropes again. Just as I feel I've made a little progress, the door flies open and he stalks in.

"Good evening, Doctor. Are you comfortable?" He asks facetiously as he sets a paper bag on the ground with an evil twinkle in his eye. I nod at him, feigning comfort. But in fact, my back is hurting and my fingers are still numb from the tightness of the rope.

He reaches in to the bag and I hear metal jingling. With a smirk, he pulls his hands out and holds up two sets of handcuffs. I glare at him, because I can't speak. I know he sees fear in my eyes and I blink it back, trying to not give him the satisfaction of my fear.

"Reinforcements, Doctor." He answers my unasked question. "You got out of the ropes last time, that won't happen again." He says as he snaps one set of cuffs on my ankle, securing me to the leg of the chair. He then fastens the other set before grabbing one more set from the bag. He stalks around me, his eyes scanning from my face to my feet, an erotic look in his eyes. I follow his eyes, giving him my best 'eat shit' look I can muster with duct tape across my face.

As he continues to circle the chair, I realize he's as stupid as he's acting. The chair I'm sitting in is not fastened to the concrete. "What an idiot." I say to myself, thankful I couldn't say it out loud. He pulls up a chair in front of me and straddle it, the back of the chair to his front.

His eyes are a dark brown, almost black. Dark hair and olive skin, like me. I can almost see myself in his face, the similarities are uncanny. We stare like this at each other for a long time, saying nothing. His putrid breath wafts across my nose, causing a gagging sensation. I swallow it back down, because puking with my mouth sealed would be instant suffocation and I refuse to die that way.

"You're still wondering who I am, right?" He asks, cocking his head slightly and his upper lip crooking up. I nod, because that's all I can do. His dirty finger rises and traces the edge of my chin, almost gently. I close my eyes and squirm at his touch. He presses it to the underside of my chin and roughly lifts my head up to look at him. "Open your eyes, bitch. Look at me. Always look at me. I want you to see the monster you've created." He growls at me. "Yeah, I'm a monster, Doctor. I kill women that look like you, that want to be like you. You drew yourself in to this situation twenty years ago and I'm here to make sure you pay for what you've done. I will get my revenge, once and for all."

My body starts trembling not because of his words, but because of the murderous look in his eyes. I know now that I need to fight for what is right and get myself out of here. Because if I truly am in Chicago, Gabe will never find me.

He steely eyes bore in to my soul as he stares me down, his fingers gripping my chin harder and harder. I feel his finger nail penetrate the skin and a drop of blood drips down my chest. My body is shaking now, even though I'm fighting for control. He gets in my face and his breath clogs my senses.

"You. Will. Pay for what you did, Doctor. You will pay, again and again. I will show you no mercy, Doctor. And maybe, if you're a good little girl, I'll tell you who I am. But for now, open your mouth." He says as he rips the duct tape from my face.

He stands and unbuttons his dirty jeans, sliding them down. His erect penis springs free and bobbles in my face. "OPEN YOUR MOUTH BITCH!" He screams at me, pinching my jaw hard so that I have no choice but to open up.

"How can you be sure I won't bite your dick off, asshole?" I spit in his face. I immediately regret it, because that could have been a way out for me. But I hold my regard and stare at him as his cock rests on my bottom lip. He hasn't showered for days and the smell makes me nauseous.

I gag and heave before my stomach empties all over his stomach.

"YOU LITTLE WHORE!" He yells as he stands back, my vomit rolling down his pants leg. "You just bought yourself trouble." He says as he removes his pants so that he's completely naked from the waist down. He picks up his pants and throws them at me, the stiff denim landing in a thud on my lap. "You can hold on to those while I go change. But don't think you're out of the woods yet, Doctor. I've heard you give good head, and I plan to find out just how good you are.

If you pass the test, I might let you live."

He slams the door behind him and I wriggle just enough to get his jeans off of me. They hit the floor in a thunk, but the odor still fills my nose. I fight off another bout of nausea and manage to calm my stomach, and my thoughts. He walked out without taping my mouth up, so I am free to speak - or scream, but I decide against it. I look around my feet and see that I could easily get out of here, the handcuffs only wrapped around the legs, and the chair is not secure. A rocking motion and I can free my legs. But do I do it now and risk him walking in? I shake my head no, I think I need to wait until he least expects it. He's going to have to sleep at some point, so I sit there and stare at the walls, waiting for him to return.

Long seconds drag by before I see his shadow under the light of the door again. My heart rate picks up and beads of sweat tickle the back of my neck. He was angry when he left before, so I can only imagine how his mind must be now. In my professional experience, I figure he will come back in clean and with a different attitude, on the outside. Inside, his mind is boiling and he's ready to kill. But he also knows that if he comes in here smelling like he did before, I will probably vomit all over him again and he won't be able to complete his task of raping me.

I'm unable to get my hands free, but I will be able to get my legs free should he try anything.

My Sanshou training will come in handy for this, and he won't know what hit him. Well, he'll know it when he's having my foot surgically removed from his ass.

The door knob slowly turns and the door opens, and I was right. His hair is wet, he's clean shaven and wearing clean clothes. The overwhelming scent of his cheap cologne flows into the room. I take a deep breath, because it's better than the moldy vomit smell in here. His eyes are glowing with evil, and strangely, romance. What does this creep think he's going to do? Woo me into sleeping with him? I stare back at him, anger flowing from my eyes. His lips curl in a seductive smile, baring his crooked teeth.

"Now, Doctor. I hope you're ready for me." He spits at me while he stalks towards me, his fingers toying with the hem of his shirt, that smirk curling his lips. He stands in front of me, his abdomen in my face. I cringe back and slam my eyes shut, cause I don't want to see what he's about to do. "Open your eyes." He says as I feel him get closer to me "You're going to finish what you started earlier. And you won't complain one bit, bitch." He lowers his zipper and his cock rolls out of his jeans. I turn my head away, clamping my mouth shut. But he grabs my chin and pulls it forward, pressing in to my cheek. My mouth opens, even though I try hard to keep it shut.

"You can fight me all you want, Doctor. I like it rough. But no matter how hard you fight, you will suck my dick."

He slides his cock in to my mouth and I struggle not to gag on it. But he pulls back and releases his cock from my lips, only to raise his hand and punch me in the face. The sound of his fist connecting with my jaw echoes in the room and spit flies from my mouth. I taste blood and I lick the droplet away. Before I can focus, he jams himself in my mouth and grabs the back of my head. In order to avoid being punched like that, I let him use my mouth how he wants. But he better be prepared for what he might have to endure if he...... "Shit!" He screams as he pulls back, releasing his filth all over my face. I clamp my lips shut to avoid consuming any of it, while ribbons of fluid splash across my face.

I resist the urge to gag and sit as still as possible, eyes closed and taking deep breaths through my nose. Before I can open my eyes, his fist comes back and slams against my jaw again.

"THAT'S IT BITCH, DAMN!" I hear him scream before my world goes black again.

Chapter 17
Gabe

"Andrews! I need to know who that tag is registered to! What the hell is taking so long?" I scream as I beat on his desk. "Get that tag run now!" I beat on the desk one last time before turning towards the door, pulling my phone out.

I scroll through the contacts and find the Delta Airlines number, quickly pressing the send button. "I need the next flight out of New York to Chicago O'Hare." She puts me on hold and comes back with the flight times out of both JFK and Newark. Mo is looking at me over his shoulder, shaking his head. I know what he's thinking, he's thinking I'm jumping the gun. We don't know for a fact she's in Chicago, but my gut instinct tells me she is.

"Hold tight, Gabe." He mouths to me. I tell the rep I'll call her back and slide the off button.

"Got it!?" Andrews says as he hangs up his phone. "Vehicle is registered to a Luis DeCarlo, out of Lincoln Park, Illinois."

"Shit," is all I can say. "Mo, he's dead right? I saw the coroner's report. Syd shot him point blank, twenty years ago. How can....."

"Relax, Gabe. Just because the car is registered to him, doesn't mean it was him. Andrews, what about the APB? Did anyone get a lead on where the car was going?" Before he can answer, Mo's phone rings. I watch him as his face lets me know we got a lead. "Right, I'm on it. Get Chicago PD over to that address and wait. If he just left New York, we've got about eight hours to get there, and we'll be waiting for him. But, do not engage until the Feds get there, you got it?" And I follow his phone with my eyes as he shoves the phone in his pocket. "Let's go.

Andrews, you're driving."

We pile in to the car, Andrews throws the blues on while we speed through traffic towards JFK airport. We arrive in about thirty minutes and make our way to Delta airlines counter, flashing badges in order to get to the front of the line. "We need two tickets on your next flight to Chicago." Mo tells the attendant.

"Sure, the next flight is at five eighteen, sir. Shall I reserve your seats?" She asks.

"Shit, that's three hours, Mo. We need to get there before Syd does, be there waiting for her."

I say to Mo, who is scanning the departure boards above our heads.

"Shit, that's the closest flight, Gabe. No other airline has one this close, we're just gonna have to book it and hope we get there in time."

I was not happy that the next flight was three hours away, then we have a three hour flight.

Then on top of that, we'd have the thirty minutes to Luis' house pending we don't hit any traffic.

"Guess we don't have any choice, book them ma'am." I say to the attendant.

She finishes up and hands us our boarding passes and we make our way through security towards the gate. We both wait impatiently for word that maybe one of the Feds has tagged the car along the way, but that doesn't happen.

We make our way through security, our badges allowing us to pass with our weapons, but not without a fight and a phone call to FBI HQ in Virginia.

Once we're in the air, Mo opens his laptop and connects to the on-board Wi-Fi. He links via VPN to his office computer and opens a file labeled "DeCarlo". I'm looking over his shoulder and he turns the screen towards me. "I have Luis DeCarlo's file here from when we started this investigation. He's dead for sure, but we have to figure out who is driving his car. What did you find out on Sydney's brother, Franco DeCarlo?"

"He holds two jobs and was accounted for when all three girls washed up. He's not considered a suspect, at this time. That could all change once we get to Chicago. Has CPD been to Franco's house and questioned him?"

Mo nods, "Yeah, he's clear for now. But now, he and his mother are worried and I'm afraid they might start sticking their noses where they don't belong." He pulls up his email program and shoots an email off to CPD, asking for a car to head out to the DeCarlo residence and make sure they stay put. "All we need is for Franco and Gloria Watkins to get in the middle. They may not be close with Sydney anymore, but they like to get their fingers dirty. When Syd disappeared as a young girl, they were right in the middle of it. Gloria tried to defend her husband, the rapist of her daughter in court. It was almost as if she condoned it, allowed it. Franco was the same way, testified in court that his father could have never raped and murdered those women and especially not his own daughter."

"Wait, murdered what women? I don't remember him being charged with any other crimes."

"No, but the deaths of two of his victims were suspicious. Samantha Brockman's birth mother committed suicide and Sophia Fishman's mother died during childbirth. Both families requested investigations be opened and further tests performed on the bodies, but the police ruled them both accidental. The files were closed and sealed, never to be reopened. Until now."

"What do you mean, until now?" I ask him.

"I've requested those files be reopened, and further investigations done. The two girls murdered were Luis's daughters....."

"Wait, is it possible he had other children from other victims?"

"That's one thing we're looking into. It's been twenty years, so who knows? At the time, only three victims were identified. Belinda Franklin was Samantha's mother and Jessica Bailey was Sophia's mother. The deaths occurred 3 months apart and since they couldn't be connected at the time, they were closed. Then another woman, the only one to wash up in Lake Michigan was never connected, until now. Her file was pulled and sure enough, she recently had given birth, but no one ever reported her or the baby missing. We are now assuming she was victim number three. And Sydney was the fourth victim, his own daughter. The only one that survived.

That tells me someone is out for revenge, we just have to figure out who."

"Even though the babies had the same father?" I ask.

"Yeah, but since the mothers were dead for different reasons, they couldn't pin anything to him. Jessica had a very difficult delivery and lost a lot of blood, she basically bled to death. And Belinda's was ruled a suicide as she was found in her car in the garage, doors closed and the engine running. Nothing suspicious about either death. It wasn't until both daughters washed up that things started to get confusing."

"Was Luis listed on either birth certificate?" I ask Mo.

Mo shakes his head, "No. Each one listed the mother only, with father as unknown. We checked into that already. CPD is looking into any birth records listing Luis DeCarlo as the father. So far, only Sydney, Franco and her sister Sylvia comes up. They are also checking into possible aliases for Luis. Not a lot was done in regards to investigating him after Sydney shot him. They figured he was dead, he couldn't hurt anyone again, so the investigation was closed."

"You mentioned Franco and Gloria tried to defend him, correct?" I ask.

Mo nods his head, "Yes, but nothing ever came of it. The courts never even considered investigating, the forensics pointed to Luis all the way, hell - his body was right there and his semen was found in Sydney. It was obvious that he raped her and planned to kill her. He fucked up though, and lost the ultimate battle, his life.

"And now, Syd is going through it all over again." I say as my body tenses up and my mind prepares for a fight. I have to stay focused and positive. She got out alive the first time, and she's a much stronger woman now than she was then. Hell, she was just a girl the first time. No girl should ever have to endure this once, let alone twice. I silently will the plane to move faster, because I feel we are running out of time.

I feel a nudge on my arm and it's Mo. "We're at the gate. I hope you got rested up, because we've got a fight on our hands." He says as he hands me his phone. There are three text messages waiting for him once he could turn his phone on.

"Car is waiting out front, CPD cruiser."

"Car is parked at the DeCarlo residence. No one appears to be home."

"Blue, 1993 Honda Civic matching tag in driveway at residence on South Halsted Street, Chicago."

"Fuck! That's the same address, Mo."

"Same address as what?" He huffs out as we run through the airport.

"The same address, Mo. He took her back to the scene of the original crime. Fuck, we've got to get to her, NOW!"

We locate the CPD Crown Vic parked on the curb, blues on. We climb in and I rattle off the address to the cop behind the wheel.

"Yes sir, we are already on scene."

"Then go. Hurry."

The driver steps on the gas, lights and sirens blaring. Cars get out of our way and we speed down I90 through the city and down towards the south side. We're about ten miles out when my phone rings.

"Torres."

"Gabe, it's Detective Ryan Wilbanks, Chicago bureau. You guys en route?"

"Yeah, what's the latest?"

"Well, we have SWAT on scene and surveillance at the DeCarlo residence. DeCarlo house is quiet, but it appears someone is home."

"Do NOT...I repeat, do NOT engage until we get there. We're about ten minutes out. Tell your men to stay put and do not engage."

"No sir. But, the longer we wait the......"

"I know, wait. She's a strong woman. If she's still alive, she'll stay that way."

God, let her still be alive.

We merge on to I94 and then exit on to South Lafayette. We head on to South Halstead off of W 71st Street and stop about six houses down. The street is quiet and I see no emergency vehicles. "Where are they?"

"On South Emerald, one street back. There's a vacant lot back there and guns are aimed at the house. We've evacuated the immediate area. You may not see us, but we're here."

"Good. I'm heading towards the house on foot, you guys keep my back will ya?"

"Wait Gabe." Mo tells me. "You're out of your jurisdiction, NYPD has no say here, so you'll have to stay back."

"What the fuck? I didn't come all this way to stay back, you find a way to get me in there, Mo. Or I'll break the fucking rules and deal with it later. You got it?"

Mo just looks at me. He knows I know the rules, but right now those rules can go fuck themselves. We stare at each other in silent unison.

I grab my phone and call Chuck Matthews.

"Matthews, it's Torres."

"Gabe, what's going on? You're in Chicago right? Any word on Syd?"

"Not yet, but I have something I need to say."

"Um, okay. Go ahead."

"I quit."

"Gabe, wait. What? You're quitting? Like this? You can't be......."

"Chuck, hear me! I fucking quit!"

And I end the call, looking eagerly towards Mo. He reaches out his hand and shakes mine vigorously. "Welcome to the bureau. Now let's go get this guy, and your girl."

Chapter 18
Sydney

Tears puddle in the corners of my eyes and I can't stop them. I'm so tired and weak and....what's that sound? I open my eyes and look around the room. My captor is over in the corner warming up the tattoo gun. I shake my head in fear, "Please don't mark me. I'll do whatever you want, just don't use that on me."

"Aww, the little doctor is begging now. Good, I like beggars." He croons as he stalks towards me, wheeling the machine behind him. He revs the gun like a motor, taunting me. I flash back to when my father engraved my skin, giving me a constant reminder of my past. I shake off the thoughts, because now is not the time to give up. He hunkers down before me, pressing a finger against my cheek. The remnants of his release stuck to my skin like glue. He shoves his finger in my mouth, "Suck it, baby. Take it all."

He squeezes my cheeks around his finger, but I hold back from sucking. This angers him and he punches me in the stomach, "You have a hard time listening don't you? I said SUCK IT!"

And he smacks me again, this time across the face. I stifle a scream because I don't want to seem weak to him, though he's slowly breaking me down. As I suck on his nasty finger, he reaches down and squeezes my breast so hard it hurts. He pinches my nipple and I suck in a breath from the pain. "You like that don't you, you little whore. You made our dad a happy man, didn't you?"

I bite down hard on his finger and he yanks it out of my mouth, hitting me again. "Damn, you're a feisty bitch. No wonder dad liked you the best."

"What the fuck are you talking about?"

"Yeah, bitch. Don't look so shocked, big sister. I'm Luis DeCarlo's demon spawn, just like you. Surprised?" He says as he walks back to the tattoo gun, turning it on. "And now, we're going to seal the deal." He says as he grabs my hair and yanks my head back, exposing my neck.

I feel the needle stab the sensitive skin under my ear as he starts to inject ink in to my skin. I squirm and fight him off the best I can, but he's holding me down. I can't even rock the chair to get my legs loose. What feels like hours goes by while he continues his masterpiece behind my ear. The buzzing and pricking sending my brain on a tailspin of emotions.

Suddenly he stops, turning the gun off. He grabs the duct tape, the shrill sound of him tearing off a strip and he plasters it to my face. "Not a word, or I'll kill you now instead of later."

And he walks to the small, rectangular window. "Shit. We've got company babe. Maybe I'll finish this off with a gang bang, eh? What do ya say? You up to it?" He says as he starts to undo my hands and legs. "Nah, you're mine Doctor. All fucking mine, now let's go."

He re-secures the handcuffs on my hands behind my back and drags me out into the other room, through the kitchen and into a mud room. He plants me in the corner and I get a glimpse of myself in a mirror there. My hair is a wild mess, my face is dirty and bloody, sticky with his residue. A trickle of blood sliding down the side of my face from behind my ear, where his artwork now lives. My eyes are wild and frantic. If he takes me out of here, I'm as good as dead.

In fact, if he takes me out of here I would prefer to be dead. He gets away, I might not ever be found. I can't live this way, I won't.

But the fact that this guy is my brother throws me off. How did he fly under the radar for so long? We knew about my sisters, the ones that......wait. He killed them both, and the other girl, making me number four again. I want to ask him questions, but with tape across my face I can't.

We have the same features, but........ "Let's go." He says quietly, bringing me out of my thoughts.

He grabs my hands behind my back and shoves me out of the back door, making sure I'm a shield for him. Parked there next to the blue Honda is a newer model, black sedan. It's very simple and doesn't stand out. He opens the back door and shoves me in, face first. Then he gets in, the engine roaring to life before he jerks the car forward, sending me in to the floor board of the car.

"Get up bitch! Get where I can see you!" He screams.

I struggle with this task, as my hands are cuffed behind my back. But I manage to roll myself in to the back seat and struggle to sit up.

"No, lay down. If they start shooting you might get hit." What?

He's protecting me? Then he answers my unasked question.

"Killing you is my job, not theirs."

Gabe

"They're on the move! Let's go!" I say as I run towards what appears to be a man in the bushes. I know the car just left, but maybe he has an accomplice and I refuse to let anyone get away. "Freeze!" I scream at the obviously male body, dressed completely in black. But the man doesn't stop, so I cock my gun and aim. I hold the gun steady and continue, "Mo! Get your men following that car! I'll take care of his........"

"GABE NO!" I hear Mo yell behind me. "PUT YOUR GUN DOWN!"

I hear him, but I'm not listening. The man runs through the brush and before I can stop myself, my finger pulls the trigger. One shot and the man falls to the earth screaming.

"Damn it Gabe! What the fuck are you doing?" Mo says as he takes my gun from my shaking hands.

"He....he, shit. He might know where this bastard is taking Syd and I....I...shit, I fucked up."

"We need EMT's in the back yard, we have a man down from a gunshot wound." Mo barks into his radio.

"I'll deal with this later, right now we need to go after that car."

"Wait Gabe, we've got unmarked cars at the end of every street, he's not going to get very far. Let him get away for now, we'll get him down the street."

"Are you fucking kidding me? We've got him where we want him, now let's roll!"

"Gabe," Mo says, "If we jump him now, he's prepared for it. We need him to let his guard down a little before we make our move. If he's armed, which I expect he is, anyone that gets in his way is a dead man. He kills a cop or a fed, he won't live to stand trial. I want this asshole alive, Gabe."

"Well, we'll just have to agree to disagree, Mo. I want him anyway I can get him, dead or alive. It makes no difference to me." And I turn to follow the car on foot, whether Mo likes it or not.

"Gabe, think about it. You get in his face, both you and Syd are dead. You really ready to take that chance?"

I stop dead in my tracks, because I know he's right. "Fine, we'll play this your way. But if he gets away I'm holding you personally responsible."

He nods before grabbing his radio, "He's on the move. Black Ford Taurus, drive out plates on the back. Follow quietly behind and let's see if we can figure out where he's taking her.

Hold your fire, do not shoot. We have an innocent in the back, any stray bullets could hit her. Follow quietly behind and keep me posted on your whereabouts. We'll catch up soon."

I follow Mo into the house, guns pulled. He slides in, back against the door and motions me in ahead of him. I take the right side and slither up against the wall. Three other men come in behind us and head through the house, finally confirming that it's empty. "Agent Morrison?" A CYPD officer calls from the other room. I follow Mo and the officer is standing in a dungeon.

Cinder block walls, concrete floors and only a small window.

"This must be where he held her. Get forensics here to get some prints run." Mo says as he reaches in his pocket and pulls out gloves, tossing me a pair. "Don't touch anything. Forensics will be here soon." He says, and I look at him like he's crazy.

"Mo, I've been a cop for years, I know the protocol."

He grins back at me, "But you don't know Federal protocol. Now, don't touch anything."

"Got it, boss."

"Jesus, there's blood over here, Mo." I say as I hunker down to my knees, the droplets splattered on the concrete floor. I see a few drops on the leg of the chair too, has to be Syd's blood. I feel my own blood start to boil, because now I'm convinced he hurt her. "We have to stop him, Mo. He'll kill her."

I don't think he even heard me, because he was on his phone again. "Flint? You still got the car in sight?" And silence, but the look on his face told me the asshole got away. "Fuck! How'd you lose him?" His head drops, chin pressed to his chest. "Damn it Flint! This is fucked up.

Find that car, now!" He screams as he shoves his phone back in his pocket. "Let's go. If my men can't do this correctly, then I will." And he turns to head out, passing the forensics team as they come in carrying their equipment. He stops and turns back to them, "I want this room cleaned out and every piece dusted for prints. I want the blood on the floor tested as well as that grimy pair of jeans on the floor." He says as he spots the denim lying there. "Those are men's jeans, Gabe."

"Yeah, I figured. Why do you think........shit?" I shake my head. "If he raped her, I'll kill him Mo. I'll kill him with my bare hands." I whispered.

"You'll have to go through me, Gabe. I'll let you have sloppy seconds and then we'll take him the long way back to the station. He'll wish he was dead."

"He will be when I'm done with him."

Mo jumps in the driver seat and I fold in to the passenger seat while he prepares to take off.

"He was last seen on I65 South, headed towards Indianapolis." He says as he gets on his car radio. "Get Indy State PD on the lookout for a Black Ford Taurus, dealer drive out tags. Get as many road blocks as you can."

Mo hits I94, blues and sirens blaring, and we finally exit on to I65 South, towards where he was last seen. "Do we have any idea who this bastard is?" I ask, effectively breaking the silence.

"Not yet, forensics is gathering evidence at the dungeon. We'll know soon enough. At least we know she's still alive.....or was....." He breaks off, watching the road. Traffic is slowing and Mo beats on the steering wheel, frustrated at the lack of common sense of people. I look ahead and see an accident up ahead, tractor trailer jack knifed across three lanes of highway. Smoke billows in to the air, but we are too far back to see anything else. Mo moves over in to the emergency lane, traveling slow but passing all of the stopped cars. People are out of their cars, walking around and looking ahead trying to figure out what is going on. We are far enough out of the city to where we shouldn't be in traffic, but apparently some stupid driver decided to take it upon himself to put a damper in our commute.

As we approach the accident scene, we see what is causing the smoke. A black sedan is on its side, wheels still spinning in the air. The smoke is coming from the car, and not the truck.

"Shit." I say as I look at Mo. "You seeing what I'm seeing?"

"Yeah." He says as he pulls forward to the accident scene, the car radio in hand. "We need cruisers and an ambulance to I65 South....." he looks over at his GPS, "Right at Ridge Road.

Also need two tow trucks, one to pull a big rig out of the road."

He pulls to the side, far enough to be out of the way and we both exit the car, running towards the car. There are people standing around, but no one is doing anything. I get angry cause some people just prefer to look the other way and not get involved, but I fly in head first to that car. I climb the passenger side and look through the shattered window. Empty. What the fuck?

"Mo, there's no one in here." I say as I climb back down. I turn to look at the people standing in the roadway looking like a deer caught in headlights. "Who was in this car?" I ask. No one speaks, they just look at each other like they have no clue.

"WHO. THE. FUCK. WAS. IN. THIS. CAR?" Mo screams as he flashes his badge at the crowd of people.

"Umm…" A faint female voice speaks from the back. "It was a man and a woman, they climbed out and ran that way." She said, pointing towards the side of the road. "The man pulled the woman over the wall and they disappeared, sir. It……umm, it looked like the woman was handcuffed, sir." She said, fear radiating out of her eyes. "She also looked scared and was bleeding. The man finally picked her up and carried her away."

"SHIT!" Mo yells as we both run for the side of the road, looking over the median wall down about what looks like a fifteen foot drop.

"No, sir. Over there……" she points down a bit. "They jumped into the grassy area and ran that way. He was pulling her behind him. She kept falling, but he'd drag her back up. He pulled out a gun sir, and held it to her head before he picked her up and carried her away. I called 911, but no one has gotten here yet, sir. No one except you, sir."

She was nervous and stuttering, but she was giving us information that we needed.

I scanned the area and saw an auto repair shop about a half a mile off of the interstate, the direction that the young woman said they ran towards. I ducked back to the car, grabbing the radio. "Dispatch, this is Agent Gabe Torres, FBI.....I need units at the auto repair shop on Ridge Road, right off of I65 and I need them yesterday.

"Sir? Agent who?" The dispatcher responded. Shit, I forgot the FBI doesn't know me yet.

Mo reaches in and grabs the radio from my hand, glaring at me. "This is Special Agent Jason Morrison, do what Agent Torres said, please. We need all available units and SWAT at that mechanics shop NOW!"

"Yes Agent Morrison. Units are in route now."

He slams the radio down and turns a circle in the road, looking for an exit to get down to Ridge Road. "Shit, damn access road. I'm better off on foot, Gabe." He says as he tosses me the keys. "I'm headed over there, you take the car, turn around and get there as soon as possible."

And he's gone, leaving me standing there holding the keys.

"NOW TORRES!" Mo screams at me as he runs towards the grassy median.

Sydney

The car is hauling ass down the highway, I'm face down in the back seat, because it hurts to lay on my back. I can't see out the window, but I can tell we are speeding. Good, maybe he'll get pulled over by the police and this will all be over. I close my eyes and wait, because that's all I can do.

I feel the car move rapidly from lane to lane, and I try and lift my head to look out. "Head down bitch!" The guy screams at me. My brother, shit. Maybe I can get him talking and he'll lose his train of thought.

"How are you my brother? What's your name?" I ask quietly and calmly from the back seat.

"What a question? I would assume that our father deposited his sperm in one of his wenches and out I came, that's typically how it happens. Now, no more questions." He says as the car swerves to the side.

Well that went over well. "What's your name?" I ask again, a little bit more determination in my voice.

"NO MORE QUESTIONS! SHUT UP AND LAY DOWN!"

I slam my head down on to the seat, pain shooting up the back of my neck. No no no, now is not the time for a migraine. I take a few deep breaths and close my eyes, but before I can relax the car spins out and rolls, throwing my body throughout the car, limp and lifeless. Without my hands free, I can't brace myself for impact.

The car rolls side to side so many times I lose count. I hear myself screaming and I hear him screaming as well, but his is an angry scream. Mine is full of fear, my vision in slow motion as my life flashes before my eyes. I see light, then dark, then light again. The crunching sound of metal and the shattering of glass explodes across my face.

When the car finally comes to a rest, I'm on my side against the door, my head on concrete through broken window glass. I feel warmth trailing down the back of my head, the smell of blood filling the car and I try to fight off the darkness that wants to consume me. I realize then that I want this to end now, one way or the other. I'm done fighting the darkness that consumes me. I had a brief flash of light that filled me as I think of Gabe, but now the darkness is back, stronger than ever. I can't live this way anymore. I won't. I close my eyes and pray to die, right here and right now.

I feel my body go limp and my head presses harder against the concrete under me. My hands still bound behind my back and pain shoots through my shoulder. I blink open my eyes and glance to my side, seeing that my shoulder is dislocated and my arm is hanging limp. It's bent at the elbow, but I can't move it. Before I can register what is happening, I'm lifted through the open door above me. "Gabe." I whisper, no strength in my voice.

"You wish, bitch. Now get up!" My brother yells, "NOW!" And I'm jerked upright and pulled through the open door, carelessly set on my feet. My legs wobble and the world spins around me. "You didn't think I'd leave you here to die did you?" He laughs. "No, you will die a slow and painful death, at my hands." He whispers in my ear, "But I plan to have some fun first."

And he tugs me behind him towards the side of the road. I hear people yelling behind us, trying to get us to stop running. I plant my feet firmly on the ground, because I decide right then and there that I am not going with him. But he's too strong and he pulls me forward, my knees going down and scraping against the blacktop of the highway. He drags me forward, ripping the skin off of my knees and exposing my flesh. He stops and looks back at me, a murderous look in his eyes.

"If you don't get up, I will kill you right here on the street." He says as he pulls a gun out of his pocket, a gun I didn't even know he had. He presses the barrel of the gun to my temple and presses his lips to my ear. "I have no problem putting a bullet in your head."

"Do it." I taunt him. "Do it now. Please." I beg.

He laughs out loud, "Yeah, okay." And I hear the safety release, the hammer engaging. I start to feel relief, because I know that darkness is soon coming and I won't have to deal with this anymore. But sirens in the distance pull him out of his trance and he locks the safety back. "Not yet, bitch. You aren't getting off that easily."

And he puts the gun in his pocket, then throws my limp body over his shoulder and runs. My head bouncing against his back. I look back at the people standing in the road and see the trailer of the truck on its side and silently hope the driver of that truck is okay. Then the darkness finally overcomes me.

Chapter 19
Sydney

The sound of dripping water awakens me. As I try and focus on my surroundings, I realize that I'm still alive. "Damn it!" I say with a weak voice. I'm face first on cold tile, my cheek pressed against the floor and my arms still around my back. My right arm is numb and I can't move it, confirming that my shoulder is still dislocated. I try to roll over, but the pain shoots down my back. I grunt through the pain and manage to get to my side, taking in my surroundings. As my eyes adjust to the darkness, I realize I'm in a bathroom. A hotel bathroom.

The smell of piss and soap causes my eyes to burn. One solitary glow coming from the light switch on the wall that puts off an orange glow to the room. The orange light goes off, then comes back on flickering like strobe lights.

I manage to sit up and gather my bearings. The dripping from the shower raking on my pounding head. My hair is stuck to the back of my neck, glued there from the dried blood. The throbbing gets worse as I try and stretch my neck, but I roll my knees under me and use what little strength I have to stand up. As I do this, the cuffs fall off of my hands and clank loudly on the tile floor. "Yes!" I whisper, not wanting to alarm my brother of my freedom. I take one of the flimsy white towels and fold it tightly, pressing it between my lips and teeth. I bite down on the towel as I press my shoulder against the wall, effectively pushing the joint back in to place. I stifle the scream and mumble curse words around the towel, but I can finally move my fingers. I stand stock still, listening to the sounds around me. All is quiet and I decide to peek out of the bathroom to see if I'm alone.

 I look back at the shower, because I would really love to clean this sticky blood off of me and wash away the last few hours, or days. But I don't know how much time I have and if I'm alone, this could be my only chance to escape.

 I slowly turn the knob and pull the heavy door back, the hinges creaking as it opens. The glow from the television lights my way as I step around the corner. At first I think I'm alone, but then a voice comes from my right. "Aww, she's awake."

 I stop, dead in my tracks, my blood boiling and my muscles tensing. I honestly thought I might be alone and could get away. I should have known he'd never make it that easy.

 "Where are we?" I ask.

"You ask too many questions. Now, come sit next to me. It's time I took what belongs to me." He says as he pats the bed next to him. I shake my head, because there is no way I'm crawling on that bed next to him. I scan the room and eye the door and figure now is as good a time as any.

My feet start to move towards the door, but before I can reach the knob an arm wraps around my waist, pulling me backwards. He grabs my mangled hair and pulls me back against his chest.

Pain shoots down my shoulder in to my fingers, and the stinging in my scalp makes my eyes water. He places his lips against my ear and yanks my head back against his chest. I realize now how much taller than me he is. His other hand reaches around my face and his fingers press against my chin, freezing me against him. His right leg comes around and wraps around both of mine, effectively trapping me. He's strong and I'm weak. I flash back to my Sanshou training, but I haven't the energy to fight him. "Please......" I whisper.

"Ooh, I like begging. Please what?" He growls in my ear.

"You're hurting me." I cry out, tears streaming down my face.

"Oh yeah?" He growls again, pulling my hair even harder. "You haven't seen hurt yet, my precious sister. Your pain has been nowhere near mine, but it's time you feel the same pain I've felt for my entire fucking life."

"I...I'm sorry, I never knew about you. I'm sorry......"

"Shut up bitch!" He yells as he pushes me forward, my chest now pressed against the wall.

His body is behind, pushing me flat. I cry out as the air whooshes from my lungs and his cock presses against my ass. "No! Please don't do this!" I cry out.

"Don't do what, big sister. Fuck you like daddy did? Don't shove my cock down your throat until you gag, like daddy did? Come on whore, give it up to me like you gave it to our dear old dad."

"I didn't fuck him......he fucked me!" I cry out as I manage to get my leg free, kicking back and pulling his knee forward. His leg buckles and bends, pushing me back to the wall, my knee cap cracking the plaster.

"Nice try." He breathes in to my ear. "You're pretty strong for a girl, but you'll never overcome me." He says as he pulls my hands back behind my back, jolting my shoulder and I cry out in pain. I feel blood on my knee, dampening the denim of my jeans that are ripped and shredded in places from him dragging me across the pavement.

He forcefully turns me to face him and the sheer terror in his eyes leads me to believe he's dead serious. I stand my ground and glare back at him, strong willed and scared shitless. I bring my injured knee up, the crunching sound of bone on balls echoing through the room. "Argh!" He screams, bending over and releasing me. "You fucking whore!" And he straightens, pushing me back against the wall, the air again leaving my lungs, my head cracking against the wall reopening the wound there.

He curls his hands around my head, pulling my face forward towards his. "You'll pay for that." He whispers as his lips come crashing down on to mine, hard enough to push my teeth through my flesh. His tongue snakes in and I bite down hard, drawing blood. He pulls back and then his fist comes crashing across my face. Flashes of light flicker in my eyes and I stumble backwards in to the table, falling in to it and pulling the table down in an effort to hold myself up. He reaches down and grabs me, collecting a handful of my t-shirt in his hand and jerks me to my feet, my shirt ripping in the process. He stops and stares at my chest, my breasts barely contained in my bra. His fingers then trace the bottom band of lace and he rips it off of me. He grabs both breasts and squeezes so hard I cry out again. "No, please don't........" and his mouth is back on mine, pressing harder in to my lips.

His foot sweeps out and kicks my feet out from under me and I go backwards in to the table again. He doesn't let me go, so he goes down with me and his body is on top of mine. I push against his chest trying to get him off of me, but he's too heavy. His long arm comes out and grabs both of my hands, securing them above my head and pressed against the floor behind me.

He wraps both of my wrists in one hand while his other goes for the zipper on his jeans. He pulls his pants down to his waist and then goes for mine, his nimble fingers tugging my zipper and yanking my jeans down, lifting his body off of mine as he rips my panties off.

I relax and close my eyes, because I know what's about to happen. Maybe if I stop fighting, he'll get this out of his system and let me go. His grimy fingers snake between my legs and penetrate me. "Dry as a fucking bone. Good." He says as he pulls his hand back and lifts his body, lining himself up with me.

"NO, PLEASE!" I scream out! "NOOOO!"

Then the sound of crashing wood and a deep male voice stops him in his tracks, his heavy body is pulled violently from me and the thud of his body hitting the wall on the other side of the room, a grunt coming from his throat. I try and focus on the room and I see him. Gabe.

He pulls me to him, wrapping his strong arms around me and I sob in to his shoulder. "SHHH, baby. I've got you." He whispers in my ear. "Let's get you out of here." He says as he tries to pull me to my feet, but before he can straighten, shots are fired and his limp body falls on to mine. Warm fluid spills from his body across my chest. "GABE!" I scream. "NO!! GABE!"

"Look at that, Doctor. Your cop friend came to save you. Too bad he didn't succeed." My brother stands above me, aiming his gun at me with shaky hands.

"Just shoot me too, little brother. Put a bullet in my head and put me out of my misery." I tell him, as I try and find Gabe's wound. I follow the trail of blood and find it, right through his shoulder. I take my ripped shirt and hold it against the gaping wound above his heart. "No no no, please don't......."

"Quiet bitch!" He says as he peeks out the window. "Shit." He mumbles as he locks the door.

I can see that point is fruitless as the lock is shattered, but he's panicking and trying anything to keep from being captured. His back is to me, and Gabe's Glock is lying next to me, having become dislodged from his fingers as he moved to help me. I manage to grab the gun and hold it in shaky hands.

"You didn't really think I'd let the good detective stop me, did you?" As he turns towards me, engaging the hammer again. Then time seemed to stop as the gun clicked. I squeeze my eyes shut and wait for the pain, but no bullet discharges. I raise Gabe's gun, aiming it at my brother, then squeeze the trigger firing three shots. Blood sprays in to the air and splatters against the wall, his body jerks back and he leaves his feet as he goes back in to the wall. I fire another shot and his face mangles, the entire left side of his face painting the wall behind him. The door to the hotel room flies open again and three cops are there with guns drawn, two pointed at me and one pointed at my brother. "NO, GABE IS SHOT! HELP HIM PLEASE!" I scream as I drop the gun and the lights go out.

Chapter 20
Sydney

The smell of chloroform invades my nostrils, closing my throat. I can't breathe and suddenly I'm choking on air. My mind starts spinning and as the darkness overwhelms me, I fall to the floor, gasping for my next breath. My heart rate increases and my limbs go numb. I can't move and my face is wet. I pull a weak arm up and brush the stickiness off of my face. Blood. Oh my God! I press my hand to my temple, feeling the gash that has ripped open as my face planted hard on the concrete. Lights are flashing in my eyes and I struggle to focus. "What in the hell happened?" I whisper as I look around the dungeon.

I scan the room and see him. My father, lying on the ground in a puddle of blood. I crawl on my hands and knees towards him, dragging the chair that I'm tied to with me. Why? I don't know, but I have to see him. I need proof that he's dead. I grab the man's head and roll his face towards me. "Why daddy why?" I cry out, the tears stinging the cuts on my face. I brush the hair out of his face, but then his face morphs. My eyes blur and a swimming feeling overwhelms me. I can suddenly no longer hold my head up straight, but I manage a glimpse and see that it's actually Gabe. "Gabe? No!!!"

Sobs tear through me, my chest heaving and I struggle to suck in oxygen. My body goes into panic mode and I start to shake uncontrollably. My body convulses and trembles as I curl next to his body, resting my head on his bloody chest. "Oh God! I'm sorry, Gabe! I thought....I thought......." I take another deep breath, "I thought you were someone else......I never......shit, oh God I never meant to hurt you!" My tears dropping on to his chest. I hear sirens in the distance and I pray silently, that they are coming for us. I force my body to relax and press my cheek against Gabe's warm skin. Wait, he's still warm. I jerk my eyes up and look at him, a dull throb snaking through my head. My vision blurs a little and as I focus on his body, I realize he's breathing. "Gabe?" I cry out.

I turn to my right side, to get a better focus on him and gently press my fingers against his neck. A pulse. It's weak, but I feel it. I look around his torso looking for a phone so I can call 911. Thankfully it's in his pocket and with shaky fingers I dig it out. But before I can press 'send', I realize the sirens are getting louder and louder. Then they suddenly stop, the silence causing a void in the room.

The door to the dungeon flies open on a slam and I scream in fear. "HELP ME! PLEASE!" I plead with whoever has just come into the room. He could be another bad guy, but at this point I don't care. If they can help Gabe........

My body is pulled away from Gabe as a uniformed officer sinks to his knees next to Gabe.

"Get a medic in here stat! We have an officer down!" I hear him bark in to his radio as I'm pulled off of him. Two EMTs come in and someone is hovering over me asking me questions, but I can't hear him. All I can hear is the cop and the EMT calling out vitals and other information.

"Ma'am, are you okay?" I vaguely hear, but I can only nod my head.

I watch the EMTs work on Gabe, talking to each other and barking out orders. I hear one of them call out for a defibrillator and I feel my body start to shake again. A hand touches my shoulder and I pull away, "NO! LEAVE ME ALONE!" I scream as I watch in horror as the EMT tries to revive Gabe.

"Clear!" He shouts as I watch Gabe's body jerk upwards, his chest rising and his head rolling back. The EMT looks at a small monitor before pressing the paddles to his chest again.

The electrical surge that blasts through his body jerking him up again. After a third time, the monitor shows a straight line running across it and the EMT drops his head, shaking it back and forth. "Call it." He says as he stands and walks away, taking his rubber gloves off as he disappears.

"No!! Wait! He was still alive a few minutes ago! Please! You can't give up! Gabe, NOOOOOOO!!!" I scream and cry as I try to crawl to his lifeless body in front of me. But strong hands pull me back. I fight with him, jerking my arms out of his hold, wrestling with a man three times as strong as me.

I'm placed on a stretcher and wheeled out of the room, my nose instantly clearing with the fresh air outside. But my nose is the only thing that is clear. I'm sobbing, my body jerking and heaving.

"Sydney, wake up babe. I'm here, it's okay."

I hold my breath, because I hear a male voice, strong and clear in my head. I wait to hear it again, because I can't be sure I heard it in the first place. But nothing, I must have imagined it.

The tears again start to squeeze out of my eyelids, and the shaking comes back.

"Sydney, baby. Wake up."

I pause again, my mind now drifting between fantasy and reality, warm light seeping between my eye lids. I take a deep breath and force my eyes open, fearful of what I'll see. I blink away the cobwebs and finally focus on the beauty that is right in front of me.

Gabe

"Welcome back, baby." He whispers to my cheek as he gently presses his lips against my skin.

"Gabe?" I choke out with a weak voice.

"Yeah, baby. It's me."

"Oh my God, you.......you're......." I suck in a breath.

"Alive, sweetheart. I'm alive, and so are you."

He moves back a little to allow me to focus and I see his beautiful face. I try and lift my right hand to his face, but I can't move it. It's taped up or something and.....I realize I have another hand.

My left hand slowly comes up and I press my palm against his face, his eyes my focal point.

"Gabe?" I ask again, not believing what I am seeing. "Am I dreaming?"

"Not anymore, babe. I'm right here."

I brush my thumb along his stubble covered cheek, my eyes roaming over his face, his nose, his lips. I scan his body and see the bandage over his shoulder and chest and realize his shirt is only half on.

"You were shot." I breathe out, my fingers now trailing along the bandages on his shoulder.

"Just a flesh wound. I'm fine." He says as his eyes close.

"But you.......shit, I don't know. Tell me what happened?" I ask.

"Later babe, you need to rest." He says as he sits back in his chair.

"You're sitting here bandaged up like a mummy and I'm in a hospital bed, and you won't tell me what happened?"

"You don't remember?" He asks.

"Some of it. Did he.....?" I ask, not sure I want to know the answer.

"No, thank God. I stopped him before that happened. But we can talk about all of that later, right now you need to rest.

Agent Morrison will have questions for you later and we need you rested and focused."

"Agent Morrison?" I ask.

"Yeah, my boss."

I ponder that thought for a moment, because I thought Matthews was his boss.

He smirks at me, his lips curling in a devious way.

I look at him with questioning eyes, but I don't speak.

"I quit the NYPD."

I try and sit up, but there are so many wires crossing my body that I'm afraid to move. He reaches down and presses a button, rising the head of the bead.

"You quit? Why?"

"We'll talk about that later." He stops as someone walks into the room. My eyes don't leave his and we stare at each other, a connection being made with only our eyes.

A nurse makes her way to my bedside, wheeling her portable station with her.

"Oh, hi Doctor DeCarlo. I didn't realize you were awake. I'm Angie and here to take your vitals, then I'll notify Doctor Kane that you're awake. How are you feeling?" She asks as she wraps the blood pressure cuff on my good arm. I nod at her, but don't answer her question.

She finishes and types it all in on her station and then leaves, "Doctor Kane will be in shortly." She smiles as she pulls the door closed.

I look over at Gabe, his head laid back and his eyes closed. He looks exhausted. "Gabe?" I whisper, not wanting to wake him up if he's asleep. He opens his eyes and lifts his head, looking at me with sleepy eyes.

"Yeah, babe. You okay?" He asks as he sits up.

"I think so. Why don't you go home and get some rest?"

"No way, not until I know you're okay."

"I'm fine Gabe. Thanks to you."

His eyes flash and he smirks at me. "You're one tough lady, Doctor DeCarlo." He says as he comes over to my bedside, pulling his chair with him. He sits down and takes my hand. "But you never should have run off without me."

Oh, so he's sticking around to lecture me huh? Well........

"I couldn't find you, Sydney. Within seconds you vanished and........" His throat catches.

"Within seconds you were gone."

"SHHHH, I'm fine now Gabe."

"But you almost weren't, Syd. God, when I came out of my house and you were gone......" he chokes back a sob, his eyes glassy with tears he's struggling to hold in. He drops his head and swipes a stray tear off of his cheek. "When I couldn't find you........." and he begins to sob, his upper body shaking and trembling.

"Gabe." I whisper. "I'm so sorry Gabe. I should have never....."

"No, you shouldn't have, but......" His eyes softening and his head shaking. "But it's over now. You're fine, I'm fine....we can move on, get past this."

"But is it really over Gabe? I won't be able to get past it until I know what happened. The guy.....he told me he was my brother. Who was he really?" I ask.

He stands up and walks to the window, looking out on the world below.

"His name was Stephan DeCarlo." He says. "He was a victim of your father's crime spree years ago, just like Samantha and Sophia. His mother drowned in a pool of her own blood when your father strangled her with barbed wire. Then he tossed her into Lake Michigan. She had already delivered Stephan and your father had no more use for her. Stephan was raised in foster care and was a tattoo artist in Chicago."

He stops and takes a deep breath, then turns to face me.

"He started studying Criminal Justice at Chicago State, which gave him access to sealed records. Apparently he had a friend in the records division of CPD as well, so he studied his father diligently."

He looks up at me, waiting for me to ask questions.

"How did you find all of this out?" I ask.

"Stupid idiot." He chuckles. "He carried ID with him, correct ID instead of a fake one. He never tried to hide who he was, and was raping and killing these young girls. The first two were your half-sisters."

"Revenge?" I ask.

He nods.

"But the third girl, was she......."

"No, that was his actual girlfriend. He needed another victim....."

"To make sure I was number four."

He nodded.

"Shit."

"Yeah, but that's not all."

What else could there be? Before he can continue a man walks in carrying a file. "Doctor Decarlo, I'm Doctor Kane. How are you feeling?" I nod at him but my mind is reeling from what Gabe told me.

"I'm going to go get a cup of coffee, Syd. I'll be back." Gabe says as he leaves the room.

The doctor checks me out, and I finally find out the extent of my injuries. A grade three concussion, dislocated shoulder and multiple contusions on my knees, wrists and head. But I'm told I'm going to be fine and can probably go home in a few days. He tells me I was dehydrated which was why I'm still here with an IV plugged in to my arm. "Once you're re-hydrated you can go home." He says as he smiles.

He heads towards the door and then turns back to me. "That man's in love with you, I hope you realize that. He's not left your side all night." And he smiles before leaving the room. He hardly said anything while checking me out, but then he says that? Internally I shake my head, because I know there's no way Gabriel Torres is in love with me. It's too soon, and too much has been going on. But then that internal head shaking turns in to a smile. A weak smile at that, but I can definitely feel my lips curling up just a little.

I lean my head back and press the button to lower the bed. I'm exhausted and I close my eyes to sleep. But my mind is in a flurry with all that I have consumed over the last few days. The sights, the smells, the pain. And fury, I realize I'm furious. At who or what, I have no idea. But I'm angry. Why did my family have to be so fucked up? My own father and brother, a brother I never knew I had. One that was just as deranged as my father.

I wrap my hand around my neck to massage the tense muscles and my fingers graze on a sore and tender area behind my left ear. Probably just one of my many contusions the doctor mentioned. But as my finger rubs the tender area, I realize the skin is raised. I rise the bed up again, so that I'm sitting and then twist my aching body sideways. My feet hit the floor and I grab the IV stand, using it to hold myself up. It's a futile attempt as the stand starts rolling and my legs can't move fast enough. I grab on to the side of the bed and steady myself, calmly waiting for some strength to come back in my legs.

When I finally get my balance, I slowly move to the bathroom and I gaze at myself in the mirror. I'm a hot mess for sure. My eyes are swollen with bags underneath. A scab just above my lip and traveling up towards my nose, and a bright red patch of skin below my ear, where my fingers found tender tissue.

I pull my hair back and turn my head and my eyes spot the jagged black lines. "Fuck." I whisper. He fucking marked me. I angle my head to get a better look and that's when it hits me.

My mind flashes back to the moment he pressed the needle in to my skin. "Son of a bitch!" I say in a slightly higher voice.

"What are you doing?"

I jump at the sight of Gabe standing behind me looking like he wants to kill someone, possibly me.

"Shit, you scared me."

"I asked you a question, what are you doing?"

"What are you my father?" I say and immediately realize what I've just said. I know I can't unsay it, but the pain in his eyes tells me I've fucked up. "Gabe, I'm sorry........."

He turns away and leaves the bathroom, the door to the hospital room clicking as he closes that too. "Shit, nice going Syd." I say to myself as I look back to the mirror. The tattoo is a smaller version of the creepy one that snaked up Stephan's neck. I get closer to the mirror and focus on it, the serpent behind my ear.

My knees give out on me and my body falls in slow motion to the floor of the bathroom, the IV stand tumbling over and yanking the tube out of my arm. The sound of metal clanking on the floor and blood spurts across the wall. The sight of it makes my stomach churn and I close my eyes to avoid the images. But once I do, the images are much worse. I shake them off and take a deep breath. The tile floor is cool, but the room is spinning and nausea waves over me. I take a deep breath and do my best to relax before the dizziness takes over, darkening my vision.

Chapter 21
Gabe

"How could she say that?" I say to myself as I storm down the hallway of Mercy Hospital.

"Mercy? Lord, have mercy on me please." I continue the conversation to myself as I exit the front door into the bright sunshine. I lean my head back, taking a deep breath and focus on the warmth on my face.

As I pace the entryway to the hospital, I continue my self-argument. "Damn it! I sat with her for two solid days while I waited for her to wake up. Then she accuses me of acting like her father? God, how could I be so stupid?"

"Gabe?"

I turn and see Mo walking towards me. "Hey Mo," is all I can muster before turning my back to him. I start to pace again when Mo claps me on my back.

"You still here?" He asks me.

"No, I'm a figment of your imagination." I spat back at him, but he chuckles.

"Sydney doing better?" He asks, cutting to the chase.

"She's awake, if that's what you're asking."

"Yeah, that's good. How is she?"

I scrub my hands down my face, realizing I need a shower and to shave, but I turn back to Mo. "I guess she's all right. The doctor was seeing her a little while ago and then......."

"Then what?"

"Nothing, just drop it okay?"

"Gabe, we've been friends a long time. And, you work for me now, so spill it."

"Shit, I'm probably over reacting. It's nothing, I'll figure it out."

"Gabe." Mo says with a warning hinted in his tone.

"Really, just something she said. I'm sure she didn't mean it, but it hit me the wrong way and I walked out on her. I really can be an ass sometimes."

"Yes you can, but you need to think about what you've both just gone through. Hell, you were shot for Pete's sake."

"A flesh wound, Mo. I wasn't *really* shot." I smirk at him.

"Well, you were still hurt. And on my watch, so that is unacceptable. Now, tell me what's really bothering you." He says as he nudges me over to a bench to the side of the door. "Sit."

I do as I'm told with a growl and Mo chuckles beside me.

"Tell me what happened."

I look at him like he's grown horns. "You were there, Mo. You know what happened."

"No, I mean in the last few minutes. What did she say?"

"She accused me of being like her father." I say as I lean back.

"Surely she didn't mean that."

"No, I'm sure she didn't, but it hit me the wrong way I guess. Then I walked out on her. Shit, I'm so stupid." I say as I stand up to go back to her room. "I have to fix this."

"Wait, Gabe. Sit back down and take a breather. Think about what to say before you go back in there. You both have been through hell and your tempers are short right now."

I know he's right, so I sit back down taking a long pause.

"She saved my life, Mo."

"And you saved hers Gabe."

"But I was angry that she ran off so quickly."

"Sounds familiar." He says.

I look at him in shock, "What do you mean?"

Mo rests his elbows on his knees and stares at a crack in the sidewalk.

"You did the same thing, Gabe. I gave you a strict order NOT to enter that hotel room without backup, but you charged along and busted in that door before anyone could stop you. How is that different?"

"It isn't." I respond shaking my head, knowing he's got me by the balls.

"You two are two peas in a pod, Gabe. But you need to give her some time to sort all of this through. She probably woke up confused and in self defense mode, so cut her some slack."

"I know, I know. But when she......damn it, I know she didn't mean it. But fuck if it didn't slash me right down my chest."

He places his arm on my shoulder. "Go to her, Gabe. Don't let her down like her own family did."

"Speaking of, any word on her brother, Franco?"

"Yeah, he's gonna be fine. Though it may take some time for him to heal.

"Okay, and her mother and sister?"

"Sister is good, mother still in hospital on suicide watch. You didn't tell Syd what happened did you?"

"Not yet, but I will as soon as she's strong enough. Right now, I think she'd retreat so far into her shell that she might not recover. Once things have calmed down a bit, I'll tell her."

Mo nods and stands up, "Well, I'll let you two work this out and come back later to talk to Syd. Call me when she's rested up."

"I will." We shake hands and Mo strides off to his car. I stand and stare at his back as he walks away, my mind going back to yesterday when I found Syd in that room, her brother's grimy body over hers. I shiver at the thought of what he was about to do. I know I shouldn't have barged in there without back up, but when I heard her scream I knew I couldn't wait. And I would do it all again the same way. No regrets. But when she finds out about Franco, God help us all.

I shove my one good hand in my pocket as I head back into the hospital. I need to get back to Sydney and apologize for walking out on her. I know she didn't mean what she said, it was just a phrase that we all use at times. But coming from her, knowing what her father did and the man that he was, made it feel like a stab in the back.

I take the elevator back up to the fourth floor and make my way down the hall, only to stop dead in my tracks as I see the cluster of people outside her room. Press? No, couldn't be. This hasn't gotten out yet, so it can't be there. I made sure last night that no press were to become involved, at least until all the puzzle pieces were put together.

My feet start moving faster and as I approach her room, I'm stopped by Doctor Kane.

"What's happened?" I ask, my breath short from running.

"Doctor DeCarlo collapsed in the bathroom, she hit her head again and we had to stitch her back up."

"Shit, I shouldn't have left her. I saw her in the bathroom and.....never mind. Can I go in?"

"Yeah, but help me keep her in bed please? She's still dehydrated and needs to rest."

"I'll do my best, but she's hard headed. When she wants something, she goes after it. She might not like me trying to stop her."

"I know, but try. Yeah?"

"You got it Doc. Thanks."

I slowly and quietly open the door, peeking in on Sydney back in her bed. I knock loud enough for her to hear me, before I step into the room. She looks up at me and attempts to smile, but I see she is upset.

"Hey. Can I come in?"

"Of course. Gabe, I'm sorry......."

"SHHHH, no need to apologize, Syd. I shouldn't have walked out on you like that. It's just....."

"Gabe, sit."

"Demanding aren't we?" I chuckle as I pull the chair up beside her bed.

She lifts her hair, showing me the ink that has been printed on her neck, something I hadn't seen yet. "Did you see this?" She asks.

"No, I didn't" I say as I lean in closer to her to get a better look. "Fuck."

"Yeah, fuck is a good word." She giggles.

"You're laughing at a time like this?" I ask her, confusion written all over my face.

"Sure, what else am I going to do? Like father like son, eh? Angry, evil men feeling it necessary to mark their territory. I remember him doing this while we were still in the dungeon. I didn't think he finished before he dragged me out to his car." She laughs. How she can be humorous during a time like this is beyond me. But it doesn't last long, before I can sit back down she's crying.

In between sobs she starts to talk. "I'm starting to remember everything, Gabe. Something I'm not sure I want to do." She looks up at me, her eyelashes glistening with tears. "You said earlier there was more, what is it?"

"Sydney, I will tell you everything, soon. But not now, you need to rest, and so do I. I'm going to check into a hotel and have a shower, I'll be back in a little while, okay?" Her eyes are angry, but also tired. I know she wants to know everything and I plan to tell her, just not yet.

"Get some sleep babe, I'll be back before you wake up."

She nods and lays her head back, closing her eyes, her long lashes resting on her high cheekbones. She's beautiful, even beaten up and torn apart. I want to stay close to her, keep my hands on her to make sure she doesn't vanish on me again, but I need a shower and a nap myself.

If I am going to be taking care of her, I need to get my own strength back. And, I need to figure out the best way to give her the news about her family. At least they are all okay, but she's not going to like what I have to tell her.

I kiss her on the forehead and she doesn't open her eyes. So I leave the hospital and make my way to my rental car in the parking lot. The Hyatt is just around the corner, so I'll head over there and see what they have available.

Thankfully, they have a suite available, something that Sydney can come to once she's released, which will hopefully be in a few days. I know she's probably going to want to get home as soon as possible, but at the same time she's gonna want to be near her family, her mother and sister, when she finds out. Or maybe not, knowing their history. I hate keeping things from her, but she's just not strong enough to take this right now.

I walk into the room and glance around, moving straight for the bedroom. I drop my bag on the floor and crawl slowly on to the bed, not even pulling the covers down. As I relax, my shoulder starts throbbing and I know right then, I will not sleep without assistance. I reach over the side of the bed to my bag and retrieve the pain pills I got at the hospital. Typically, I would work through the pain, but I need rest right now, so I pop a pill and swallow tightly without water.

I lay my head on the pillow, but not before setting the alarm on my phone. I don't want to sleep long, as I need to get back to Sydney. I set it for two hours and lay back, closing my eyes.

My mind flashes back to the events of the past few days, and then focus on the pain in Sydney's eyes when I walked out on her in the bathroom. For as long as I live, I never want to see that kind of pain in her eyes again. I realize then, that I want to be the one to take away her pain. I want to be the one to love her unconditionally, without regret. I want to be the one to stand by her, to help her love again. To bring her back to the here and now, and show her that there's still good in this world, in light of all of the pain. I just hope that she can forgive me when she finds out the truth.

Chapter 22
Sydney

Hours pass and I'm still lying in this damn bed, alone. "Where is Gabe?" I ask myself as I glance at the clock on the wall. "He said he'd be right back, but it's been five hours." I shake my head. "Guess I scared him off. No man wants to get involved with a woman like me. I put him in danger and he ran. Can't blame him I guess."

The nurse comes in to check on me like she does every hour, on the hour, driving me bat shit crazy. I did manage to get some sleep, so it was probably good that Gabe wasn't here. He needs rest too, so I try and calm myself down and relax some, though I'm starting to worry. Gabe holds to his word and......no, never mind. I scared him off and that's probably better for us both.

I grab the remote control and turn the television on, searching the stations for something interesting. Something to keep my mind off of things. I come to a halt on one of the local news stations, because something catches my eye......oh shit.

Flashing lights and crowds of people fill the screen. My body tenses as I turn the volume up.

We are on scene at the One Stop Motel on Pulaski Street where two men, one believed to be a police officer, have been shot. A man was holding a young woman hostage and she was found lying under the victim's body. The woman gained control of the officer's gun and fired at her captor. The captor was found and pronounced dead on the scene. The officer, Agent Gabriel Torres with the Federal Bureau of Investigations, was wounded in the shoulder, but was said to be in stable condition at a local hospital. The female victim, Doctor Sydney DeCarlo, is also said to be in stable condition at a different area hospital. The name of the deceased has not been released yet.

Doctor Sydney DeCarlo was kidnapped, beaten and raped by her own father twenty years ago, right here in Lincoln Park. It was determined then, that the then thirteen year old girl, fired the shot that killed her father, Luis DeCarlo. When asked if the two cases were related, we were told "no comment at this time."

We'll be here on the scene through the evening and will provide updates as we have them.

Shit. Gabe told me he kept the press out of this. But realistically, I know he couldn't do that on his own. The people of the press are vultures and will dig and dig until the........wait, what's that? The reporter on scene at the motel is back on, what the fuck?

We have just found out that a Lincoln Park woman and her daughter were found bound to each other in their home early yesterday. Fifty-three year old Gloria Watkins and her daughter, twenty-five year old Sylvia DeCarlo, were tied back to back in the basement of Ms. Watkins home. The woman's son, Franco DeCarlo was found a mile away with a gunshot wound to his back. It is believed the son was shot by Agent Gabriel Torres, the man found wounded in the motel room early yesterday. We will continue to update you as information is received.

"Son of a bitch! He shot my brother? What in the hell was he thinking? How could he shoot him? Fuck! I need to get out of here." I say out loud as I slowly lift my body out of bed. I move slowly towards the small cabinet in there and pray my clothes are in there. I exhale a breath as I see a plastic bag full of my personal belongings. "Thank God." I say as I grab the bag. The clothes are dirty and bloody, but I sure as hell can't leave in a hospital gown. I pull the stiff jeans on and carefully remove the gown, pulling my t-shirt over my head. I can't even think about putting a bra on right now.

Once my shoes are on, I look around the room to make sure I'm not forgetting anything, cause I damn sure don't want to come back to retrieve anything. "My purse, shit, I need my purse." I open the other door to the cabinet and sigh in relief that my bag is right there.

"Whew!" I say as I grab my bag and carefully secure it to my good shoulder.

Quietly, I open the door and peek out into the hall way. At this particular second, the coast is clear so I scan the hall looking for the elevator. Great, I have to go right by the nurse's station to get there, so I quickly walk in that direction. They must be on rounds, because there is no one behind the counter. The elevator doors open and I freeze. An elderly gentleman exits and I jump in before the doors close. "That was too easy." I say as the doors close.

As the elevator descends to the first floor I start to panic. What if Gabe is there waiting when the doors open. I don't want to see him. I need to get out of here quickly. The doors open and I peek out, not seeing anyone of importance. So, I start digging in my purse for my phone, but it's not there. Crap. But I spot a pay phone in the corner and I smirk, because I didn't think those existed anymore. I dig out a quarter from my bag and place it between my lips while I grab the phone book hanging from the bottom. The front door opens and I glance over, and there he is, marching in here like he owns the place. I turn my back to him and dial the first cab company I see in the book. Ten minutes, shit. "I'm sorry, I can't wait that long. Thank you." I hang up. A golden light reflects off of something outside. I peer around the corner and a yellow taxi has just pulled up. I bolt out the door and almost plow over the passenger that just got out. "Go!" I tell the driver as I climb in the back seat. "GO NOW!" I scream again.

"Lady, my last passenger hasn't paid me yet."

"Don't worry about that, keep the timer running. I'll pay their fare if you can get me to the airport in ten minutes."

"Which airport, lady?" He asks, pulling out in to traffic.

"O'Hare." He groans, but he continues.

I know inside I need to be going to my mother and brother, but I just can't. Not after all they've put me through over the years. While we still talk occasionally, I haven't been to visit in years and I plan to keep it that way. They blamed me for our father's death, not even caring what he put *me* through. All they can think about is the fact that I killed him. My life was never the same and to have my own family blame me, sent me over the edge. Once I finally was able to leave home, I never looked back.

I pull myself out of my thoughts as he pulls in to the drop off lane and I grab a hundred dollar bill from my purse, silently saying a prayer of thanks that no one stole my money. I toss it over the seat and jump out of the car.

"Lady, your change!" The driver calls out of the window.

"Keep it!" I say and keep running towards departures and make my way to the Delta counter.

As I approach, the clerk behind the counter looks me up and down. I know I'm a mess, but I need to get a ticket and get moving. "One way ticket to New York, any airport. Whatever is closest to departure."

She nods and views her computer screen. "There's a four o'clock to LaGuardia."

I look at the clock on the wall, two forty five. "Perfect."

"Seat preference?"

"Excuse me?"

"Do you have a preferred seat? Aisle, window, first class?"

"Doesn't matter, but preferably an empty row if you have it."

She gets quiet, searching. "Okay, row 23C. As of right now, the seat next to you is vacant, but that could change."

"I'll pay for that seat too, just to keep it empty."

She stares at me for a moment. "Just do it, please."

She nods and I hand her my credit card. I'm starting to sweat, because this has taken too long and I half expect Gabe to come running in here.

"Bags?"

"Um, no. I don't have any bags."

She keeps a straight face, and I know she's probably going to call security on me. But I can't think about that right now. She hands me my boarding pass and I make my way over to the X-ray machine. I scan the corridor looking for a shop or something where I can pick up a change of clothes, but I have zero luck.

So I get in line and wait. As I approach the metal detector, the TSA agent looks me up and down. Great, nothing like a body cavity search after all I've been through. I kick my shoes off and place my bag in the rubber bin and watch it travel down the belt.

I walk through the metal arch and hold my breath. I know I don't have any metal on me, but I'm paranoid by this time that I can't be sure.

The light turns green and I grab my shoes and bag. After I've tied my laces I head towards Terminal Three. "Ma'am?" I hear from behind me. I don't turn back, pretending not to hear him.

"Ma'am! Wait!"

I stop and turn back towards the TSA agent coming towards me. "You left this in the bin, ma'am." I look down and she is handing me my watch.

"Oh, thank you so much!" I say as I continue my way to the terminal. As I round the corner I spot a Brooks Brothers store. "Thank God."

I quickly grab a pair of khakis and a cute top and make my way to the restroom to change. I glance at my tennis shoes and shake my head. Shoes will have to wait. I splash cold water on my face and run my fingers through my hair. What I wouldn't do for a hot shower and a hair brush right now.

I make myself as presentable as I can and detour back to Terminal Two where my flight will depart from. I pass a store that stocks cell phones and accessories. But before I go in, I spot the clock on the wall. Three fifteen. Shit, I don't have much time.

"Do you have any prepaid cell phones?" I ask the sales person

"Yes ma'am. What kind are you looking for?"

"I don't care, something cheap and quick. My flight boards soon and I forgot my cell at home."

"No worries, ma'am. Let me show you what we have."

I quickly select a Motorola flip phone and giggle internally. A flip phone? Well, it's better than nothing and it's temporary. I need to call Mom and Leslie and let them know what's going on, before Gabe sends a search party out for me.

He shows me how to use it and hands me a slip of paper with the phone number on it.

Thanking him, I leave and get to my gate, which thankfully has just started boarding. I find my seat and sit down, totally exhausted. As the plane loads, I call my mother's house, but there's no answer. "Damn it."

So I try Leslie and thankfully she answers.

"Doctor Phillips."

"Les, it's me Syd."

"Sydney? Oh my God, what's going on? I JUST SAW THE REPORT ON THE NEWS!" She screams in to the phone and I have to hold it back from my ear to keep my ear drums from blowing.

"Relax, Les. I'm fine. I'm on a plane coming home, I need you to pick me up at LaGuardia in three hours. Can you do that?"

"Sure, but Gabe just called me....."

"Do NOT tell Gabe where I am. As far as you know, you don't know anything. Got it?"

"Yeah yeah, okay. But why?"

"I can't get in to it here, the plane is taxiing and they're announcing for us to turn off our phones. Write down this number, okay?"

"Okay, go ahead."

"630-555-9834, that's my mother's number, I need you to keep trying to call her for the next three hours. Can you do that for me, too?"

"Sure, but why? What do I need to tell her?"

"Just tell her I'm okay and I'll call her when I get home. No need to go in to any other details." I tell her, unsure why I'm even bothering updating my mother.

"Well, considering I have no idea what in the hell is going on, I think you're safe."

I laugh, "I'm sorry. But I promise, I'll fill you in on everything when I see you. Flight lands at seven thirty or so. I'll call you when I'm off the plane and heading towards the exit, okay?"

"Okay, I'll see you then."

I snap the phone shut and cut an evil eye at the flight attendant motioning me to turn off my phone. I press and hold the off button and put it in my purse. The plane is moving, so I know no one else can get on, so I close my eyes and rest a little. I just hope I can sleep a little without having a nightmare. That would be all I need do is to wake up on this plane screaming and the TSA hovering over me thinking I'm a terrorist.

We finally get to our cruising altitude and the 'fasten your seatbelt' light has been turned off and I feel my body relaxing. I stare out of the small window and imagine faces in the clouds. I see Gabe in one and I blink to make the image disappear, but it doesn't work. So I close my eyes and lean my head back, the rocking of the plane luring me to sleep.

"Ma'am? Would you like peanuts or pretzels?"

Opening my eyes, I look at the flight attendant. "Umm, pretzels, please. And a Coke?"

"Sure." She says as she hands me two small bags of pretzels that could never fill up anyone's stomach, but I'm so hungry right now, this will have to do. She hands me a clear plastic cup full of Coke and as I take a sip, the bubbles tickle my nose. But the cold, carbonated drink is a relief to my dry and parched throat. I try not to gulp it, because I'm not in the mood for the hiccups.

I deposit my trash in her bag as she comes back around and put my tray table back up. I glance at my watch and see we should be landing soon. So I make my way to the restroom, squeezing into the small room and do what I need to do. I glance at myself in the small mirror and wonder how anyone let me on this plane looking like this. My face is swollen and bruised, my skin pale and gaunt. I look like I died three times already. I chuckle, because I got lucky I guess.

I get back to my seat and buckle up, ready to get off of this plane and back home.

"Ma'am?" I hear someone over my shoulder and I jump, startled. "I'm sorry ma'am, but we've landed. You're free to exit the plane now."

Shit, I fell asleep and now I have to gather my bearings. Oh yeah,

LaGuardia.....Leslie....phone, I need to call her and let her know I'm here. Hopefully she won't be late picking me up. I need to get home, showered and call my mother to check on Franco.

The anger comes back again and I can't imagine why Gabe would shoot him. My brother's a good guy, never been in trouble. But he was never the same after...... what was Gabe thinking? I start to regret running off without even giving him time to explain, but after the last few days I just need to get away from him and Illinois. Too many bad memories there and had it not been for my long lost brother, I would have never gone back.

As I make my way down the terminal to the exit, I call Leslie and let her know I've arrived and to meet me out front. I exit the doors and the cool breeze takes my breath away. I inhale and throw my head back, because it feels good to be home. I glance around and Les is parked along the curb, so I make my way to her car and climb in.

"Jesus, Syd. You look like shit!" She says as she looks me up and down. "What in the hell happened?"

"Oh geez, Les. I have no idea where to even begin. Just take me home and I'll fill you in there. Right now, I just need a moment to think." I say as I lean my head back against the seat and close my eyes.

"You're exhausted, Syd. Tell me what happened."

"Les, please. Let me have a few minute to think. So much shit has happened and……and, I was……fuck, Les. Just give me time, okay?"

I didn't open my eyes, but I can hear her exhale a breath and can sense her nodding her head.

Les continues to drive, weaving in and out of traffic before she finally pulls in to the parking garage. I open my eyes and look around. "Why are we at your place? I wanted to go home."

"You will, but not before you talk to me. You need a shower and a fresh change of clothes."

I look down at my brand new outfit. "What's wrong with my clothes?"

She chuckles, "It looks like you grabbed the first thing you found Syd. So not your style.

Come on, I have something you can put on after you have a shower. Then, we'll talk before I take you home."

Les lives on the fourth floor of a sixteen story brick building in midtown, closer to her office.

It's quiet, but you can sense the nosy neighbors as we pass them in the lobby. I know I have to be a sight. Leslie ignores them, but I feel on display and rush past her to the elevator. Thankfully, the doors open as soon as we get there.

Once in her apartment, I drop my bag and go straight to her bathroom. "Towels are in the closet, I'll have some clothes ready for you when you get out." Les says as she walks past me down the hall.

I get the water as hot as I can and step in the stall, closing the door behind me. But all I do for the longest time is stand there, thinking back to the last twenty-four hours. Kidnapped, again.

Almost raped, again. And then the man that I had started falling for shoots my brother and didn't tell me. Had he told me, explained the situation, then I might have understood. But he kept that from me and I hate secrets. And when he never came back to the hospital, well.......I don't know what to think anymore.

After washing my face and body, I wash my hair three times to try and get the blood out of it.

That's when I feel the raw skin behind my ear. The tattoo that my loving brother etched in to my skin. I find the yoga pants and t-shirt on Leslie's bed and slip into it, silently thankful she didn't provide me with underwear or a bra, because I'm good without that right now. It feels good to be clean and comfortable. My body is still sore from the events of the last few days, but my mind is clearing and I'm ready to spill the beans to Les.

I walk out into the living area as she hangs up her phone. "Who were you talking to?"

"A patient. Sit down and tell me what happened." She says as she hands me a glass of wine.

I sink down on to her leather sofa and take a long sip of my wine before setting the glass on the coffee table. I close my eyes and think back to when all of this started and finally am able to tell her the story.

"Jesus, Sydney. A brother? Where in the hell did he come from?"

"Really? That's what you ask? He kidnapped me, almost raped me, and you want to know where he came from?" I huff as I stand up and move towards the window overlooking the city.

"Apparently my dad was quite the ladies' man. Only, when he had gotten what he wanted he killed them and moved on to the next. Stephan wanted some sort of revenge on me for killing our father. Somehow he knew about the spree dad went on and decided to copy what he had done, making me the fourth victim again. He was angry that I survived and wanted me dead, and he almost succeeded. If it weren't for.....shit." I drop my head, pressing my forehead against the glass.

"What Syd? If it weren't for.....?"

"Gabe." I say as I pick my head up and turn towards Leslie, who is now standing right behind me. "He got there just in time, but Stephan shot him before Gabe could get me out of there."

"He shot Gabe?"

I nod. "Just a flesh wound, he's okay. But Gabe didn't take him completely down before coming to me, so Stephan pulled a gun and aimed it at us lying on the floor. Gabe was unconscious, his heavy body pressing me into the floor, but I was able to reach his Glock and put three bullets in my brother's head. Jesus, I've now killed two members of my own family.

What kind of crazy person does that?" I cry as Les pulls me in to her arms.

"You aren't the crazy one, Syd. There's a bad gene or something in your dad's side of the family. You were only protecting yourself, and Gabe."

"Gabe." I whisper.

"Where is he?" Les asks as she pulls back, looking me in the eyes.

"I....I don't know. He was supposed to come back to the hospital, but he never came back.

Then I saw the news report........"

"The same news report I saw?"

I nod, "He....he.....he shot Franco."

"Your other brother?"

I nod, tears streaming down my face.

"Why would he shoot Franco?"

"I have no idea, but I bolted out of the hospital before he got back. Apparently, a lot went down during the time I was held, and my fight or flight reflex kicked in and I ran. I felt so betrayed that he didn't tell me the whole story. I realize now, I should have waited and......."

I'm cut off by a knock on the door. I look at Leslie with surprise in my eyes, but she just stares at the door, a smirk curling her lips.

"Leslie?"

"Oh my, let's go see who's at the door." She chuckles as she makes her way across the room.

"Leslie, no. Please don't open the door. It could be......"

"Gabe, hi!" She says as she opens the door, standing back so he can walk in.

"No no, Les. You called him?" I question as I stare at the man standing in the door way, his right arm still bandaged.

"No." Gabe says. "I called her. I figured she would be the one you would come to first. Why did you check out of the hospital without telling me?" He says as he looks me up and down, silently confirming that I'm okay.

"How did you get here so quickly?" I ask him, confused.

"You didn't see me in the back of the plane? I figured you were headed home, so I jumped on the same flight. You were so scared for anyone to speak to you, that I just waited, and watched.

Now, tell me why you checked out without telling me." He asks again.

"I didn't exactly check out. I just.....left." I say as I turn to go back down the hall towards Leslie's bedroom. I plan to shut the door and lock it and not move for days. My best friend in the world sold me out, threw me under the bus and now I'm not sure who I can trust anymore. I was very specific in her not telling Gabe where I am.

"You're angry, I get it." Gabe says as he follows me down the hall, Leslie just standing back watching the show. "But please, give me five minutes to explain. Can you do that?"

"Five minutes? You had plenty of time to *explain* while I was in the hospital. I had to find out that you SHOT MY BROTHER from a news report. That's fucked up, Gabe. You should have told me before the press got a hold of the story."

"I know, I was waiting until you were rested and better mentally prepared to handle the truth."

"Mentally prepared? Holy shit, I will never be mentally prepared for any of this shit! Twice, TWICE, in my life I've lived a nightmare. HELL, I'M STILL LIVING IT. IT'S RIGHT IN FRONT OF MY FACE!" I scream as I slam the door behind me. But before I can figure out how to lock it, Gabe is barging in.

"Sydney, please let me explain." Gabe whispers, a tender and soft look in his eyes.

"NOW, you want to explain?" I turn and run my fingers through my still damp hair, planting my ass on Leslie's bed. It's soft and comfortable and suddenly all I want to do is sleep. So I crawl back and slide under her thick comforter and nestle my head on to her feather pillow and close my eyes. I feel Gabe sit down next to me and his fingers gently brush my hair out of my face, his fingers stopping on the tattoo engraved under my right ear.

"The letter 'S." He whispers.

"What? What are you talking about?" I look at him with curiosity in my eyes.

"The letter 'S' in the form of a devil serpent. The tattoo he put here." He says softly as his fingers brush the ink. "He marked each of those girls with their number. But you, you already had the number four, so he gave you the same tattoo he had on his neck. The first initial of all his victims, and him."

I turn my head away from him, tears pricking my eyelids and I know I'm finally on the verge of a complete melt down.

"Sydney, look at me please." He whispers.

I blink my eyes open and focus on his face. His jaw is covered in stubble and his eyes look tired. I realize then that he's been through Hell too, and I start to feel guilty. "Five minutes, please. Then I'll let you get some rest before I take you home."

I scoot back a little and prop another pillow under my head. I'm too tired to argue with him anymore, so I let him explain.

"Franco worked at the restaurant next door to 'Ink'd Out Tattoo' which is where Stephan worked as a tattoo artist. They became.....friends," he says using the quote marks with the fingers on his left hand. "At first, neither of them knew they were half-brothers. One night, they got drunk and high at Stephan's place and Stephan started talking. He told Franco about his father, not realizing they had the same father. He told him his own sister shot and killed his dad in cold blood, and that he was out for revenge. As he told Franco the story, Franco started putting two and two together and realized who he was. So, he did some research and once he confirmed his suspicions, decided to become a vigilante and bring Stephan down on his own."

I lie there staring at Gabe in disbelief, but I don't say anything.

"At first, Franco agreed to help. But only to get closer to the situation, when he should have called the authorities. Stephan was a smart man, and he got suspicious when Franco got a little too enthusiastic about Stephan's plan. So, he did his own research and figured out who Franco was and tried to stop him in is his tracks. Franco then tied up your mother and sister....."

"Sylvia. Shit." I whisper.

"Franco did that to protect Sylvia, so that Stephan couldn't get to her if his plan to get you failed."

I stare back at Gabe, lost in what he's telling me.

"There's more." Gabe continues. "When we finally got to Stephan's house, you were gone.

But there was a man lurking in the bushes and I acted too quickly. Damn rookie mistake." He says as he shakes his head. "I yelled for him to stop, but he kept moving so I fired. It wasn't until later that we found out it was Franco."

"You shot my brother." I whispered, anger lurking under my exhaustion.

"I didn't know it was your brother, Syd. Honest to God. We got him to the hospital and treated, then he was questioned. He told us everything, including where to find you. Stephan had planned all along where he would take you if his plan went awry, but totally forgot he had told Franco. Franco saved your life, Sydney. If it weren't for him being stupid, we would have never found you."

"Oh my God, Franco. Is he all right?"

"Yeah, I got him in the shoulder." He shrugs as he looks at his own shoulder. "He's gonna be fine."

"And my mother and sister?"

"They're good too, though your mother is having some issues mentally. She's in Mercy Chicago's mental health facility getting treatment for the trauma, but she's improving every day.

Sylvia is with her and doing fine."

"Oh thank God. I know I haven't been very close with them over the years, but I didn't want any of them hurt. They blamed me for dad's death, you know?"

Gabe nodded, "Franco filled in the authorities. I think they are finally coming to terms with what happened to you all those years ago and are having to deal with it now. When you're stronger, you need to go to them."

I nod, but I know it will be a while before I can do that. They never forgave me for shooting dad, even after what he did to me. I'm going to have to work on forgiving them for blaming me.

"This is fucked up, you know?" I say, trying to smile.

"Was, Sydney. It was fucked up. But it's over and now maybe you can finally move on with your life. I'm sorry I kept it from you, but I......" I cut him off.

"I know now, Gabe. And I'm sorry for taking off on you.....but so much came at me so quickly that I just reacted, without thinking."

He leans down and brushes his lips across my forehead and I see something in his eyes I've never seen before.

"I'm here for you baby, and so is Leslie. We'll both help you, but you need to get some rest.

I'll come back tomorrow and take you home." I nod and close my eyes, because I am so exhausted I can't even think anymore.

Chapter 23
Gabe

I sit with Sydney for a while and just watch her sleep. God, she's beautiful. Even battered and bruised, she's beautiful. She's been through hell, again, and I couldn't stop it. I'm just thankful that her vigilante brother got in on the game, though I wish I hadn't shot him. He shouldn't have run, damn it. I'm going back and forth with this in my mind and I know what's done is done.

Now we deal with the consequences. I'm facing a reprimand my first day on the job with the Feds and I still have to explain my actions to Chuck.

I tuck the covers under her chin and gently kiss her cheek before heading back out to the living room. I see Leslie standing by the window, a glass of wine in her hand. She hears me and turns to face me, but I'm not sure I like what I see on her face.

"How's she doing?" She asks quietly.

"She's sleeping, thank goodness. I told her everything and she seems to be okay, for now.

But I can't predict whether one of her nightmares will wake her later."

"Did you tell her everything?"

I look dead at her, because I'm not quite sure what she's asking. "Everything? I think so, why?"

"Did you tell her how you feel about her?"

I stare back at her, dumbfounded. "Umm......"

"You need to tell her how you feel, Gabe. She needs to hear that right now."

"Oh, Doctor Phillips, and how exactly do I feel about her?"

"You love her. Am I wrong?" She asks.

I look down at my boots and shake my head, "No. You aren't wrong. But there's a time and a place for that, I'll tell her when she's ready."

"You don't think she's ready now?" Leslie asked.

"You're the shrink, Doc. You tell me."

She pauses for a second as she glances down the hallway. "No, you're right. But soon, she deserves to know. She needs you, though she may not admit it right away. Be good to her." She breathes.

But before I can respond to her, there's a loud knock on her door. "Leslie! Open the door! I need to talk to you!"

"Shit!" Leslie says as she walks towards the door.

"Everything all right?" I ask, the cop coming back out.

"No, that's Joe, my ex. What in the hell does he want?" She answers as she peeks through the peephole.

"LESLIE! OPEN THS DAMN DOOR NOW!" Joe screams while he bangs on the door.

"You want me to get that?" I ask, patting my hip where my Glock sits.

"No, I got this. Give me a second." She says as she unlocks the deadbolt and opens the door.

I stand prepared to jump in if needed.

"What in the hell do you want Joe?" She asks to a tall, but thin man standing at the door. His eyes drift to me and then back to Leslie's.

"Who is that?" He asks as his chin nudges towards me.

"No one you need to know about, now what do you want?"

"We need to talk."

"No, we don't. We said all we needed to say when I tossed your shit into the hallway."

"Yeah, about that. Something's missing. I need it back."

"What are you talking about? I tossed everything you own outside, there's nothing left for you in here."

"Bullshit! Let me in so I can get what belongs to ME!" He screams. I step forward and his eyes drift to me. "You stay where you are asshole, Leslie has something of mine and I'm here to collect it." He says as he tries to push the door open. Leslie pushes it back and Joe places his foot in between the door and the jamb.

"No, Joe. You can't come in. There isn't anything of yours here, now you need to leave."

"Yeah, so you can fuck your new boyfriend, Les?"

"That's enough, Joe." I step forward. "I think the lady said you need to leave, so I suggest you do just that."

"Who the fuck are you? You have no right to tell me what to do. Leslie is my girl, not yours."

"Fuck you Joe! Now get the hell out before I call the cops."

"Ooooh, I'm scared Leslie. Go head, call the cops." He says as he backs up a bit. "But I'll be back to get what belongs to me, you can bet your sweet ass on that."

He moves back further and Leslie shuts the door, visibly shaken.

"What an asshole." I say as I move towards Leslie and ensure the doors are locked up.

"Yeah, fucking prick. I'm sorry you had to see that."

"I'm a cop, you know. I could have dealt with it for you."

"No, he's harmless. He's just pissed because I wouldn't let him keep fucking his bimbo and letting him crash here. She dumped him when I kicked him out and now he has nowhere to go.

Not my problem. He should have thought of that before he started screwing around."

"Well, you call me if he comes back, yeah? I'll have a squad car here in minutes if he tries anything."

"But how, you aren't with the NYPD anymore, are you? Syd told me you quit?"

"Yeah, I'm with the FBI now. So, I can get a squad car here within minutes okay?" I say on a chuckle.

"FBI? Damn, you move fast." She smiles.

"Long story. Listen, are you going to be okay here if I head home?"

"Yeah, we'll be fine. I'll lock up and set the alarm. I doubt he'll be back tonight since he thinks you're still here. Go on and get some rest, I'll call you if we need you."

"Okay." I say as I brush my fingers on her shoulder. She's still shaking and I don't want to leave her and Sydney alone here. But if I don't get some rest, I may just collapse myself.

I hear her lock the door behind me and the beeping sounds of her alarm keypad, so I know she and Sydney are secure. I head down the elevator and as I step off, I decide to call Mo and see if he can put a man outside, just to keep an eye out until I can get back.

"You don't ask for much do you, Gabe?" Mo asks.

"Look, I know I'm the new kid on the block, but Sydney is in there. I don't need to deal with another madman tonight."

"Yeah, okay. I'll get someone over there ASAP. You go home, get some rest and I'll see you at HQ first thing in the morning, so we can make your new job official."

"Yeah, I'll be there after I meet with Chuck."

"Ah yeah, that'll be fun."

"He'll get over it. He's known Sydney all her life, so he'll understand why I did what I did. I hope." I chuckle.

"Well, good luck with that. See you in the morning."

"Later." And I shove my phone back in my pocket. I look around and I don't see Joe lurking anywhere, so I flag down a cab and go home.

Once I get inside, I take a hot shower, replace my bandage and finally crawl in to bed. It's late and I have a long day tomorrow, but I just can't get to sleep. I pop a pain pill to ease the sting from my wound and finally drift off.

The alarm goes off sooner than I would have liked, but I stretch and roll over to shut the alarm off. My bandages stretch and the glue from the tape pulling my skin. "Damn this, it's coming off now." And I yank the tape, effectively removing the bandage and some skin at the same time. "Fuck that hurt!"

I then laugh at myself, because pulling a little tape off hurt worse than the gunshot wound.

"Pussy." I call myself as I climb out of bed.

Another shower and now I'm dressed to head to NYPD HQ. Chuck is waiting and I need to face the music, though I have a feeling the argument isn't going to be pretty. The cab lets me out on LaFayette Street and I walk in, Olivia is behind the window. "Hey Gabe. Go on back, Chuck is waiting."

"Thanks." I say as I pull open the heavy steel door and make my way down the cold hallway.

I reach the door, but before I can knock, the door opens and a highly upset Chuck stands there, one hand on the door and the other on his hip.

"You're late. Sit down." He barks.

I decide to save face, so I do what he says and sit. The door slams behind me and I know the fun is about to begin.

"You quit! Mother Fucker, YOU CAN'T JUST QUIT OVER THE PHONE!" He screams.

"It was the only way I could help Sydney. I was outside of NYPD jurisdiction......."

"Yeah, about that. You'll be reprimanded for trying to intervene with a federal investigation."

"No, I won't."

He looks at me with confusion and I smile back. "You're looking at the FBI's newest agent, Chuck."

"What the fuck?"

"Yeah, signing on the dotted line today. I'm a federal agent now. No more grunge work with the NYPD. I'm out, Chuck."

"You've got to be kidding me. Just like that huh?"

I nod, "Just like that."

"Well, shit. I don't know what to say now. You've got me by the short and curlies, Gabe.

We'll miss you around here. The Fed's got them a good man, just try not to shoot another innocent man on your second day." He laughs.

"You know about that eh?"

"I know everything, Gabe. Mo filled me in on *most* of the details last night. Speaking of, how is Sydney?"

"She was fine last night, I'm picking her up after I meet with Mo. Then I'll know for sure.

She stayed at Leslie's last night. Oh, by the way. I'm going to get some info on Leslie's ex-boyfriend. He came around last night and caused some trouble. I need you to look into him for me, can you do that?"

"Yeah, sure. Just send me his info and I'll check him out. Was he violent?"

"No, not really. But he would have been if I hadn't been there. Leslie was shaken up, but she locked up tight behind me so I assume they're fine."

"Yeah, we didn't get any calls for domestic issues last night, so I assume so too." He stands and holds out his hand. I grasp it and shake, "Good luck with the Feds, Gabe. NYPD will still be here when you get ready to come back."

"Right, I'll keep you posted on that Chuck."

"Oh, and take care of Sydney. She's fragile right now. I find out you hurt her, and you'll answer to me, Gabe. Federal Agent or not, I can still take you."

I laugh out loud, "I'm sure you can Chuck. I'll watch my back."

"You do that. Oh and Gabe?"

"Yeah." I say as I turn back to him.

"Good job in Chicago."

"Thanks man. Take it easy, I'm sure we'll be in touch."

I head over to FBI headquarters and meet with Mo, signing the papers and getting an update on Sydney's family.

"Franco was released from the hospital last night and he's with his mother and sister at Mercy. She should get out today, but will continue treatment on an outpatient basis. Seems this really has taken a toll on her."

"Yeah, Sydney said her family blamed her for Luis' death. Guess it finally hit home that Luis brought it on his own family. That has to be hard to admit to after all these years."

"Yeah, but it's something. Hopefully the entire DeCarlo family can now heal and move on.

Franco is the hero in all of this, had he not gotten involved we'd still be looking for Sydney."

"Or found her body washing up on the banks of Lake Michigan."

"Yeah. Well, welcome aboard Agent Torres. I'm looking forward to solving more crimes with you, my friend. But watch that trigger finger, eh?"

"Yeah, no problem."

"Now, go get Sydney and get her home. You have some making up to do." He says as he waggles his eyebrows.

"Ha, yeah. There will be no making up of that kind for a bit. She needs time to recover both physically and mentally. She's been through Hell, a Hell that has stayed with her for twenty years. Her insecurities and fear are not going to go away quickly."

"No, but she has you and Leslie to help her. Be good to her."

"Why does everyone keep telling me that?"

"You know why Gabe. Lots of people love her and want to protect her, she's going to need you to help her get through this. Be there for her and just love her."

"I will."

I head out and walk across the street to the flower shop, hoping that something like that will help Sydney feel better. Yeah, right. Like flowers can heal deep wounds. I know how stupid it sounds, but she's seen so much hurt, fear and evil the last few days that maybe a pretty arrangement will help.

I pick out a vase full of lilies, daisies and fresh greenery. Bright colors and strong fragrance should ease her pain a little, even if just for a moment. As I wait for a cab to stop, I call Leslie and confirm that they are in fact, okay. Sydney slept all night with no nightmares, and they are talking over coffee right now. I feel better knowing that asshole Joe didn't go back last night and pull a stupid stunt like he did earlier. I'll try and get more info on Joe once I get to Sydney and get her home.

Chapter 24
Sydney

Leslie opens her door and there stands the most beautiful man I've ever laid my tired eyes on.

The man that rescued me and saved my life. Well, one of the men anyway. I need to check in on Franco soon and thank him. And smack him for getting involved with that asshole that almost killed me.

"Hey Leslie. How is she?" I hear him ask.

"I'm right here, Gabe, and I can hear you." I smile as I walk towards the door.

"Babe, you look beautiful." He says as he kisses my cheek. No one has ever called me 'babe' before him, and I'm finding I like it. "Did you sleep well?"

I nod, "Yes. For the first time in...years, I think."

"No nightmares?"

"No, thank goodness."

"These are for you." He says as he hands me the vase of flowers.

"Thank you, they're beautiful."

"Beautiful flowers for a beautiful woman."

I find myself blushing, which I do easily anyway. But I take the vase and place it on the table as Leslie locks the door again.

"Everything quiet last night?" Gabe asks Leslie.

She cuts her eyes to me, but nods to Gabe.

"What's going on?" I ask Leslie, but she just walks away towards the kitchen.

"Les?" I ask as I follow her.

"Nothing's going on Sydney, he was just concerned."

I know Leslie, and I know she's keeping something from me. But I let it go, for now.

"You ready to go home?" Gabe asks.

"Yes, I am. Leslie, thank you so much for picking me up at the airport and letting me crash here last night. I'm sorry I've been such an inconvenience."

"Shut up, Syd. You are never an inconvenience. You're my friend and I love you, but don't you ever try to keep shit like this from me again. I know where you live."

I laugh and it feels good, because I haven't laughed in forever. Laughter is the spice of life, without it you'll go mad. I know now, that I'm going to be fine. It might take while, but I'll be stronger than I ever was. I feel freer than I've felt in years, almost like my psyche knew my nightmare wasn't over yet. But now I feel closure, though I know I have a long way to go. You don't just kill two people and get over that right away, but with my friends and my man beside me, I know I can conquer anything.

My man? I'm not sure where that came from, but he's seen me go through Hell and knows the prior Hell I've gone through, and he's still here. That says something. What, at this point, I can be sure. But time heals all wounds, they say.

"Let's go babe." Gabe whispers as he takes my hand in his.

I give Leslie a hug and she hugs Gabe back, whispering in his ear. I wonder what she said, but I don't ask. They obviously have some sort of secret going on and I'll get it out of one of them eventually, but now is not the time. Right now I want to go home.

The fifteen minute cab ride takes thirty minutes, but we finally get back to my place. Gabe sits on my sofa and pulls me down in to his lap, his fingers brushing my cheek. I close my eyes and press my face harder in to his hand, absorbing the comfort of his warmth.

"Where are your bandages?"

"I took them off. Bleeding has stopped and the tape was pulling on my skin." He answers.

"Can I see?" I ask, tugging the hem of his shirt up.

"Are you sure? It's not pretty."

I nod and pull his shirt over his head, watching him grimace at the pain that still lingers.

I examine the wound, lightly brushing the puckered skin around it.

"I'm sorry." I say quietly.

"Sorry for what? Sydney, you didn't cause any of this. You have nothing to be sorry for."

"If I had just stayed with you at your house, none of this......."

"SHHHH, stop it. What's done is done, now we work on getting past it. It's over and no one will ever bother you again, that I can promise you."

"I've said this before Gabe, don't make promises you can't keep. We both know the world is unpredictable and no one knows the future."

"Well then, I promise you this. I promise to do whatever I need to do to make sure you're protected. I'll never let anyone hurt you, not again."

I smile at him and he smiles back.

"How did we get here?" I ask.

"Where?"

"Me, sitting on your lap in my apartment. We just met recently, but I........" Stop it Sydney, it's too soon to start pouring you feelings out. I'm still an emotional wreck, but I need to feel him.

"But what, Syd. Tell me what's on your mind."

I shake my head, "Never mind. It isn't important."

"Bullshit, everything about you is important."

"When I was in that basement, Stephan......forced me to do things I didn't want to do. I felt so ugly and dirty, so weak. I never want to feel that way again."

"I know baby, and you never will."

"Make love to me."

I can't believe I just said that, but it's out there.

"What?"

"You heard me, Gabe. I need you to bring *me* back to life. I know it's soon, and the wounds are still fresh. But I need to feel beautiful again. Take away the ugliness and bring back the beauty, Gabe. Please, I need that to feel whole again."

He stares at me for a moment while my fingers trace his hard stomach, my eyes glued to his wound. He reaches up and presses his fingers against my chin, turning my face towards his.

"Are you sure, Sydney? I don't want to hurt you."

"You'll only hurt me if you say no. I need to feel your body on me, I need to feel you inside me. I need to feel alive again, and only you can do that to me. Please, Gabe. Bring me back to life."

He brushes his lips over mine in a tender kiss, his tongue swiping the seam of my lips. I immediately feel my body relax as I part my lips and take him in. The kiss is soft, sweet. But as our mouths are fused together, our breathing picks up and the kiss becomes frantic. My hands are pressed against his chest and I feel him hardening under me. I grind myself on him, but before I know it he's picking me up and flipping us, so that I'm on my back and he's hovering over me.

Our lips stay locked and he puts his weight on me and my body begins to throb. I ache for him and I need him inside me. "Now Gabe, please." I beg.

He lifts my t-shirt over my head and his eyes go to my breasts, before his large hand cups my flesh. His thumb brushes over my hardening nipple and that throbbing heads between my legs. I reach down and unbutton his belt and his jeans, shoving them down his hips, exposing his erection.

He stands up and pulls his jeans all the way off, so that he is completely naked and staring down at me with heated eyes. I move to remove my pants and he shakes his head. "That's my job." And he tucks his thumbs under the elastic and slowly pulls my pants over my hips and legs, tossing them to the floor.

We're both naked now, and suddenly I feel vulnerable lying under him. "Are you sure, Sydney?"

I nod, because I need this. I need to feel loved and wanted, after feeling so hated for so long.

"Yes, please."

He gets on his knees and draws a finger through my folds before sinking his middle finger inside me. My back arches and I suck him in further, my juices spilling on to his fingers. His thumb presses against my clit and I feel my eyes roll back in my head. "Look at me Sydney."

And I open my eyes, focusing on Gabe's face. "At any point this is too much, you stop me baby."

I nod, but all I want is to feel him inside me. He positions his body and I feel him at my entrance. He pushes slowly inside and I feel my body come alive. I place my hands on his shoulders and keep my eyes on his, so that he can see that I need this. I need him to make love to me. And he knows, I can see it in his eyes as he sinks deeper and deeper in to me.

His body drops and his weight is on me. I trace my fingers down his back and cup his ass as I pull my knees up and back, his cock sinking even deeper inside. He pulls back and strokes back in, over and over until we're both sweating and panting. His cock hits that sweet spot inside and I feel my body tensing. Gabe must feel it too cause he looks down at me searching for confirmation that I'm all right.

But before I can nod at him, my sex clenches and I explode as I say his name, "Gabe!" He picks up his speed and his thrusts get harder and harder, his lips finding mine and he breathes my name as he cums.

"Did I hurt you?" He asks against my ear, his hot breath sending tingles down my spine.

"No Gabe, you loved me."

He pulls back and looks at me with surprise, and I realize I've stepped over the line. I need to work on not getting overcome with emotion.

"You're right Sydney, I do love you." He whispers as his hand gently cups my cheek and he kisses me before I can respond.

"You love me?" I ask.

"More than you'll ever know. I know it's soon, I know it's probably too much right now, but I wanted you to know."

I smile against his mouth, "I already knew."

"How?"

I chuckle as he sits up, his body separating from mine.

"You came for me, Gabe. I knew when you came barging into that grimy motel room, I knew then you love me."

He smiles before he says, "I knew it long before that Sydney. Long before that."

His eyes stay on mine as he waits. I know what he's waiting for, and while saying those words scare the shit out of me, I know it needs to be said.

"I love you, Gabe. Thank you for saving me and for loving me."

He smiles as his lips press against mine, harder and deeper than before. He rolls us over and cradles me in his arms, his fingers tangling in my hair. But we don't speak, not for a while. We just lay there in each other's arms.

Then a thickness invades the air, but neither of us speaks. Reality has come back and discussions need to be had, but right now it's just us.

"We'll take this slow, Sydney. You have a long road ahead of you. CPD still needs your statement, since you split before they could speak to you. And you need to go visit your family, to make peace with them."

"And I have a tattoo to get removed." I say brushing the ugly serpent behind my ear.

"What about the one on your hip?" Gabe asks me.

"I'll keep that one, it symbolizes my survival. But this ugly snake has to go." I chuckle.

"I can take you to Chicago, when you're ready." He whispers.

"I know. We'll go soon, but not right now. Right now, I just want to lay here with you and not think about the past. Our future is ahead of us, and that's all I want to focus on right now.

You and me. Not Franco, not Stephan and certainly not my father. Right now, in this room there's you and me. No one will ever come between us, not again Gabe."

He kisses me on the top of my head.

"No, never again."

The End

Other works by Christa Lynn

Running from Destiny - Book 1 of the Destined Series

Accepting Destiny - Book 2 of the Destined Series

Please visit me on Facebook:

https://www.facebook.com/pages/Christa-Lynn-Author/186996248141318

Or Follow me on Twitter @ authorclynn

Continue reading for a glance at Running from Destiny.

Running from Destiny

Chapter 1

"C'mon, you're going with me." Heather told me as she packed for her trip to Miami.

"No, Heather, I'm not. I have to work. I can't just take time off on a whim like you can. I have bills to pay and a job I need to keep." I replied with a bit of sarcasm in my voice.

I am Ally Sanders, and I have no life.

Well, not an interesting life anyway. I'm overweight, single and broke. I've got a decent job as an Administrative Assistant to the CFO of Robertson Industries, but it barely pays my bills.

And that's just the way I like it.

"C'mon Al, live a little!" Her eyes bored into me.

"Heather, you are a model slash fashion guru heading into one of the most important times in your career. You'll be there primping and scooting along that runway having the time of your life. What exactly am I supposed to do while you're off being beautiful and living your dream?

I don't belong in that world, and you know it." I sighed.

"Stupid, that's what you are, Ally. You're a gorgeous woman, and I'm totally surprised that a plus sized modeling agency hasn't gobbled you up." She glared at me while she said that, I just chuckled under my breath.

"Yeah, okay. Whatever you say Miss Optimistic." I said back to her. "I'm not exactly plus size, either H. At least I don't think I am. Am I?"

"See, that's your problem Missy Miss, no self-esteem what-so-ever. Your glass is always half empty instead of half full. You need to get off your ass, have some fun, forget that bastard Ryan, and move on. He was an idiot and wouldn't know the first thing on how to treat a lady. You're better off without that douche bag."

Heather Langley is always so uppity. She's also anxious, exciting and lives life without regrets. I envy her, because I'm the exact opposite. Maybe that's why we're such good friends.

She has no problems calling me to the carpet.

She's tall and thin, probably five foot six and built like a brick shit house, whatever that means. Tan, sleek and a natural blonde. I know, because she could care less who sees her naked.

I, on the other hand, am five foot three and a size fourteen with big boobs and a matching big butt. No figure whatsoever. Heather is an hourglass. I'm just a glass, a plain ole water glass.

But I am happy with who I am. Most of the time anyway, or at least I thought I was. The only thing I've got going for me are my eyes, a light blue with golden flecks scattered about.

I've got shoulder length straight brown hair which is all one length and quite plain compared to her long blonde locks that settle at the small of her back. Damn, we really are the polar opposite of each other. But we have been friends since high school, when Michael Jameson purposely slammed into me in the math hall, just so I'd drop my books and look like an idiot.

She came to my rescue, cussing at the stupid jock that thought he owned the school. The whole football team thought they were God's gift to women when, in fact, they were all assholes.

But, the majority of the cheerleading squad swooned and giggled whenever they were around.

Heather helped me pick up my books and papers that had spread over the entire hall way.

She then proceeded to ask me to join her and the other cheerleaders at their table at lunch. I was flattered, but in way over my head. I thanked her for her help and then politely declined lunch knowing how awkward that would have been. But she insisted and defended me to all the other giggly, whiny cheerleaders. It turned out to be the best day of my life, so far anyway.

We ended up at the University of Georgia together and our friendship continued to bloom through exams, bad boyfriends and crappy one night stands. We were both there for each other when we needed it the most, which was often.

"C'mon girl, you have never taken a vacation. Your boss is a gem, I'm sure he wouldn't mind you taking a long weekend to hit the baddest city in the world. Take a chance, Al. Live a little would ya?" Heather begged.

I glared at her with steely eyes. I'm good at that. She flinched, but smiled when I finally agreed. "Fine, what should I pack?" I responded on a huff.

"Well, for starters, you will pack nothing that is in your closet. You wear frumpy suits and long skirts that cover all of your assets." She said while peering at my ass. "So, we're going shopping."

"No no, H, I can't afford to go shopping. I am already struggling to pay my credit card bill off from that damn washing machine I had to buy last month when it flooded the laundry room."

I was determined to win this argument, even though the look on Heather's face said otherwise.

"Fuck that, come on." She grabbed my hand and pulled me out the door.

The next thing I know we're at the Mall of Georgia. I called my boss and told him I was taking some much needed R&R and would see him on Monday. Surprisingly enough, he was all for it. "Enjoy, Ally. You deserve it. Have fun, be safe and I'll see you on Monday."

Being an administrative assistant, my boss was on speed dial so he could be reached at any given moment. Which was great, but I too was on his speed dial, meaning he could call me at any given time, at any given hour. I didn't mind it usually. As I said before, I have no life. I had no idea how my life was about to change.

We shopped until we dropped. Dillards, Nordstrom and every little boutique store in between. I may be short and round, but Heather has this fashion sense about her that had me wrapped me in clothing I would have never bought for myself. I have to admit, I looked and felt good. I guess her Fashion Design degree is paying off for her.

Skinny jeans, cute ruffled tops, shorts and the most amazing cocktail dress. "What do I need this for, Heather? I'll be in the hotel the whole time you are out strutting your stuff."

"Oh hell no you won't, you're going to be sitting at the bar with me, in that HOT little number and those black strappy sandals that you have right there." She pointed at the Nordstrom bag in my hand, "And you're going to have a good time. Maybe even get laid." She gleamed, so sure of herself.

"Ha!! Laid? Are you kidding me?" I exclaimed. "I am not getting laid, no way, no how.

End of story." I glared back at her.

"Hmph, we'll see about that." She smiled coyly back at me.

After a quick bite to eat in the food court, we headed home. My apartment is across the street from the mall, but since traffic is so heavy in the evenings, we drove her little Prius and it still takes us 15 minutes. We could have walked in that time.